The Legend of the Caribbean

Brian Hallaway

Table of Contents

Copyright

Published by Defiance Press & Publishing, LLC

Bulk orders of this book may be obtained by contacting Defiance Press & Publishing, LLC. www.defiancepress.com.

Defiance Press & Publishing, LLC
281-581-9300
publishing@defiancepress.com

Chapter I
Williamsburg, Colony of Virginia

The night sky was cloudless and bright, and the full moon illuminated the town with a bluish light. The town was asleep. There was no sound except an occasional gust of wind blowing through the trees. It was close to midnight when footsteps on a cobblestone road interrupted the silence. Four soldiers were taking a pair of criminals to the gaol. The prisoners wore dirty, blood-stained clothes and walked barefoot. Every once in a while, a soldier would nudge one of them with the butt of the musket or yell at them for moving too slowly.

They navigated the moonlit streets of Williamsburg until they reached the gaol. There, they were met by a guard. The soldiers explained to him that a ship sailing for England had made a stop in Virginia and saddled them with some prisoners.

"Sure, we'll find a place for them," the guard said. "Harrison, get over here! We've got a couple more scumbuckets to babysit."

The prisoners were taken to separate cells. The younger of the two, a black-haired, brown-eyed man, ended up in a small room where another prisoner was already asleep.

"Your trial's tomorrow, first thing in the morning," the guard named Harrison said. "And the execution right after that."

He locked the door and walked away.

The noise woke up the other inmate. He was a cheerful young fellow with a round face that was partially obscured by a prison beard.

"What do we have here," he said. "I have a roommate now. Welcome, welcome."

The new arrival lay down by the opposite wall.

"My name's Robert Blakewell, or simply Rob. I'm in here 'cause I couldn't pay off a few debts. What are you in for?"

The new guy just stared at the ceiling.

"Do you have a name?"

There was a long pause, but eventually the guy blurted out two words.

"James McDougall."

"Well, nice to meet you, James. Welcome to the Williamsburg gaol."

No response.

"Say, are you from around here?" Rob asked.

James slowly shook his head.

"Then welcome to the beautiful Williamsburg. Not much to see from where we are, though."

"Do you *have* to talk so much?"

"I'm just keeping conversation. Since we're going to be roommates from now on."

"Did you hear what the guard said?"

"Yes." Rob scratched his arm. "Why?"

A few minutes passed in silence. James stared at the ceiling. His eyes had not adjusted to the darkness yet, and he couldn't see anything. Rob sat and watched the silhouette lying on the floor. They could hear each other's breathing.

"Look, I'm sorry if I was being annoying," Rob said. "I've been here all alone for a while. And when a man is alone for a long time, he starts talking to himself. I know, because I've been doing it for the last few days. Don't know about others, but for me it didn't take long. I was told that when a man talks with himself, that's the first sign he's losing his mind. Prison does these things to people."

He expected James to say something, maybe to express understanding, maybe call him a lunatic, but the new guy didn't seem to be paying any attention.

"James?"

"What?"

"Are you listening?"

"Sure."

"Do you want to say anything?"

"No."

"You know, you might be the worst conversation partner I've ever had."

"Whatever."

"Come on. Tell me something about yourself. What are you in for?"

"Doesn't matter. What are you in for, Rob?"

"I've already told you, I had debts I couldn't pay off. I borrowed some money from a friend, who I thought I could trust, but then I couldn't pay him back. And then one day that bastard decided he wanted the money back immediately, and I couldn't pay him, so he took me to court and now I'm here. Funny, isn't it? I pay debts by getting into more debt, to avoid going to prison for debts, and then I end up in prison anyway."

Rob lay down on the floor. There was another long silence.

"Why don't you want to talk about it?"

"About what?"

"About why you're in here."

"Just leave me alone."

"Look, we're all bad people here. We've all done bad things. You probably couldn't hold a candle to some of the lads that came through here."

"What difference does it make now?"

"Fine. Be like that."

Rob tried to fall asleep, but sleep was all gone. He just looked at the ceiling, listening to guards chatting outside. He couldn't make out the words. After a brief conversation, the guards each went their own way.

"It was something really bad, wasn't it?" Rob said. "The thing that guard said. You must've done something ugly. Not that I care. Whatever it is you did, I won't say anything. We're all bad people in here."

"You sure you want to know?"

"Yes."

"Piracy."

Rob sat up.

"You're a pirate?! Well I'll be damned! I've met many colorful characters in my life, but I've never had a chance to talk face-to-face with a real pirate. People tell legends about you."

"About me?"

"I mean, about pirates. I hear stories all the time, even in prison. Your exploits have traveled far. Can you tell me some stories?"

"About what?"

"You know, about pirate life."

"Not much there to tell. It's like being a sailor, but with more shooting and blood and drinking."

"And money?"

"Yes, there's some money."

"How much did you make when you sailed?"

"I don't know. I wasted most of it. There's really not much to tell." James hoped that the conversation would end right there, but even in the dark he could see the enthusiasm in Rob's face.

"It can't be. There has to be a ton of great stories. What ship were you on? Who was the captain?"

"Does it really matter?"

"It does to me."

James sighed.

"*Howling Doom*."

Rob's eyes went wide.

"What?!" he said. "You were on the *Howling Doom*? Are you telling me you sailed with Heartless Harry?"

"Yeah."

Chapter II
Kingston, Jamaica

Not long after Jamaica disappeared beyond the horizon, the crew of the *Valiant* heard a scream followed by a loud thud. Everyone on the lower deck jumped.

"What the fuck was that?"

James ran up the ladder to the upper deck. Sailors were gathering around something. Mark Bishop was among them.

"What happened?"

"Barton fell off the mainmast," Mark said. "He's dead."

"Shit."

James went back to the lower deck. Everyone looked at him.

"Well?"

"Barton fell off the mainmast."

"He's dead, isn't he?"

"Yes."

"Great," Ashleigh said. "Absolutely fucking perfect. First day on the trip back, that son of a bitch decides to learn to fly. We're already short a dozen men."

"Make that thirteen," Wilcoxon uttered.

Ten minutes later, Phelps came down.

"Funeral. Topside."

The doctor had already wrapped Barton's body in a tarp and tied a cannonball to the legs. The *Valiant*'s captain, Jonathan Spencer, took it upon himself to deliver the eulogy.

"Hurry up, you dimwits!" he yelled. "I want to get this over with!"

The crew finally gathered on the upper deck, most of them shielding their eyes from the bright Caribbean sun.

"It's going to mess up watch rotations," someone whispered. "Just when it seemed that things were not so bad..."

"Do you think someone pushed him?" said a different voice.

"Calm down, you idiot, he was probably just drunk."

"Of course he was drunk, why wouldn't he be drunk? Hell, I wish I was drunk right now."

"He was trying to unfurl the main royal," Morrison said. "To be honest, I'm not sure why it was furled in the first place."

"Gentlemen," the captain said, "may I ask you to shut up and pay attention?"

The crew finally became quiet. Captain Spencer waited a little before starting.

"We are gathered here today to mourn the death of a great friend and great sailor. It is a sad, sad day for the *Valiant*, for… uh… It's sad that we all have lost a dear friend today. A good shipmate. And… And today, we return this sailor back to the sea. Lord, accept his soul into your heavenly kingdom. Let's have a moment of silence for the late Jacob Barton."

"His name was Jack, not Jake," Phelps said.

"Quiet!"

They stood in silence for a few seconds.

"Now, Mr. Phelps," the captain said, "since you're too stupid to understand what a moment of silence is, would you like to use your muscles instead of your brain and throw the body overboard?"

Phelps slowly picked up the body, lifted it off the deck and unceremoniously threw it overboard.

"Lord, have mercy on Mr. Barton's soul. Amen. The funeral is over, you may return to your duties. Mr. Phelps, you've earned yourself ten lashes."

"What?!"

"You heard me. Keep your mouth shut next time. Everyone else, back to work!"

"You heard the captain," said Golightly, the boatswain. "McDougall, I'll need you to take over Barton's duties."

"Yes, sir," James said.

"Well, what are you waiting for? Get on the fucking mainmast and unfurl that damn royal. Bishop, you too. Get moving!"

James and Mark hurried to the shrouds before the boatswain exploded. As soon as they started climbing, a huge wave hit the ship on the larboard side and the *Valiant* suddenly rocked and straightened out again.

"Shit! Mark, you still there?"

"Right behind you. We almost took water on that one."

"I almost ended up overboard."

"If you do, I'm taking all your stuff."

"What stuff?" James said. "I'm not sure if they'll even pay me after this is over."

"I'll find your family and tell them that you left all your belongings to me."

"My family's dirt poor. You think I'd be here right now if I had money?"

They got to the top of the mainmast, cut the gaskets, and let the sail fly. They coiled the gaskets and stood there, on a footrope, holding on to the yard. Ahead, for miles upon miles, lay the Caribbean Sea. Wind howled in their ears.

"It's got its moments," Mark said.

"What?"

"This job. It has its moments."

The mast suddenly swung to starboard.

"And then it tries to kill you," James said.

"You want to enjoy the view some more or do you want to go down?"

"Down."

They climbed down the shrouds to the deck.

"Hurry up, ladies," Golightly yelled. "I need you down here! Captain said brace the yards."

Phelps was hugging the foremast and loudly cursing while Ashleigh was giving him his ten lashes. Ashleigh's face showed no remorse and maybe even some amusement.

"Ten. You're free to go," he said.

"Cocksucking piece of shit."

"Hey, don't blame me, I'm just following captain's orders. If you don't like the whip, learn to keep your mouth shut."

"Fuck you."

The whip had ripped Phelps's shirt. He was quietly mumbling curses. James overheard only "cunt" and "shithead."

"Phelps, get to work!" Golightly yelled. "Man the starboard fore brace! McDougall, why the fuck are you standing around?! You too!"

The *Valiant* was making its way north towards the Windward Passage.

Around sundown, the sailors sat down to eat. The dinner consisted of a mishmash of vegetables and some gray stuff the cook called "meat."

James emptied his plate, drank some water, and got into his hammock. He was used to the smell and the noises, and he fell asleep quickly. After what felt like a few moments of actual sleep, something woke him up. Phelps was tugging on his arm.

"What's going on?"

"You're standing watch," Phelps whispered.

"What? Wait, what time is it?"

"Three o'clock. They changed your rotation because of Barton."

"Shit. All right. Is your watch over?"

"Yes. Wind is pretty strong, otherwise nothing interesting."

"How's your back?"

"I'll live."

"Can you sleep on it?"

"I'll sleep on my side."

"All right. I'll see you in the morning. Get some rest."

"Thanks."

Topside, he found Mark at the helm. The sea was choppy, and the ship rocked back and forth. The weather was nice and cool.

"How's it going?" James said.

"I've never been at the helm before."

"How does it feel?"

"To be fair, I expected something more. I mean, it's not bad, but I kind of thought that steering the ship would be a little more… interesting, I guess."

"Not as fun as expected. Perfectly describes everything about being a sailor."

"Yeah. Although Kingston was nice."

"It's a nice city."

"If I could've stayed there, this whole trip would've been not that bad."

"I like the Caribbean," James said. "It's beautiful out here."

"And the weather's great."

"Yeah."

The sky in the east was slowly getting brighter. By the time their watch was over, it was bright enough that lanterns could be put out. James woke Wilcoxon and went back to his hammock, but couldn't fall asleep. He just lay there until everyone else got up, and then went to the galley for breakfast.

The day started with a report from Donaldson, the first mate.

"We were taken off course during the night because one of you fuckheads couldn't steer the ship straight. We got a little too close to Hispaniola, but that shouldn't be a problem. We'll be going through the Windward Passage sometime today or tonight because we are once again *way* behind schedule. We should've been there by now. Anyway, that's it for today. Get to work, and try not to fuck this up any further."

"I think that was you," James whispered to Mark.

"Yeah, it was probably me. Well, nothing can be done about that now."

The crew went back to work.

A couple hours later, they heard Stevens shouting from the crow's nest.

"Sail! Larboard bow!"

For a moment, everyone stopped what they were doing to look at the small white dot in the distance. As it got closer, they could see it was a brig, about the same size as the *Valiant*. It was headed west-southwest at full sail.

"I don't think that's a Spanish ship," Donaldson said.

"Looks English to me," the captain agreed. "Hopefully they're bringing some good news."

"Or a few extra crewmen."

"Stop it. We'll be fine with what we've got."

"Captain, with all due respect, we are at least a half-dozen short. At least. We need about a dozen."

"No, Mr. Donaldson, we do not. I do not want to hear that talk again, are we clear?"

"Yes, sir."

"And no mention of this to the other ship's crew. We'll make it back to Portsmouth just fine with the crew we have."

"If nobody else dies."

"Nobody is going to die, Mr. Donaldson."

"What if somebody–"

"I'll say it again: Nobody will die on the way back. There is no need to think that way. Are we clear?"

"Yes, captain."

"Good. Now raise our colors."

"Yes, sir. Raise the colors!"

Ashleigh and Mills rushed to the stern and unfurled the enormous red flag with a small Union Jack in the upper left corner.

James looked at the brig to see if it was indeed English, but it wasn't flying any colors. The ship was now close enough to discern the pole at the stern.

"Why haven't those idiots flown their colors yet?" the captain mumbled. "Are they stupid or just lazy?"

Golightly came and stood next to James and looked at the approaching ship.

"Do you see any colors?"

"No," James said. "They've yet to fly any."

"Shit."

"What?"

"We're fucked. We are so fucked. It's too late."

A minute later, they saw movement at the stern of the brig. Two men raised a black flag.

"Pirates!" the captain yelled. "Pirates! Battle stations! We're not going down without a fight!"

"Captain," Donaldson said, "let's just surrender the cargo peacefully."

"Mr. Donaldson, if you say that again, I will shoot you myself! Now get to work!"

"Yes, sir. Ashleigh, get the muskets! Everyone else, load the larboard guns!"

"We're fucked," Golightly said. He sounded tired. "We're completely fucked. Even if we somehow survive, we'll be crossing the Atlantic even more shorthanded than we are now, and with a damaged ship. It's done."

James looked around the deck to see if there was anything he could do, but every cannon was already crewed. He went down to the lower deck, where he found Ashleigh, Mark, and a few others loading the pistols and the muskets.

"James, get over here, help us load these."

Mark handed him a couple of pistols.

"How do you think this will go?" James asked.

Other crewmembers started moving powder and shot to the upper deck.

"We're going to paint the sea red," Ashleigh said. "It won't be pretty. Hopefully the pirates will leave us alone when they see we're not an easy target."

"The guns are ready, sir!" the first mate yelled.

"Wait for command!"

The ship went silent. James heard nothing but the breathing of his friends and the sound of ramrods shoving ball and powder into barrels.

Phelps and Stevens came down the stairs.

"Are the pistols loaded?"

"All of these are."

Both grabbed as many as they could and took them to the upper deck. Then they came back, grabbed the remaining few weapons, and left. Ashleigh, Mark, and James were alone in the hold with a loaded pistol and a knife each.

"What do we do now?" James said.

"We'll wait here," Ashleigh said. "We'll go topside if they need our help. Honestly, I'm not gonna risk my life defending whatever trash we have in the hold. The pirates can have it for all I care."

They sat and listened to the waves hitting the hull, waiting for hell to breakloose, wondering how far away the pirate ship was. James was clutching a pistol in his right hand and had his finger on the trigger. The grip was getting sweaty.

A cannon fired, followed by a crash as a chain shot tore through the foresail yard and cut some of the rigging along the way.

"ALL CREWS, FIRE!"

Multiple cannons blasted at the same time, followed by a couple of others a second later. The upper deck was shrouded in thick white smoke. The pirates fired again, this time the cannonballs crashed through the side of the ship, destroying everything that got in the way. One shot hit the bulwark just beside a gun port and bounced off and hit the cannon, destroying the carriage. The gun couldn't be moved and the crew were unable to load it.

"LEAVE IT!" Donaldson shouted. "GRAB A MUSKET AND SHOOT!"

Someone was screaming in pain. A few shots were fired from muskets. The *Valiant*'s cannons erupted again, once again filling the air with smoke. Another blast from the pirates' cannons tore more holes in the hull and killed several more sailors.

"CAPTAIN'S DEAD! THE CAPTAIN'S DEAD!" James couldn't make out whose voice that was, but it didn't matter. Captain Jonathan Spencer was no more. He looked at Mark and Ashleigh for some reassurance, but all he saw in their faces was fear.

A couple more shots were fired by the crew. The pirates answered with a dozen of their own. One smashed the bowsprit, another crashed into the hull just below where James, Mark, and Ashleigh were sitting, and they could feel the hit resonating through the planks. Another cannonball went through the gunwale and flew by inches from Phelps's head while he was swabbing the cannon. The same shot sent dozens of wood chips flying everywhere, and one hit Phelps in the left eye, and he fell to the deck and rolled around in pain, covering his blind, bleeding eye with his hand.

A body rolled down the stairs. It was Mills. James, Mark, and Ashleigh rushed to help him, but he was already dead. Grapeshot had hit him just above the ear.

"What do we do with him?" Mark asked.

"Let's just move him somewhere else so he doesn't get in the way."

Ashleigh and Mark grabbed Mills by the hands and ankles and carried the body away and put it in the corner. Then they came back and sat in the same spots, looking at the stairs.

"FIRE!" they heard Donaldson yell. "FIRE! THOSE BASTARDS DON'T KNOW WHAT THEY'RE IN FOR!"

Morrison and Phelps came down the stairs. Phelps was bleeding from the eye.

"What happened?" Mark asked.

"He got hit in the eye. Where's the doc?"

"With a musket ball?"

"I don't know. Where's the doc?"

"We didn't see him," Ashleigh said.

"He's not with you?"

"No."

Morrison went looking for the doctor. Mark helped Phelps to the corner and sat him down next to the body of Mills.

"Who's that?"

"That's Mills. He took one to the head. Sit down, you'll be fine. Morrison went to get the doc. Try to relax, all right? Everything will be fine."

Morrison came back. He was reloading his pistol.

"Doc's dead."

"What?"

"He got hit with a cannonball. I almost threw up when I saw what's left of him. We are fucked."

"How's it going up there?"

"We're fucked."

Morrison ran back up the stairs. The *Valiant*'s cannons fired again. The pirates' cannons weren't firing in volleys anymore. Instead, cannonballs and grapeshot were hitting the ship every few seconds, nonstop.

"DONALDSON'S DEAD!"

"THEN WHO'S IN CHARGE?"

"GRANGER!"

"GRANGER'S ALSO DEAD!"

"FUCK! JUST SHOOT AT THE FUCKING PIRATES!"

The *Valiant*'s cannons fired less and less often, while the pirates fired almost automatically. Their crew was a well-oiled machine.

"DON'T LET THEM BOARD THE SHIP! DON'T LET THEM BOARD THE SHIP!"

Wilcoxon came down the stairs. He was hit with a musket ball in the left elbow, and the wound was bleeding heavily.

Ashleigh took off his shirt and tied it over the wound. It made Wilcoxon cry out in pain. The shirt immediately turned crimson.

Mark led him to the corner and sat him down next to Phelps.

"They're preparing to board the ship," Wilcoxon said. "We won't last much longer. It's over. Where's the doc?"

"Dead," Mark said.

"Shit."

"How many dead topside?" Phelps asked.

"Half the crew, give or take. Captain's dead. Donaldson's dead. I saw Golightly get his leg blown off."

"Jesus…"

"Yeah, we're fucked. Best we can hope for is that they let us live."

"The boat's in bad shape," Ashleigh said. "We probably wouldn't make it far."

"We could take the lifeboats, make some kind of sail and get back to Kingston," Mark said.

"That's the best we can hope for."

The cannon fire ceased. There was a lot of pistol fire and shouting.

"They're boarding," Ashleigh said. "God help us all."

The pirates were tossing ropes with grappling hooks to bring their ship close enough to the *Valiant*. The crew tried to cut the ropes, but anyone who drew a knife was immediately cut down by musket and pistol fire.

"Reload and fire! Shoot them while they're climbing!"

They fired, but their shots were inaccurate and hit either the ship or nothing at all.

The pirates laid planks between the ships and started crossing over. A broad-shouldered pirate with a long brown beard was the first to land on the deck of the *Valiant*. He was right next to Morrison, who pointed his pistol up and fired. The ball went through the pirate's lower jaw and came out of his skull, and he collapsed. Morrison grabbed the gun out of the man's dead fingers and fired it at the second pirate to board the ship, destroying the man's pelvis. The ball came out the other side and hit the *Valiant*'s quartermaster, Trevor Mulligan, who was crouching behind a cannon.

"Aim at the stairs," Ashleigh told Mark and James. "Anyone from our crew passes, any pirate gets shot."

They held their guns up. Neither could get a good grip with their sweaty hands. James glanced at the injured in the corner. Phelps still had his hand over his injured eye. Wilcoxon wasn't moving. He had bled out.

More and more pirates came onto the ship, firing their pistols and swinging cutlasses. Those remaining on deck were wildly swinging swords and knives, not fighting but trying to keep death away for a moment longer. The pirates quickly shot or stabbed most of them. The sailors posed little challenge.

Morrison flipped the unloaded gun in his hand and tried to hit a pirate with the brass cap on the pistol's grip. The pirate evaded the strike and pointed his own gun at him. Morrison dropped the weapon and raised his hands. It was over.

"Do you like money?" the pirate said.

"What?"

"I said, do you like money?"

"Yes?"

"How about you join our crew?"

"I... sure."

"Welcome aboard." He put away the pistol and shook Morrison's hand.

A few pirates were finishing off the wounded and the survivors, using their cutlasses so as to not waste powder. Several others went down to the lower deck. The first one to get down the stairs took a ball to the chest from Ashleigh's gun. Mark fired at the same time, but his shot missed. James still had his pistol aimed at the stairs. The second pirate fired and hit Ashleigh in the neck. James aimed and pulled the trigger, but nothing happened. He pulled the trigger again and the result was exactly the same. Nothing. The pirate drew a second pistol.

"Drop it, boy."

James placed the gun on the ground and put his hands up. He realized that he forgot to pull back the hammer.

More pirates came down the stairs. One was checking on Mills, Wilcoxon, and Phelps.

"This one's dead. This one's also dead. You, let me see that... Oh fuck. Yeah, this one's alive, but his eye is all fucked up."

"Finish him off."

The pirate quickly drew a knife and stabbed Phelps.

"Take these two to the deck, we'll see what to do with them."

"Stand up, both of you. Keep your hands up. Upstairs, let's go."

"Wait," another pirate interrupted. "Where's the ship's doctor?"

"Dead," Mark said.

"All right. Go."

They were led to the upper deck. It was littered with bodies of their crew. Golightly indeed had one of his legs ripped off by a cannonball, as Wilcoxon said. A few pirates were standing around Captain Spencer's body.

At the stern, they were told to sit down next to Morrison and Stevens. Both were tired and covered in blood, but neither was seriously wounded.

"Where were you?" Stevens asked.

"Lower deck," Mark said.

"Anyone alive down there?"

"No."

"Wilcoxon?" Morrison said.

"Bled out."

"Phelps?"

"They stabbed him."

"So it's just the four of us."

A tall, broad-shouldered man calmly boarded the ship. He had a thick brown beard and bushy eyebrows. He had a cocked hat on his head and he wore a French officer's coat over his shirt. The coat was dark blue with lots of intricate gold ornaments on the skirts and cuffs, and in a few spots there were old blood stains. The sleeves only covered half of his forearm.

The captain.

A pirate reported that they found coffee and indigo in the hold and that the four men at the stern were the only survivors.

"Put them to work," the captain said.

The pirate approached them.

"You're going to help us move the cargo. Don't do anything stupid or you'll end up like the others." He kicked Granger's body. "Let's go."

They went back to the darkness of the lower deck.

"We were told to help out with the cargo," Stevens told the pirates in the hold.

"Good. Grab those boxes, take them to our ship."

One by one, they moved the boxes to the pirate brig. At one point, a pirate stopped James on the way back to the lower deck.

"Where do you keep the sails and line, that kind of stuff?"

"I'll show you."

He led the pirate to the hold.

"All right. Can you help me move these?"

"Sure."

"Thank you."

After a couple of hours, everything of value was removed from the *Valiant*. The quartermaster—the shortest guy in the crew—personally checked the holds.

"All right, we're done here," he said. "Everyone back to the ship."

James, Mark, Morrison, and Stevens followed the pirates to their ship.

"Gentlemen," the quartermaster said, "we have gained several new crewmen."

The pirates clapped.

"Gents, you are no longer slaves to your captain. You will never have to deal with that shit again. On this ship, you are free men. You are equal to others. You will get your fair share. Welcome to the *Howling Doom*."

Another round of applause and cheers from the crew.

"My name is Jacob Thatcher, I will be your quartermaster. You, what's your name?"

"Adam Stevens."

Thatcher shook his hand.

"Welcome, Mr. Stevens. You?"

"Charlie Morrison."

"Welcome, Mr. Morrison."

"I saw him fight," one of the pirates said. "This man is not afraid of anything."

"Well, Mr. Morrison, it seems you impressed Mr. Hammond here. If he says you're brave, then you must have the balls of an elephant. Welcome aboard. You, what's your name?"

"Mark Bishop."

"We found those two hiding in the lower deck," someone said.

"Really? How do you explain that, Mr. Bishop?" Thatcher said.

Mark was silent.

"Give me a reason not to throw you overboard right now. Come on. I need my crew to have my back. I need to know you won't go and hide the next time we go into battle."

Mark and James were still silent. Everyone in the crew was looking at them. It was even more awkward because Thatcher was up to Mark's chin.

"Well, in that case, we're going to do a little test. Mr. Ashborne, may I borrow your knife?"

A pirate handed him a large blade. Thatcher then drew his own.

"Mr. Bishop, you and Mister… say your name, idiot."

"James McDougall."

"You will fight Mr. McDougall. Winner proves himself worthy, loser goes overboard."

Thatcher handed each of them a knife.

"Make some room, gents, make some room."

The pirates cleared out a large area amidships. The quartermaster grabbed Mark by the upper arm and dragged him to the other side.

"All right, are you ready? Answer me, you dolt."

"Yes."

"Mr. McDougall, are you ready?"

James nodded.

"FIGHT!"

Mark seemed just as dumbfounded as James. They both slowly approached, looking each other in the eyes but also glancing at the other's knife.

"KILL! KILL HIM!"

James couldn't tell which one the pirates were rooting for, and soon all the cheers and shouts and chants turned into a jumbled noise that his ears could hear but his brain couldn't—or wouldn't—comprehend. He just watched Mark's every move, trying to figure out some way for both of them to survive, to convince the pirates that they were both able and willing to fight without anyone dying. Mark had to be thinking the same thing.

They were now close enough to where they could reach each other. Mark was carefully moving to his left, and James did the same. They circled for a while, watching each other's movements, until suddenly Mark lunged at James and tried to stab him, but he got out of the way and the circles resumed. James realized that the attack wasn't supposed to be successful; Mark only wanted to make it seem as if they were actually trying to kill each other.

James decided to repay the favor and lunged at Markin thesame clumsy, predictable way, and his blade missed completely. Once again Mark attacked, seemingly aiming for the left armpit, and James easily dodged that one too, then swung the knife to hit Mark's blade, as if they were sword fighting and he had just made a parry. Another swing that was too short to reach James's abdomen, and another slash, this time close enough to connect with Mark's ribs, but doing little damage, just enough to cut the skin and draw a little blood. James looked around to see if the pirates would consider that to be enough, but they didn't want a bit of blood, they wanted a corpse.

One pirate yelled something into his ear, but James didn't understand any of it. He watched as Mark wiped the blood off with his handand realized that Mark probably didn't understand his plan. James had turned the staged knife fight into a real one.

He wanted to give Mark some kind of sign to let him know that it was not serious, just a light scratch, that he still didn't want either of them to die. But he could see it in Mark's expression, the anger, the fury, the determination. He knew the next attack won't be clumsy or slow. Mark was out for blood.

James watched the knife as his friend moved closer. Mark lunged at him again, and this time James had to knock the knife out of the way with his left hand to avoid being gutted. Another lunge, and James barely evaded that one by jumping backwards. The ship rocked, and he almost lost his balance.

They were moving in circles again. James was trying to think of a way to land a solid attack, but then Mark attacked again, this time going for the right hand and the knife. James pulled the hand out of the way, and Mark followed with an immediate stab to the chest, which James barely managed to block with his left hand, slicing one of his fingers in the process. Without thinking about it, he thrust the knife into Mark's body. Both friends were equally surprised when the blow landed. James's knife went into Mark's side all the way to the handle. James pulled it out and backed away.

Mark fell to his knees. Only then James realized that this whole time the entire crew had been cheering, and now were celebrating his winning blow.

"I think we have a winner," Thatcher said. "Congratulations, Mr. McDougall. Welcome to the *Howling Doom*. Can I get my knife back now?"

James handed over the knife. He looked at Mark, who was pressing on the wound with his hand, but blood was running through his fingers.

It's not a deep wound, James thought. *He'll live. It will take a few weeks to heal, but Mark should be fine. He's strong as an ox.*

The man known as Mr. Hammond walked up to Mark and tried to drag him away, but he resisted.

"So you want to play?!"

Hammond pulled out his knife and stabbed Mark in the abdomen six times and kicked him in the head. Blood was flowing on the deck. The man named Ashborne took the opportunity to get his knife back.

"You goddamn little shit!" Hammond uttered under his breath. He grabbed Mark by the legs and dragged him to the side.

"Help me out!"

Another pirate grabbed Mark's wrists and they tossed him into the water.

"We had a fun time, now let's get back to work," Thatcher said. "We have places to be and riches to make."

Morrison approached James, who was still standing in the same spot.

"Hey, are you all right?"

"Yeah… Yes, I'm fine."

Another pirate walked up to them. He was skinny and had curly blond hair.

"Welcome to the crew, fellas. Name's Roger Davies. Come on, I'll show you around. And I'll get you some rum, you both look like you could use a drink. Don't worry, first day is always hard. You'll get used to this boat."

Chapter III
Williamsburg, Colony of Virginia

"Unbelievable," Rob said. "A pirate from the *Howling Doom*. You have to tell me everything. I want to know it all."

"There's nothing to tell," James said. "We were pirates. We robbed people. Then we spent the money on whores and booze."

"But your captain was Heartless Harry Wright."

"So?"

"You *must* have some stories about him."

"Not really."

"Are you joking? You served under the–"

"*Served*? What do you mean, *served*?"

"You know what I meant."

"We served no one but ourselves."

"All right. You *sailed with* the most feared pirate crew in the whole world. They tell stories about *Howling Doom* throughout the thirteen colonies, England, and even Spain."

"Do they?"

"Yes! I've met a Spanish sailor in Norfolk, he said that in every place he's ever been, everyone knows about Heartless Harry."

"Impressive."

"The man is a living legend! Come on. Give me something. There have to be stories about him."

"The stories you've already heard are probably more entertaining than anything I could tell you."

"Tell me anyway."

James was quiet for a while, and Rob patiently waited. There was a squeak of rusty hinges. Someone had opened and closed the door to the neighboring cell.

"Well?" Rob said. "What's he like?"

"I'm not sure what to tell you."

"What does he look like?"

"Somewhat tall. Not extremely tall, but taller than most."

"Six feet?"

"I don't know."

"Taller than you? What's your height?"

"I don't know."

"How old is he?"

"Probably in his forties. Don't know for sure. Nobody knew."

"Is he big?"

"Broad shoulders. Big chest. A belly. Yeah, somewhat big. Had a beard."

"Keep going."

"And he had that look on his face that made it seem like he was constantly angry about something. Deep voice. But he didn't speak much."

"Have you ever had a conversation with him? Man to man?"

"No, he only barked orders at me a few times. He wasn't much of a conversationalist anyway."

"Where is he from?"

"I don't know."

"Is it true that he had a family back in England?"

"I don't know, Rob. Stop asking me about his personal life."

"Right. You're right, sorry. So… What's it like standing in his presence?"

"What?"

"Is it intimidating?"

"Maybe at first."

"I would probably soil my pants if I had to speak to him. I mean, there's a reason he's called Heartless Harry. He could probably kill me in more ways than I can count. Have you ever stood in front of him fearing that he might shoot you if you do something wrong?"

"If a pirate captain killed his men for every little thing, he wouldn't have a crew. I never had to fear that. I just did what I was told to do and used common sense. It's just ship stuff."

"That's it?"

"That's it."

"I feel like something's missing there."

"It's just like any other ship. Don't get in trouble and you won't be punished."

"So he wasn't very strict about rules?"

"We didn't have many rules. Being a pirate is about enjoying life, rules just make it more difficult."

Rob went quiet for a while to ponder the next question.

"Why did they start calling him Heartless Harry?" he asked.

"I don't know. It was probably before I got there."

"Did you – I mean, the crew – call him that?"

"No, we called him captain."

"Of course."

There were voices chatting outside the cell.

"New shift of guards," Rob said. "Must be midnight."

He looked at James, who was still lying in the same position, staring at the ceiling. He hadn't moved an inch the whole time, didn't even turn his head at any point to acknowledge his cellmate.

He's a strange one, Rob thought.

"Is Heartless Harry really like they say?" he asked.

"I don't know what they say."

"Well, they call him heartless."

"I never got the chance to open up his chest and look inside."

"Is it true that he once had a man submerged waist-deep in the water until the sharks ate his legs?"

"I don't know. I never saw or heard anything like that."

"What *do* you know about him?"

"He was no saint, I can tell you that."

"Why are avoiding questions? Hell, if I was on Heartless Harry's crew, I'd be telling everyone about it. I'd want everyone to know I sailed with the meanest group of men since… I don't even know. I would let everybody know that I'm not someone to mess with, you know?"

"It's nice that you think so highly of them."

"What do *you* think of them? Your crew, I mean?"

"They were pirates."

"And?"

"They were just like any other pirate crew. They gambled, they drank, they robbed, they killed. Every pirate crew did that. *Howling Doom* was just one of many."

"But still…"

"What?"

"They don't tell stories about other crews like they do about the *Howling Doom.*"

"Or maybe the storytellers just don't know any other pirate ships."

"Maybe it's just that Heartless Harry is the most successful."

"All right, I'll give you that. Few other pirates have done it for as long. Or as successfully."

"What makes him better than others?"

"I don't know. Maybe ruthlessness."

"Maybe instincts?"

"Maybe luck?"

"People always say that. Whenever someone is more successful than them, it's always, *Oh, he was just lucky.*"

"Think whatever you want."

"What was it like to see him in battle? I can imagine him fighting some Spaniards or Frenchmen on the deck of a ship, sword in hand…"

"He preferred the pistol," James said. "And in battle fighting face to face was stupid. We all tried to avoid that. It's much easier and safer to stab someone in the back when he's not looking."

"Does your captain fight that way too?"

"We all did that. Because we all wanted to stay alive. We were pirates, not Knights of the Round Table."

Silence fell again as Rob ran out of questions.

"They say that Harry ruled with an iron fist. Is that true?"

"Who says that?"

Chapter IV

Cartagena de Indias, Kingdom of the New Granada

James woke up with the worst hangover of his life. Memories of the previous day were fuzzy. James slowly made his way to the deck to find Roger. He seemed like the most agreeable in the whole crew.

"Good morning. Feeling better today?"

"I guess."

"Good. Last night you got free because you're new, starting tonight you'll be standing watch."

"All right."

The breakfast wasn't very appetizing, but still somewhat better than what he ate on the *Valiant*.

"I should probably catch you up with how things work," Roger said. "You remember Jacob Thatcher, the quartermaster." He pointed to the shortest man in the room. "Here he is the second to the captain. Any problems you have with someone else, you go to him. And if he tells you to do something, you do it, and you do it quickly."

"Got it."

"Then there's the bosun, Mr. Jack Hammond."

Hammond was a handsome man with blond hair and a short beard.

"In charge of sails and rigging, like everywhere?"

"Yes. The man sitting to your left is Will Ashborne, the navigator."

Ashborne, a handsome twenty-something guy with long black hair, put down the knife and shook James's hand.

"How's the first day of being a pirate?" he asked.

"It's all right, I guess."

"You'll get used to it."

"So where are we going, Mr. Ashborne?"

"Panama. We're taking Porto Bello."

"Over there is Nathan Clarke," Roger continued. "Used to be a slave in Virginia, now he's the first mate. Second mate is that Spaniard sitting next to him, Carlos Manzanares. We have quite a few Spaniards here. Over there is the surgeon, Antonio Ortega."

Ortega didn't even glance their way and just calmly ate his food.

"We got him from a Spanish ship a year ago. He wanted no part of it, but now he's more or less one of the boys. He's pretty good when he's not drunk. And next to him is the carpenter, Jim. I'm not sure if he even has a last name, everyone here knows him as Jim. I think that's it for a start."

"Phillips?" Ashborne said.

"Right. That brawny fella over there. Ben Phillips, master gunner."

"And the captain?"

"The captain's name is Harold Wright. Some people call him Heartless Harry. I don't think anyone's called him that to his face. In battle, the captain has authority over everything. When not in battle, you'll mostly be taking orders from the quartermaster."

"All right."

"Any questions?"

"No."

"Can you shoot a musket?"

"I've never fired one. Just pistols."

"I'll teach you. Your friend Morrison killed one of our crew yesterday, Andersen. The bright side of that is that you'll be inheriting Andersen's musket. And we won't be confusing him with Anderson anymore, so that's nice. Who knew that Andersen getting his head blown off would be a gift that keeps on giving."

James didn't know whether to be happy about getting a musket or to express condolences.

"Ashborne," Roger said, "how much more 'til we're in Porto Bello?"

"No more than a week from now. Even if the wind is against us, we'll be there at least a day before we're supposed to meet Whitaker and Stafford crews."

"Good."

After breakfast, Stevens and Morrison approached.

"Hey, McDougall," Morrison said, "how are you doing?"

"Fine. And yourselves?"

"Aside from Stevens getting a little lost, everything's swell. Did you hear where we're going?"

"Panama. I talked to Ashborne, the navigator."

"We'll be sacking Porto Bello," Stevens said. "We're about to make *way* more money in one day than what they would've paid us for the whole trip to Kingston and back. Can you imagine? Yesterday we were poor sailors. A week from now we'll be rich."

"And we have a captain who isn't a complete idiot," Morrison added. "That alone is priceless."

On the upper deck, they were stopped by the boatswain, Jack Hammond.

"What did you do on the previous ship? I need to know what you can and can't do."

They quickly explained how things were done on their ship. Hammond asked a few questions, and was satisfied with the answers.

"Just do what you're told and don't fuck up, and you'll be fine," he said. "And don't get drunk on the job."

"We had one drunk fella fall off the mainmast right after we left Kingston," Morrison said.

"Well, don't be like him. Stay alive, don't fuck up, and you'll get rich. Right now just stay around here, we might need to brace the yards soon."

They hung around the main deck for a while, mostly talking to the other crewmen. The *Howling Doom* had a large crew, and there wasn't enough work to keep everyone busy. James got into a conversation with a Portuguese sailor named Rodrigo Guimaraes, who had joined after his captain peacefully surrendered to the *Doom*. Rodrigo was the only one to join the pirates. His captain called him a coward and promptly received a knife blade to the chest from Thatcher.

Hammond gave the command to brace the yards. The bracing went much smoother than James had expected, mostly because there was more manpower. The job was done twice as fast as his previous crew's best time.

Only then he noticed that the captain had shown up on deck. He was wearing the same French officer's coat.

"What do you know about the captain?" James asked.

"He doesn't like people getting into his business," Rodrigo said. "Not very talkative. Most of the time he just lets Thatcher run the things on the ship."

"How long have you been on this ship?"

"I'm not sure. I think at least a year."

Captain Wright was talking to the helmsman. The helmsman answered a few questions and was left alone. The captain went by James and Guimaraes, and for a moment James thought Wright was going to address them, but he just walked right past them.

"Mr. Thatcher," Wright said. "Report."

"We've replaced or patched up most of the parts damaged in the last battle. A few more things to do, but the important stuff is all done. Jim is patching up the last hole in the gunwale, so she be back to her old shape before lights out."

"Good."

"Mr. Hammond talked to the new crewmen. They're caught up and good to go."

"Thank you, Mr. Thatcher."

The captain went to the bow, said a few words to Clarke, the first mate, and went back aft.

"Mr. Ashborne, what's our course?"

"Almost directly southwest. We should pass Cartagena within three days, if the wind keeps up. Right now we're going nine and a half knots."

Wright nodded and looked out to the sea.

James's first day on a pirate ship was unremarkable. It was mostly the same things he had done on the previous ship, except here the crew was in a good mood. That night, he and Roger snuck into the galley for some rum and got drunk.

The second day, Ben Phillips, the master gunner, introduced him, Morrison, and Stevens to the way cannons were used on the *Howling Doom*, where the powder and shot were kept, and explained the subtleties of round shot, chain shot and grapeshot. The rest of the day he volunteered for whatever job that needed doing. James stayed up late to take his turn standing watch – he even had his turn at the helm – and once it was done, he drank some rum and went to sleep. He did not sleep well and had another hangover.

In the afternoon, a call came down from Abraham Johnson up in the crow's nest.

"Sail, larboard side!"

Without any rush, Wright went to the bow of the ship and took a spyglass out of his pocket. He looked at the ship in the distance for a few minutes, then put the spyglass back.

"Captain," Thatcher said, "what's the plan?"

"Tell the helmsman to take us south-southwest. If it's worth taking, we're taking it. We'll have to wait and see what we're dealing with."

"Yes, captain."

The message quickly spread and there were more and more pirates coming to the upper deck and standing around. Some of them were talking, but most just quietly watched the approaching ship. Thatcher was barking out commands to the crew.

"Mr. Manzanares," Thatcher told the second mate, "Mr. Guimaraes, you too. Listen. Depending on how the situation develops, we might need one of you to play the captain. Come up with fake names for yourselves and the ship, cargo, destination, everything. Make it believable."

"Aye, sir."

"Hopefully we can just scare them into giving up their cargo. Didn't work the last time, did it, Mr. McDougall?"

"I would've surrendered, but it wasn't my call," James said.

"Either way, I'll need you manning one of the guns. Did Phillips give you instructions?"

"Yes."

"Good. Scott, Milford, I need you to help the new guys with the guns."

The *Doom* moved closer and closer to the other ship. Wright was watching it through the spyglass, only putting it down to rest his eye.

"It's a brigantine," he said.

"Can I see it?"

Wright passed the spyglass to Thatcher.

"I think they're flying Spanish colors," he said. "We'll get a better look when it's closer."

Roger came up from the lower deck carrying two muskets.

"Hey, Rog."

"Why did it take you so long to tell me we're about to fight?" He poured some black powder down the barrel of one musket and pushed it down with the ramrod.

"Where were you?" James asked.

"In the hold. What are we dealing with?"

"A brigantine."

"English, Spanish, French?"

"Thatcher says he saw Spanish colors."

"This should be fun." Roger started loading the other musket.

"What are you going to do with two muskets?"

"I'm going to take out the helmsman. If I miss, I won't have time to reload."

"You're going to take out their helmsman?"

"Sure. I've done that before."

"But we still don't know if we're taking that brigantine. The captain hasn't said anything yet."

"I know this crew. We're going after it."

The ship was getting closer, and the mood on the *Howling Doom*'s deck gradually changed. No more jokes were being told. Laughter was replaced by a rare nervous chuckle. Conversations died down. Everyone's eyes were drawn to the sails in the distance.

Thatcher brought his own spyglass. He and Wright were both monitoring the ship.

"That's Spanish colors for sure," Thatcher said. "It looks like a juicy target. Might even have some silver in there. Prepare to take her! We have ten minutes, let's go!"

"Load larboard guns!" Phillips commanded. "Milford, Morrison, chain shot. Everyone else, ball."

James ran to the nearest cannon. He didn't want to man it, but he was worried that he might be labeled a coward again. The *Howling Doom* carried twenty-four cannons; this one was at the larboard quarter. James was joined by a pirate by the name of Nicholas Scott. Together they loaded the gun.

"Stay down," Scott said.

They sat down on the deck, looking out through the gun port. They could see the Spanish brigantine slowly getting closer.

The ship was eerily quiet. There was no talking, no jokes, no commands from the captain or quartermaster. James looked around and saw Roger with his two muskets, sitting on the mainsail yard and leaning against the mast. James gave him a thumbs up and he responded with the same.

Pirates who weren't manning the cannons were preparing to board. All of them had one or two loaded pistols and either a cutlass or an axe. Some had ropes with grappling hooks.

They were now so close to the target they could almost make out the crew's faces. There was still no command to attack. James wiped his hands on his pants. He looked at Scott, then at Johnson and Abernathy, who were taking cover behind the bulwark. All of them seemed focused. If they were scared, they weren't showing it.

"Wait for it," the captain said. "Now. Raise our colors."

Up came the plain black flag. James saw the brigantine's crew come alive and start running around the ship.

"I don't think they're planning to surrender," Scott said.

"DO NOT shoot unless you get the order," Thatcher yelled. "We might be able to take that ship and sell her."

Scott picked up the linstock.

"They're loading the guns!" someone shouted.

Up on the mainsail yard, Roger carefully aimed his musket at the helmsman and fired. The ball destroyed the helmsman's pelvis and he collapsed.

The brigantine fired a cannonball that flew above the pirates' heads, hitting nothing but water on the other side.

"Chain shot, fire!" Phillips yelled. Two cannons fired, each sending two chain-linked balls spinning towards the rigging, cutting ropes and ripping sails.

"ALL GUNS, FIRE!"

James covered his ears as Scott lit the fuse. The cannon fired, releasing a plume of thick white smoke. There was no time to check where the shot landed. James grabbed the swab and shoved it all the way into the cannon, moved it around and pulled it back out, and Scott poured more powder down the barrel and threw in a rag. James took the rammer and shoved the wad all the way down. Scott inserted the ball, followed by another wad, and James again shoved it all the way to the breech of the cannon. Scott primed the touch hole with powder. Abernathy helped them push it into firing position, and Scott lit it with the slow match on the linstock. James covered his ears again, and again the cannon fired, and there was more and more of that thick white smoke hanging over the water between the two ships. They started reloading again.

Meanwhile, Roger, who was still sitting on the yard and still had one loaded musket, carefully aimed and after a good minute of waiting had a good look at the brigantine's first mate. He fired, and the man fell down. Roger took his muskets and climbed down the shrouds to join the battle.

Ben Phillips ran over to James and Scott.

"Load grapeshot from now on!"

"Aye, sir!"

Scott lit the fuse and the cannon fired once more. They loaded it again, this time with smaller balls that were meant to injure or kill the crew.

Scott lit the fuse and the cannon fired again, and the grapeshot killed a Spanish sailor and injured their boatswain. The *Howling Doom* had a few holes left by the brigantine's guns and a couple of pirates were lying dead, but the Spaniards were severely outgunned.

All of the *Doom*'s cannons were now shooting grapeshot. The Spaniards responded with lots of pistol and musket fire. One musket ball went through the cannon port and hit the deck boards, missing James by an inch. It made a loud crack as it flew by. James looked at the hole with splinters sticking out, then at his knee which was a mere inch away from being mangled. He realized it could've left him peg-legged for life. That is, if he even survived. Then Scott smacked him over the head.

"What the fuck are you looking at?! Swab the cannon!"

It brought James back to reality. He grabbed the swab and shoved it down the barrel and turned it a couple of times and pulled it out. They loaded the cannon with grapeshot once again, and fired, hitting one Spaniard in the chest as he was running towards the stairs to the lower deck.

The pirates began throwing grappling hooks.

"Don't let them cut the ropes!" someone yelled. It was a familiar voice, but it was overwhelmed by the noise and disappeared before James could figure out who gave the command.

He saw Scott and Abernathy pull out their pistols, and he did the same. There was still the same white smoke floating in the air, despite strong wind. James wasn't entirely sure what he was supposed to shoot at, but then he saw a Spanish sailor stand up and try to hit the rope with a sword, only to take a musket ball to the stomach. Then his brain finally figured out what the order meant. He was supposed to shoot anyone who attempted to slash the rope. James aimed the pistol at the brigantine and waited for a target. The ships were getting closer to one another and the smoke was being carried away by the wind. Shooting someone from that distance was reasonable, maybe even easy for a good shot.

The Spaniards didn't want to risk their lives. A few tried to cut the ropes by just sticking one hand out, but couldn't quite reach it. One of them went too far and stuck his head out, and immediately James and a few others fired. As he pulled the trigger, he saw that one ball smashed right through the sailor's skull.

"BOARD! BOARD!"

James sat down to reload the pistol while all around him pirates were jumping and climbing into the brigantine. Abernathy jumped on the cannon, then on the gunwale, and disappeared in the white smoke. Scott finished reloading and did the same. James looked around and saw that everyone was boarding the Spanish ship, and followed them. He stepped over a dead body. It was Stevens. He had been hit in the thigh and bled out on the deck.

The Spanish ship was full of pirates stabbing and shooting everyone, and cannons—some loaded and some empty—were forgotten. The first pirate to cross over was cut down by fire from Spanish muskets. He fell into the water and was gently floating away, carried by the waves.

Jack Hammond waited until over a dozen pirates crossed over to the other ship, then quietly made his way to the bow of the brigantine. He climbed aboard almost unnoticed and immediately shot the first sailor who spotted him. Then he drew his cutlass and stabbed the nearest Spaniard, who was reloading a pistol.

At the stern, Nathan Clarke did the same thing. He safely made it across to the brigantine, then started wildly hacking and stabbing every Spaniard that was in his way.

The Spanish were in trouble. They were outnumbered and losing ground, but they still fought with everything they had. With no time to reload their weapons, the sailors swung their muskets like clubs or drew their knives and flailed them wildly.

Morrison attacked the Spanish captain with his cutlass, but the captain turned out to be well trained. Morrison quickly realized that he was in trouble. He was deflecting blows that came so fast that he couldn't lose focus even for the half second it took to draw a pistol. A few seconds into the duel, the captain managed to slash Morrison's forearm, and used that momentary distraction to sink the rapier into his stomach. Morrison dropped his cutlass and fell to his knees. The captain pulled out the sword and grabbed a pistol from his opponent's belt and fired. The ball hit a pirate, Adam Bell, in the upper right arm. Bell fell to the deck screaming in pain, his hand on the wound, blood running between his fingers.

"Take the captain alive! We want the captain alive!" Thatcher was screaming. He was lost somewhere in the whole mess. The Spaniards were yelling among themselves in Spanish.

Hammond took a blow to the face from a sailor swinging his heavy musket. The hit chipped one of his teeth. Blood was coming out of his mouth.

"You son of a bitch!"

Hammond attacked the sailor, who tried to swing the musket again, but he caught it and hit him with the pommel of his cutlass. The sailor let go of the gun, and Hammond tossed it aside and stabbed the man several times and stomped on his head when he collapsed.

"Goddamn little cocksucker!" He spat blood on the corpse.

Meanwhile, James was at the stern of the brigantine, unsure of what he was supposed to do. The deck was a complete chaos, with Spanish sailors and pirates everywhere fighting to the death. He couldn't join the battle, or at least felt that he would be useless, as there were so many pirates already on deck that he couldn't reach any Spaniard. He watched as Clarke and some sailor started wrestling and went to the ground, but Clarke managed to get his right hand free and he smashed his opponent's head into the boards of the deck over and over until the sailor went limp. Another Spaniard tried to hit Clarke over the head with the butt of his pistol, but he evaded the strike, pulled the man to the ground, drew his knife and slashed the man's throat. Immediately a bucket's worth of blood spilled on the deck and the Spaniard twitched for a few seconds and then stopped moving altogether.

Clarke grabbed his cutlass and went against the captain, who easily blocked every strike, but from the other side came Phillips, and the captain had nowhere to go.

"*¡Nos rendimos!*" he shouted. "*¡Rendimos!*"

The fighting stopped and the sailors slowly put down their guns and put their hands up. Hammond saw an opening and stabbed one of them.

"What the fuck are you doing, Hammond?!" Thatcher yelled. "They surrendered!"

"So?"

"That means fighting's over."

"I see an opportunity, I take it."

"Opportunity? Just—just don't kill anybody for a while, can you do that?"

Captain Wright crossed over to the brigantine.

"Captain's here!"

The Spanish captain and a dozen surviving sailors were kneeling amidships. Wright quietly looked them over.

"I'll need someone who speaks Spanish."

A pirate named José Manuel Pereira came forward.

"I'll translate, captain."

"All right. Who is the captain?"

Pereira repeated it in Spanish. The captain raised his hand.

"What is your name?"

"*Capitán Fernando de Espinosa.*"

"What is the name of the ship?"

"*El Triunfo.*"

"What port?"

"*Barcelona.*"

"What do you have in your hold?"

"*Café, tabaco, y azúcar.*"

"Any other cargo on this ship?"

"*No. Nada.*"

"I think that's bullshit," Thatcher said. "I bet he's hiding something. He fought like hell, he wouldn't risk his life for coffee and sugar."

"There has to be something else," Wright said. "Probably silver. Tell him that he better tell us what he's hiding or we'll have to get the answer out of him."

"*Señor, nosotros no tenemos–*"

Thatcher slapped him.

"Stop lying," he said. "Pereira, tell this fucker that we'll kill what's left of his crew one by one until he gives us something more than cargo. Where does he keep the silver?"

"*Señor, por favor…*"

"Mr. Hammond, take one of these bastards and kill him."

"Blade or gun?"

"I don't care, just make it look impressive." Thatcher turned to the rest of the crew. "Get to the hold and start moving the cargo while I deal with this."

Hammond grabbed one of the sailors by the hair and dragged him away and made him kneel in front of de Espinosa. He then drew one of his pistols and without any hesitation shot the sailor in the head, covering the deck with blood and brains and skull shards.

"You really thought you could just say no over and over and we'll leave you alone? Ask him again. Where do you keep the silver?"

The captain was silent.

"Mr. Hammond, bring another one, but don't shoot him yet."

Hammond finished loading his pistol and brought another sailor in front of the captain.

"Get him down," Thatcher said. "If his captain still won't talk, shoot this one in the knee. Got it?"

"Got it."

"Tell him that if he won't give up where he keeps the money, this man here loses his leg."

The captain started explaining something in rapid-fire Spanish.

"Do it, Hammond."

Hammond pulled the trigger and the ball went through the back of the sailor's knee, destroying ligaments and most of the patella. The Spaniard screamed in pain. His reflex was to put his hands on the wound but at the same time he was afraid to touch it. Blood was gushing on the deck.

"You did this, captain," Thatcher yelled. "Tell that to him. You did this. We didn't want to do this, but you made us. We gave you a choice, give up the money or we destroy this man's leg, and you made the choice. You had a choice, and you wanted to keep the money. You," Thatcher pointed at Johnson. "Drag this one-legged shit away."

Johnson did as he was told. There was a thick trail of blood left on the deck.

Milford approached the group.

"Captain, we found a few barrels of rum. What do you want us to do with it?"

"Mr. Milford, do you need someone to hold your hand?" Thatcher said. "Take it and put it in the hold. What are you waiting for? Go!"

He turned back to the Spanish captain.

"Why do you treat your crew like that? They fought for you. These men here are the ones who survived. They're the toughest, the best fighters. They deserve to go home. They fought for it. But you don't care. You'll watch them die. You'll watch them die like dogs because you care more about the silver than about these men. You surrendered not ten minutes ago, remember? You surrendered so they wouldn't have to die, and yet you'll watch them being killed one by one instead of giving up some money that doesn't even belong to you. What kind of captain are you? What kind of captain is willing to surrender to pirates? What kind of captain chooses money over his crew? You're a snake. That's what you are. A snake and a coward. You never cared about these men. You just used them. They trusted you, they followed you, they died for you, and you betrayed them. Because they're just pawns to you. And now that they're of no use, you'll just throw them out to protect yourself. You're pathetic. Pereira, did you get all that?"

"Aye, sir."

"Get over here. Tell these men this. Gentlemen, I am interested in learning where your captain keeps the silver. I saw you fighting and I know all of you are good fighters. You deserve better than to die like dogs on the deck of this ship. Your captain doesn't care about you. He'd rather watch you die than part with his money, and when you return to Spain, he will likely blame all of this on you. He doesn't care. We just need one man to speak up and give us the location of the captain's money. That man will be greatly rewarded. The rest of you, well, we'll see. Some of you might end up like your friend over there." Thatcher pointed to the sailor whose knee had been destroyed by Hammond. He was dead.

"If any one of you knows the location, speak up right now."

The sailors were quiet. One of them glanced at his crewmate.

"Mr. Johnson, take this one," Thatcher said. "I saw one of them looking at him. He knows something."

Johnson grabbed the Spaniard by the hair and pulled him aside.

"Álvarez–" the captain started, but Wright punched him in the face and knocked him down.

"Tell me, where does your captain keep his money?"

"*No se.*"

"Don't bullshit me. Where is the money?"

"*Señor, lo juro por Dios, no miento. No lo se.*"

Thatcher drew his pistol and put the end of the barrel against the man's forehead.

"Where is the silver? One."

"*Señor, por favor…*"

"Two."

"*No lo se.*"

"Three."

"*Por favor…*"

Thatcher pulled the trigger and the sailor's brains and blood splashed on the deck.

"Say what you want about the Spaniards, they're a tough bunch," Thatcher said. "How many more times do we have to do this, captain? You were supposed to say that in Spanish, Mr. Pereira."

"I'm sorry, sir."

"Pay attention. Mr. Hammond, Mr. Johnson, Mr. Abernathy, I'm going to need your assistance. Mr. Pereira, tell the captain that if he refuses to cooperate one more time, we'll kill all of his remaining crew."

The captain was begging in rapid-fire Spanish.

Thatcher looked at the three pirates with their cutlasses drawn.

"Do it."

They immediately stabbed three sailors. Then Hammond stabbed another one, Abernathy slashed the throat of a fifth one, and Johnson swung his cutlass into the neck of a sixth one, but it got stuck and he had to push the corpse off with his foot. One of the remaining three sailors was quietly praying, one was crying, and one jumped up and tried to jump overboard but somebody shot him. Hammond and Abernathy finished off the remaining two.

"Where did that dolt think he was going?" Hammond said. He looked over the side and saw the body floating in the water.

"Throw them overboard. Don't stand around, help them out!" A few other pirates came to help and they quickly tossed the remaining eight bodies into the sea.

Thatcher drew his other pistol.

"Now it's just you, captain. Stand up!"

"Don't shoot him in the leg," Hammond said. "He'll just bleed out like the other one."

"I'm not stupid, Jack."

"Break his legs," Phillips yelled.

"With what?"

Clarke approached and handed Thatcher an axe.

"There we go. Thank you, Mr. Clarke. Wait! Grab one of his legs and hold it up."

Clarke did as he was told.

"Pereira, tell him that if he doesn't give us something, we'll break his legs."

"*No, señor, por favor…*"

Thatcher turned the axe around, swung it, and hit the captain's knee with the back of the axe head. There was a loud crack and the Spaniard's leg now bent inwards.

"TALK, YOU LITTLE SHIT!" Thatcher yelled over the captain's cries.

"*Una… una gaveta…*"

"*¿Dónde?*" Pereira asked.

"*Mi escritorio.*"

"He said something about a drawer in his desk."

"Finally." Thatcher put his gun to the captain's temple and pulled the trigger.

"Let's go check his desk."

Thatcher and others went to the captain's cabin.

Inside, he and Hammond went through the drawers. Others came in to watch.

"Papers… More papers… Here we go!"

He found a small canvas wallet. Hammond cut it open and spilled the coins on the desk.

"That's it?! That's all he had? I thought the Spanish were loaded with silver!"

"So that's why the captain wouldn't talk," Roger said. "He couldn't understand what fucking silver we were talking about."

"Mr. Davies, shut the fuck up," Thatcher said. "Did anyone check the captain's pockets?"

Johnson was the first to get to the body.

"Pockets are empty," he reported to Thatcher. "But he has some nice rings."

"Take them."

Johnson took the axe from Thatcher and chopped off the captain's fingers and removed the rings.

"I'm glad we didn't throw him into the sea," Johnson said.

"You can do it now," Hammond said.

With the captain overboard, *El Triunfo* was clear of its original crew.

Wright ordered everyone to take anything of value from the ship. James joined a few others in the search. Aside from some medical supplies, the ship was pretty much empty.

"Is there anyone else down there?" Thatcher asked when they returned to the upper deck.

"No, sir. We're the last group."

"Did you find anything else?"

"Nothing. The afterhold is taking water."

"How much?"

"It's probably three feet deep."

"Good. I'll need two volunteers to go in with axes and make it go down quicker."

Roger raised his hand, and James decided to do the same.

"All right. Here's an axe, there was another one somewhere… Milford, give me that axe. There. Go make that hole bigger. I want this boat underwater by sundown. When you're done, get back to the *Doom*. Everyone else, back to ship."

James and Roger went down to the hold. Parts of it were underwater.

"This was all done by our guns," Roger said. "Nice work."

"Hey, look. Right there, I think that wall is leaking."

"Yeah. We should be able to make a nice big hole there."

There was less water there, but it was still up to their knees. James and Roger started hacking, and soon the leak turned into a stream, and after a few more hits the hull gave in to the pressure and large amounts of water were pouring in.

"That's enough, let's go," James said. They went back up, tossed the axes to their crewmates and jumped the gap. The crew had already prepared nets for them to catch on to.

"It's done," Roger said.

"Good job, Mr. Davies. Cut her loose!"

A few pirates cut the ropes that were holding both ships together. The Spanish brigantine slowly drifted away.

"Full speed ahead!" Wright roared.

The crew unfurled the sails and the *Howling Doom* was off. James looked back at *El Triunfo*. It was leaning to its side. Another hour or two and it would be resting in the bottom of the sea.

"I think I need a drink," James said.

"We both do," Roger said. "Let's go."

Chapter V

Williamsburg, Colony of Virginia

"I've heard that somewhere."

"Don't believe everything you hear," James said. "Can we talk about something else?"

"All right." Rob pondered the next question for a while. "What's the scariest thing you've ever done?"

"As a pirate?"

"In general."

"Probably Porto Bello."

"What happened in Porto Bello?"

"We sacked it. It was a long battle and we took casualties. But we sacked it."

"What was it like to be in the battle?"

"It's an absolute mess. Gunshots. People screaming. Corpses. Blood. It's hard to describe it."

"How long did it go on?"

"It ended on the same day it started. That's all I can tell you. You don't think about things like that in the middle of a battle."

"What *did* you think about? Winning?"

"Surviving. Just doing whatever has to be done to survive."

"Like shooting the Spaniard who wants to kill you?"

"Yes. Like that."

"What's it like to kill someone?"

"It's nothing to feel good about."

"How did you get your first kill? Musket, pistol, sword?"

"Musket."

"Where did you get him?"

"What do you mean?"

"In the head? In the chest? Where?"

"It's not important."

"What's your total?"

"Total what?"

"Total number of people you killed?"

"Never counted. Don't want to know."

"Double digits?"

"Shut up, Rob."

"What is it now?"

"Ask me something else. Or don't ask anything."

"Are you always like this?"

"Like what?"

"You know, not very talkative. Avoiding questions."

"Seems to me like we've been talking for a while now."

"But you're still avoiding questions."

"Maybe you're asking too many."

"Look, I'm not a polite man, I know that. I'm just really curious. You're a pirate from a legendary ship captained by the scariest man to ever sail the seas, how can I not be curious? I get that you got yourself captured and you feel awful, but it won't get any better here. Trust me, I've been here for a while. A cellmate you can talk to is a luxury."

"Did you ever have cellmates you *couldn't* talk to?"

"When they first locked me up, there was a man here whose throat was messed up. Had this huge ugly wound on his neck. He couldn't speak, he could only make some sort of gargle. And when he breathed he made this annoying whistling sound. I couldn't sleep because of it."

James laughed.

"Sure, laugh at my misery."

"What happened to him?"

"The next day the guards took him somewhere and I never saw him again."

"What was his name?"

"I don't know. He couldn't tell me."

"Well, they're going to take me away tomorrow. You just have the worst luck when it comes to cellmates."

"I have the worst luck when it comes to everything."

"No you don't."

"Tell me more about combat."

"I really don't want to."

"Come on. Tell me about Porto Bello."

"I already told you everything."

"You haven't told me anything. Come on. Did you have a job during the battle? Like an assignment?"

"No. I just did what everyone else was doing. I shot at the Spaniards, loaded the musket, shot again. When they fell back, we charged forward, I went with the others."

"That's it?"

"That's it. I did that until the battle ended."

"It sounds like you didn't want to be there."

"Would you?"

"Sure."

"What would you do?"

"I'd lead the charge."

"You'd be dead within two minutes."

"Maybe, maybe not. Some people fight for years and never get wounded. It's all luck."

"You think you'd be one of the lucky ones?"

"I might be."

"How do you know?"

"I don't. Nobody knows until they win the battle or die."

"Don't you think surviving a battle is an achievement?"

"Sure. It's good to live to fight another day. I'm not arguing with that. But there's no glory in it."

"There's no glory in sacking a city and taking people's money, either. So I guess it doesn't matter in my case."

"There is glory in victory."

"Victory means leaving a lot of dead bodies on the battlefield."

"I'd say it's better to kill than to be killed."

"Is it?"

"Sure."

"All right, then."

"Is there anything you wish you knew back when you went into battle for the first time?"

"I don't know. Not really."

"Seriously?"

"Seriously."

"How many battles have you been in?"

"We sacked three cities and took maybe a half-dozen ships."

"That's impressive."

"Not really."

"That's nine battles you survived."

"So?"

"You really don't have any advice you'd give to a first-timer?"

"You know, I might actually have one tip."

"What is it?"

"Don't bother asking people for advice on combat."

Rob frowned.

"Why?"

"As soon as the shooting starts, you'll forget all of it anyway."

"Didn't other pirates give you any tips?"

"They did. I forgot most of it."

"What do you remember?"

"They said that the shot that gets you is always the one you don't hear coming."

"What does that mean?"

"You wouldn't understand."

"Do you have anything else?"

"Let me think."

"Take your time."

"Here's one. In a fight to the death, nothing is dishonorable."

"I'll keep that one in mind."

"Don't. It's not going to help you much."

"Any other pirate wisdom?"

"Pirate wisdom? That's a new one. Never heard anyone put those two words together. Here's another little tip my friend Rog gave me: watch the hands. Always watch the hands."

"Why the hands?"

"If someone is going to reach for a weapon, he'll use his hands. If someone wants to punch you in the face, he's going to need to clench his fists first. If you're going to hurt or kill someone, you'll do it with your hands."

"That's a good one. I'll keep that one in mind, might be useful someday."

"Most people go their whole lives without ever needing it."

"Any other advice?"

"No. I'm out."

"If you remember anything else, I want to hear it."

"That's pretty much all I can remember. This stuff wasn't really that useful anyway."

"But still, if you remember something that helped you survive in battle, I'm all ears."

"You want to survive? Don't get into a fight in the first place. That's the best way to stay alive."

"And if lead is already flying, what then?"

"Don't get hit."

Chapter VI
Porto Bello, Viceroyalty of Peru

A couple of days after taking and sinking *El Triunfo,* they reached the shores of Peru. Ashborne guided the ship along the coast, keeping land in sight but not getting too close to Spanish ground. Two days later, James and other pirates woke up to find that the *Howling Doom* was anchored just off the Panamanian coast.

“According to Mr. Ashborne, we’re about twenty-five miles away from Porto Bello,” Thatcher informed the crew. “We’re going to stay here for a few days until Whitaker, Smith, and Stafford crews arrive. Once everybody’s here, we’ll sail to within ten or so miles and attack at night. You’re free to go to the shore, but stay near the ship. We may have to leave at any moment. We’ll maintain watch on the deck, same as before.

“Mr. Milford, Mr. Douglas, you are on fresh water duty. Anderson, Pereira, Richards, you’re the hunting party. Get Mr. Beasley some fresh meat. Mr. Keene, you’ll be helping Beasley, he wants to search for fresh fruit. If you can manage to not fuck up, we’ll eat like kings tonight.”

The crew was dismissed and immediately prepared launches to go to the shore. Guimaraes handed his weapons to Pereira and simply jumped over the gunwale into the water and swam to the shore himself.

“Look at him go.”

“How’s the water?” James asked when the launch reached the shore.

“It’s great. Nice and cool.”

Hammond took off his boots and jumped out of the launch. He walked to the beach through ankle-deep water and stretched out on the sand.

“Nobody bother me,” he said.

Beyond the beach was a lush, dense forest. Anderson, Richards, and Pereira told everyone to stay close to the beach and be quiet, and went into the forest to hunt. Ten minutes later, there was a shot.

“Sounds like they got us something for dinner,” Ashborne said.

“Now we just need to wait and see if we’re eating boar or Pereira,” Hammond mumbled.

After a while there was another shot, and later all three pirates returned with two large deer.

“So they didn’t kill Pereira after all.”

Beasley, the *Doom*’s cook, drew his knife and started gutting one of the deer. Anderson did the same on the other. Richards and Pereira went back into the jungle to look for more meat.

A few pirates had followed Guimaraes and swam to the shore. Some of them were swimming laps or just splashing around in the water. Clarke went knee-deep into water and just sat down and soaked. Hammond fell asleep.

Roger brought the musket that previously belonged to Andersen, together with some powder and shot.

"I'm going to teach you to shoot. Let's go."

James and Roger went deeper into the jungle. It was quiet except for a couple of birds singing somewhere in the distance.

"Stay here." Roger went over to one tree and peeled off some bark with his knife to leave a large patch of white sapwood.

"There's not much room for target practice, but this will do. Can you see that white patch over there?"

"Sure."

"That's your target. Lay down on your stomach and put the gun on that log. You see this groove on the barrel? It's there to help you aim. Line it up with that white patch, exhale, hold your breath, and pull the trigger."

James did exactly as he was told. The hammer clacked and the musket fired, leaving James in a cloud of smoke, and the ball ended up hitting the target.

"There you go," Roger said. "Not very complicated, is it? Load it, shoot again."

James loaded the musket, aimed, held his breath, and fired. The shot landed a few inches from his previous shot.

"Very good. Again."

The third shot completely missed the tree.

"You moved the gun too early," Roger said. "You have to hold the musket firmly, but not so tight that your hands shake. Don't expect the shot. Let it surprise you. Do it again."

"How many more times will I have to shoot it?"

"Until we run out of ball and powder."

The rest of the day was more of the same: James shot at the target, Roger dished out advice. They stopped the exercise to get some food and rest James's sore shoulder, then went back to it. This time he shot at a different tree, as the first target was all shot up.

"All right, last ball. Make it count."

James took his time aiming, held his breath, and pulled the trigger. The soreness in his shoulder was becoming too much. The musket fired, and the shot landed just inside the target.

"Nice work. I'd say you're deadly out to fifty yards. We'll return to this tomorrow, see if we can make you equally deadly from a hundred yards."

For dinner, the pirates had fresh venison with guavas, pineapples, and some other exotic fruit for dessert. It was a nice change after months of salted meat and hardtack. They couldn't get enough of the pineapples, and Keene ended up making the trip to find more. After washing all of it down with some rum, James felt a blissful laziness come over him. He sat by a bonfire with a few others, watching the flames and listening to the crew sing shanties.

A little later, James went and got himself more rum, quickly downed all of it, and went to the water and let it wash over his feet. He watched the night sky for a long time before finally deciding to find himself a place to sleep. The beach was littered with sleeping drunk pirates. A couple of pirates went for a night swim. A few were still awake and talking around the fire. James picked out a spot among the trees, where he wouldn't be woken up by the first rays of sunlight, and he lay down and fell asleep.

When he woke up, half of the crew were still sleeping. Those that were awake were standing on the beach, looking at the horizon.

"What's going on?"

"Ship approaching," Douglas said. "Right there."

"I see it."

"We're waiting to find out if it's our men."

Wright showed up. He had sand all over his coat.

"Did the crew on the ship give a signal?" he said.

"Not yet."

A few minutes later, they saw one of the crewmen on the ship waving. Wright watched him through his spyglass.

"It's one of ours."

The ship, a brigantine, drew closer and eventually anchored close to the *Howling Doom*. The ship's flag was a pair of swords in a black background. It was the *Sea Dragon*.

The launches were greeted with cheers and rum. The captain, William Stafford, was on the first one. He shook hands with Wright.

"I thought Whitaker would be the first to get here," he said.

"So did I. He'll show up eventually. Until then, let's have fun."

Several pirates were sent out to hunt and a few others to find more guavas and pineapples. Thatcher grabbed Beasley, who was still asleep after getting drunk the previous night, and dragged him into the water.

"Wake up, you lazy piece of shit. We want some fucking breakfast!"

"What the fuck, Jake?" Beasley said, and coughed out some water. "You really didn't have to do that."

"We want food. Your job is to make food. Get to work!"

"All right, I'll—Where the fuck did all these people come from?"

"Stafford and his crew arrived."

"Well, they better bring their own cook here, because I'm not cooking for all these people alone."

A few hours after breakfast, they saw another ship on the horizon. The *Doom* and the *Sea Dragon* were facing broadside to it, and there was no real danger coming from it, but everyone stood there watching. Eventually, the ship, which turned out to be a small schooner, came close enough and raised a red flag with an angry skull. It was John Whitaker's flag.

The launches reached the shore and Whitaker, dapper and classy like a true English gentleman, came onto the beach and shook hands with the other captains.

"Where's Angry Mark?"

"Not here, obviously," Stafford said.

"Well, at least I'm not the last."

"Where did you get that schooner from?"

"The French. Snagged it a few weeks ago near Hispaniola. They surrendered peacefully, so I thought, hell, I'm not moving all that cargo, we're taking the ship too. I named her *Marlin*. I was going to sell her in Havana, but things didn't exactly work out."

"What happened to the old *Hunter*?"

"She was damaged pretty badly after we encountered some Spanish ship. I think it was called *San Buenaventura*, this big frigate, armed to the teeth. Started pounding us with cannonballs, so we bailed. Poor old *Hunter* was all beat up. I figured it wasn't worth repairing, so we sank her off the coast of Cuba."

"Damn. She was beautiful."

"That she was. Anyway, you got something to eat?"

"No. No we don't," Beasley said.

Meanwhile, James and Roger went further down the beach and found a good spot for target practice. They hung up a shirt they took off of Cartwright while he was still asleep, measured approximately a hundred yards, and James started shooting. He was doing well from that range, so they went back thirty paces and fired some more shots.

"You're doing pretty well," Roger said. "I think you're ready to sack a city. For two days of shooting, you've done great."

That night there was another delicious meal followed by lots of rum, and drunk pirates singing songs around bonfires burning on the beach.

James sat by a rum barrel, refilling his tankard whenever it ran dry, and listened to Phillips tell stories about his time in the Royal Navy.

He woke up with a strong headache, and couldn't remember how he ended up falling asleep in the middle of the beach. Guimaraes gave him a tankard of rum to ease the pain.

That evening, they saw yet another ship and began celebrating. It was Mark Smith's brig, the *Devil's Reject*. A black flag with a skeleton holding two swords was flying on the mast.

"Angry Mark is here," Wright said. "We've got everyone. Time to take down Porto Bello."

The pirates erupted in cheers.

"That means no rum tonight," Thatcher said. The pirates grunted and cursed. "We'll need you sober and ready to fight. Once the city is ours, feel free to drink yourself to death. Until then, no rum, no beer."

"Does this apply to us too?" said one man from Stafford's crew.

"It applies to everyone, including the captains," Whitaker said.

Devil's Reject anchored near the other ships and the launches showed up soon after.

"I see we're the last ones to the party," Smith said when he landed on the beach.

"The party's over," Wright said. "We've been partying for the last two days, now it's time to work."

"That's what you get for being late," Whitaker added.

Meanwhile, Thatcher addressed the pirates.

"Gentlemen, I have an assignment," he said. "I need three volunteers to go and scout ahead of the remaining party. Tomorrow they will meet up with the rest and relay what they know. Who wants to go?"

Pereira immediately raised his hand.

"Pereira, that's one."

One of Whitaker's pirates, a salty forty-something, stepped forward.

"I want to go, sir."

"What's your name?"

"Moses Williams."

"Thank you, Mr. Williams. That's two. Captain Stafford, I believe it would be only fair if somebody from your crew was the third."

For a while, everyone just looked around at each other, until finally one pirate raised his hand.

"I'll go. Jonathan Piercefield, second mate."

"Very good. Mr. Ashborne will give you all the information. Gentlemen, we'll see you tomorrow."

The three volunteers received a map and instructions, and left.

"Everyone else, listen up," Wright said. "Be prepared to fight. Clean your muskets, make sure you have powder and ball, you may not have the time to do that tomorrow. The *Howling Doom* will have a crew manning the cannons and will stay out of the reach of the fort guns. Other ships will stay a few miles away, a skeleton crew in each. We will land in a small cove several miles from the city and from there we'll go on foot. Make sure your boots are in good condition, because no one is going to carry you. We'll meet with the scouts about halfway through. Changes may be made at that point, depending on what they tell us. Be back on your ships tomorrow at noon. Are there any questions?"

One man from Whitaker's crew raised his hand.

"Yes?"

"Who is going in and who will stay on their ships?"

"Each ship's quartermaster will handpick the skeleton crew. Mr. Phillips here will choose the men to man the guns on the *Doom*. Anything else?"

Silence.

"Good. Be ready."

James cleaned his musket very carefully, making sure that the bore was spotless, then did the same with the pistol. He stocked up on powder and ball, and borrowed a stone to sharpen his knife and cutlass. He was done in an hour and didn't know what to do next.

"Sit down and wait," Roger told him. "There's really nothing else to do."

James left his things on the shore and went for a dip. After the attack they'd probably be back on the ship for another few weeks, and there wouldn't be many chances to go for a nice pleasant swim.

After dinner, which wasn't half as good as the previous night, James and a few others took a launch and paddled back to the *Doom*. There had always been a stench in the lower deck, and now, after a couple of nights sleeping under the open sky, it was more prominent. But the hammock was infinitely more comfortable than the beach sand.

That night, James woke up twice. He was having nightmares where he ran through a grassy field trying to evade cannonballs and explosions.

In the morning, the crew was more silent than usual. Some, including James, ate very little; a few completely skipped breakfast.

Time went by slowly. A few pirates were playing cards. Some invented other games. Some were cleaning, then re-cleaning their muskets. James told Roger to wake him up if something happened and went to his hammock but couldn't fall asleep. He just lay there, with a strange feeling in his stomach, listening to various noises around him. A few pirates tried the same thing, but James was sure not one of them managed to fall asleep either.

After what seemed like days, it was finally noon, and the four pirate ships started moving towards the city. The *Howling Doom* was the first, the other three followed.

After a while, Roger showed up.

"We're getting close to the landing spot," he said. "Did you get any sleep?"

"No."

Others got out of their hammocks too. They all went to the upper deck.

The ship was moving painfully slow.

"Ashborne?" James said.

"What?"

"Are we supposed to be moving so slowly?"

"We could do better, but the current is against us and the wind isn't what it could be. But we'll be where we have to be before dusk."

Little by little, the ships made their way to a large cove and dropped their anchors.

"Ready the launches!"

The pirates quickly got into the launches and paddled to the shore. There was no talking. Launches from all four ships kept coming. Eventually there were almost four hundred pirates on the small beach, standing around, sitting around, pacing back and forth, and staring into the jungle they were about to enter. The treetops were painted orange by the setting sun.

"Signal the *Doom*," Wright said.

Hammond took a scarf he had found on *El Triunfo* and waved it left and right. Wright watched his ship through a spyglass.

"Good. Time to go. We have to reach the city before midnight, let's move."

They marched into the jungle. There was no talking. James couldn't see who was navigating, but he trusted that the captain knew what he was doing.

He thought about the battle that was about to happen, and how quickly he went from a poor sailor on a horribly mismanaged ship to a pirate who was about to make a lot of money. He thought about Portsmouth and wondered if he'd ever return and see his childhood home again.

The jungle was dark, and when the sun set it was hard to see anything. The pirates lit torches, but they only had a few, and most of their crewmates ended up just following the light and trying to not bump into the trees.

A couple of miles in, they found a small stream, and some of the pirates stopped for a quick drink. James was one of them. The night was hot, and after walking through the jungle he was tired and sweaty, and there were still several miles to go. He quickly gulped down a couple of handfuls and kept going.

The ground around the stream was soft and wet, and their boots sank into the mud, and there was a lot of quiet cursing. Abernathy tripped and fell, and his boots and pants were covered in mud. He yelled a few curses and for that got hit over the head with the butt of a musket and was told to be quiet.

The jungle was full of strange smells and noises. Several times James thought he heard something moving in the bushes, but he couldn't see what it was. Each time he would jump and his heart would beat like crazy, but whatever was hiding in the bushes would be gone in the darkness.

After what seemed like several hours but was probably only two, they stopped. James went forward to see what was going on.

"Why are we stopping?" he whispered.

"We're supposed to meet the scouts here," someone answered.

Pereira, Williams, and Piercefield were nowhere to be seen. They had to stand around and wait.

"Put out your torches," Thatcher whispered. "Everyone, put your torches out. Tell the others."

The message quickly traveled to the end of the pack, and the jungle was now pitch black. All they could see were the sky and the stars above, and silhouettes of men and tree trunks.

After a long wait, they heard movement. Several pirates drew their pistols.

"Who goes there?" Thatcher said.

"It's us, don't shoot."

Three dark silhouettes came out of the brush.

"How did it go?"

"They're not expecting us," Williams said. "They're undermanned and unprepared. The town doesn't even have a wall. But we'll need to take over the three forts or they will sink any ship that comes close."

"How far are we from the nearest house?" Wright asked.

"About a mile. They have a lot of small huts outside the town. We'll have to navigate around them or we'll lose the element of surprise."

"How many soldiers?"

"About a hundred, maybe more. Armed with muskets."

"Do they stand watch at night?"

"Yes, all three forts."

Wright, Stafford, Smith, and Whitaker huddled to discuss the plan. No one could hear what they were whispering, but there was obvious disagreement. After a good fifteen minutes, they finally decided on a plan.

"What's the plan, captain?" Thatcher said.

"Relay this to the others: we'll split into four groups. Three groups will attack the forts, the remaining men will raid the city to keep the residents from escaping with their money. I will lead the first one, captain Stafford the second one, Smith the third, Whitaker the fourth. Start separating our crew."

Thatcher, Hammond, and several pirates from other crews were going through the crowd giving out assignments. Once they were in groups, orders came down. James' unit, number four, was given the task to go house to house and take anything of value.

"Rog, you're in our group?" James whispered.

"Yeah, I guess we'll be fighting together," Roger said. "This should be fun."

"We're moving out," Wright announced. "Stay quiet, no torches. We cannot afford to lose the surprise. Let's go."

They moved slower than before, because every step was careful and calculated. James's stomach was upset. He kept telling himself to just keep going.

The jungle ended and the pirates were in a clearing. They could see the dark shapes of houses and huts. There were a few small lights coming from the city. As they got closer, James felt a weird feeling in his chest. He took a deep breath and reminded himself that they outnumbered the Spanish. Besides, the pirates were fearless in combat and would come in unexpected. The battle could be over before he even fired a shot.

The scouts led the crew down a longer route, further away from the heart of the city. The pirates moved stealthily, making very little noise for such a big group. All of a sudden, Piercefield signaled everyone to stop. Ahead of them was a chokepoint. There was a gap between two buildings, and the only way to get through it was to go single file.

The area was getting crowded. Pirates couldn't shoot the gap fast enough, and the crowd waiting to get through kept growing. Soon half of them would be in one big bunch out in the open. James's turn came, and he followed the others through the gap. There was plenty of room for one person, but nowhere near enough for two. Once James was through, he looked around and saw that he was in the middle of the city.

Half a dozen pirates—mostly from the other crews—were hiding behind a nearby building. James joined them.

"You, what group are you in?" one of them whispered.

"Four."

"Keep going. You, what group you in?"

"I don't know."

"What do you mean you don't know? That's the only thing you had to remember!"

"Quiet, quiet!"

"What are we doing here?"

"Waiting."

"For what?"

"For the whole thing to start."

"And then what?"

"Then we fight, you fucking dolt."

Roger and Guimaraes joined them.

"This is our group, right?"

"I don't think so," James said.

"This is Captain Stafford's group."

"I thought this was group one."

"This is a goddamn mess."

"Be quiet!"

"Let's all just move towards the fort, then we'll see where we're necessary."

There was a pop somewhere in the distance.

"You hear that?" Roger said.

"Was that a gunshot?" James asked.

There was another one, then a third.

"I think it's starting," Guimaraes said. "We need to get moving."

He stuck his head out and looked around.

"Empty."

"Move."

They moved fifty feet and took cover behind a different house. Two guys ran away and joined the others.

"I think I heard something," one of the pirates said.

"What?"

"Voices."

"Our guys?"

"I don't know."

A few more pops in the distance. Then several more.

"Move up, I don't wanna miss the fun," someone said.

Out of nowhere, a tolling church bell interrupted the silence.

“What the fuck is going on?”

“They’ll wake the whole fucking city!”

In the quiet of the night, the sound of the bell was deafening.

“We have to keep moving!” one of the pirates shouted. “Go!”

He and two others ran from behind cover and immediately a musket ball went right through one pirate’s chest, came out the other side and hit another one in the arm. The third pirate managed to get behind a house without getting hit.

“Well, there goes the surprise,” Roger said.

The pirates fired back at the defenders, and now gunshots were coming from every direction. Roger unwrapped the oily rag that protected his musket, quickly leaned just enough to see from behind the corner, fired, and went back to cover. As he loaded his musket, Guimaraes took his spot and fired.

“They’re charging,” he said. “They don’t know what’s coming.”

James sat in the same spot, terrified by the gunshots, staring at the lock of his musket. His hands were shaking. He heard the musket balls flying everywhere, bouncing off rocks and hitting buildings, and the church bell tolling somewhere in the distance. Any one of those musket balls could easily end his life, and probably one of them will, it will go through his brain and the next moment everything will be nothingness, or maybe it will hit him in the stomach and he will lie on the ground in agonizing pain until death eventually takes him. The Spanish were charging, and it was only a matter of time before they find him and others hiding behind some house, and they would all get killed with no mercy or remorse, here in a foreign land, so far away from home…

He saw one of the pirates yell something at him, but his mind couldn’t figure out what the words meant. Then the man tried to take away James’s musket, but Roger pushed him away.

“Hey.” Roger sat down beside James. His voice was completely calm. “How are you doing? You know, this place is pretty nice, don’t you think? I mean, the beaches, the jungle, the sea… This must be a nice place to live, don’t you think?”

“I… I guess…”

For a moment, all the noise seemed to fade away.

“You know what place you’re really going to love? Nassau. No other place like that anywhere else. It’s a paradise. Beautiful beaches with white sand, crystal clear water… You’ll see. We’ll be going there soon. We just need to get rid of these damn Spaniards first. Right?”

“Right.”

"How about you load your musket and shoot, just like I taught you. Look right here and point it at one of those Spanish uniforms. Can you do that?"

"Yeah… Yeah, I'll do it."

"Let's not waste any time, then. Don't worry about the noise. Don't worry about the others. I want you to aim at a Spaniard and fire one good shot. Just one."

James felt easier as the gunshot sounds returned. The bell wasn't tolling anymore. James took a few good breaths and slowly loaded the musket. He stepped out from behind the building, looked down his sights, aimed at a running Spanish soldier, waited for him to stop, and fired. He saw the man fall down.

"I think I got one."

"Beautiful," Roger said. "But it would be great if you could take out a few more."

While reloading, James saw Abernathy run past. A Spaniard stormed out of the nearest house and attacked him with an axe. The very first strike shattered Abernathy's skull. Less than a hundred feet away, James aimed and pulled the trigger. Even in the dark he could see the blood splatter. The Spaniard dropped.

"He got Abernathy."

"What?"

"Someone killed Abernathy. But I got him."

"Good job. Keep going, let's show those fuckers what we're made of."

Roger peeked behind the corner and fired another shot.

"They're falling back! We have to charge, let's go!"

He ran out into the open. James and Guimaraes followed. Around them a bunch of other pirates were charging towards the Spanish, trying to stop them from barricading themselves in the fort.

As the pirates charged, James saw several men around him drop to the ground. The Spaniards were moving cover to cover and firing back. Roger, James, and others took cover behind another house, and again laid down fire. The Spaniards had to retreat.

Hardwick, the quartermaster of the *Devil's Reject*, ran over to them.

"We have men around the forts," he said. "Right now we need you to go around and start taking stuff. Don't let the bastards run away. And don't let them near wells, they will try to throw their plate into wells."

"Aye, sir. Come on!" A large pirate from Stafford's crew led the way. James and others followed.

"Check that house!" Roger, Guimaraes, and another man went to the house while James and two others followed the leader. He kicked the door open. Behind the door stood a wiry man holding a large knife. The pirate drew his pistol and shot him in the chest. The Spaniard fell to the ground, still alive but bleeding from the chest and mouth and unable to breathe. His wife and child were hiding under the table and crying.

"What do we have here?" The large pirate shoved his pistol under his belt and picked up a bottle of wine. It was really big—at least several gallons—and made of green glass. "These people know how to party. Find some mugs." He pulled the cork out of the bottle.

"Shouldn't we get going?" another pirate said.

"We have time for a drink."

They found some tankards and filled them and drank all the wine, then refilled the tankards and emptied them again.

"Man, this is strong stuff. I'll give it to the Spaniards, they know how to make good wine. All right, grab anything that's worth something and let's go."

They went out into the street and entered another house. James couldn't see what happened there, he just saw a man bleeding on the floor and his wife attacking the big pirate, who hit her with the butt of his pistol and she dropped to the ground unconscious.

"These people are dirt poor, let's move," one of the pirates said.

The owner of the next house had a pistol and the big pirate who led the charge ended up dead on the floor. The others – there were five of them already as more came to help – killed him and his wife and started ransacking the house. James left the group alone and went his own way, only to encounter Jack Hammond.

"McDougall, follow me."

He kicked open the nearest door and went in, and James followed. Two men – father and son – attacked Hammond. The son grabbed Hammond's cutlass and they managed to pin him against the wall. James drew his cutlass and drove it between the young man's ribs. Hammond pushed the father away and stabbed him in the stomach several times.

"Nice work, McDougall. I guess I owe you one."

James and Hammond quickly searched the house and found a stash of silver coins and a bottle of wine. Hammond pulled the cork out with his teeth.

"To victory," he said, and downed almost half of it. He gave the bottle to James, who chugged most of what was left. He was slowly starting to feel the buzz.

Outside, they met Thatcher.

"How are you boys doing there?" Hammond asked.

"We took over two forts, the north one will go down soon. This town is pretty much ours."

"We're going through the houses. Found a nice stash of silver there. Those fuckers almost got me, luckily McDougall was there to help me out."

"Really? Well, you've earned your share today, McDougall. Keep it up. You lads keep working."

Thatcher ran off.

Suddenly, three men came from behind the corner. Two were holding axes, one had a sword,and all of them were yelling in Spanish. James and Hammond drew their pistols and shot two of them. The third one was still coming, and without thinking James dropped his pistol and swung his musket, and the hit landed perfectly, breaking the man's jaw and knocking him down. Hammond flipped the pistol in his hand and hit the man over the head with the brass end of the grip and didn't stop striking until he saw blood.

"What the hell were they thinking?" Hammond said as he reloaded his pistol. "Three men with axes? They would've been better off if they just killed each other."

"How can three people kill each other with axes?" James said. "I mean, one is going to stay alive, who's going to kill him?"

"McDougall, what the fuck are you talking about?"

"I'm not sure anymore."

"Let's go see if we can find more wine somewhere."

"We found this huge bottle in one of the houses."

"And you're only telling me now?! Let's go, lead the way!"

They ran to the house and stepped over the dead body. His wife and child were still hiding under the table.

Hammond filled two tankards to the brim, they knocked them, spilling some of the wine, and drank.

"That is some good stuff. I'm taking the whole bottle, I don't care."

"There's the cork."

Hammond corked the bottle and carried it out under his arm. On the way out, he looked back at the crying family.

"This is some good wine you have here. *Muy bueno*." He gave them a thumbs up, turned around, and left. "*Muy bueno*."

Before they got a hundred feet, they stopped again and filled the tankards James picked up at the same house and drank again.

"This is what being a pirate is all about," Hammond said.

He carefully placed the bottle by the door of one house and they went in. They found two guys from Smith's crew already there.

"There's nothing," one of them said. "They took everything and fled. Those fuckers are quick."

"Burn the fucking place down," Hammond said.

They threw some clothes into a pile, lit a piece of paper with the flint of a pistol, and watched the fire spread.

"Let's keep going. You boys want some wine?"

"You have wine?"

"Sure."

Hammond filled the tankards and they stood there, watching the smoke come through the window, and drank wine. One of them told a dirty joke that James didn't get, but he laughed anyway.

In the next house they found a family of seven. They were poor, and there was nothing of value to be taken, so they beat up the father and left.

"You hear that?" Hammond said. "The *Doom*'s guns are quiet. We have all three forts. All that's left is to pick up the loot."

They kicked down another door. The owner threatened the pirates with a knife, so they took it away and savagely beat him until his wife offered to hand over all their valuables. One of the pirates found a bedsheet and they threw all the loot from their pockets in it to make it easier to carry. Then they left and drank some more wine outside.

The house where they started the fire was in flames, illuminating the area. The fire reached a neighboring house, and its roof was slowly burning. The four pirates could feel the heat even from a good distance away.

"It looks pretty," one of the pirates said.

"Yeah."

"There's something beautiful about fire. I really like the way the flames move. It's like… it's like a dance, you know?"

"Do we have more of that wine?"

They sat down on the ground and watched the fire and passed a tankard of wine around.

"Is the battle over?" James asked. He had just realized that there were no more gunshots.

"I guess," Hammond said. "We took the forts. Hey, thanks again."

"For what?"

"For helping me out back there."

"Don't mention it."

"No, really, thank you. You saved my arse back there. I appreciate it. You're a good man, McDougall."

Clarke showed up. He had a piece of bedsheet wrapped around his upper left arm.

"What happened?" he said, pointing at the flame.

"We found that place empty, so we set it on fire. How're our boys doing?"

"The battle is over."

"Take a seat. We found this huge bottle of wine, you want some?"

"Sure."

Clarke quickly emptied the tankard.

"Good stuff."

They finished the wine as they enjoyed the view, and when the bottle was empty Clarke took it with one hand and threw it as far as he could, and it fell on the ground and broke, shards flying everywhere.

"Back to ship," he said.

They slowly got up.

"Which way is it?" James asked.

"I'll show you."

They saw smoke coming from somewhere across the town. Someone else had started a fire too. A shot rang out in the distance.

Hammond started singing, and others joined in.

Look ahead, look astern
Look the weather in the lee!
Blow high! Blow low! And so sailed we!
I see a wreck to windward,
And a lofty ship to lee!
A-sailing down along the coast of High Barbary.

They sang until they reached the port. The *Howling Doom* was already there, and the pirates were moving their loot to the hold. They passed well over a dozen corpses, both Spaniards and pirates from all four crews. Guimaraes was among them. He was hit in the pelvis during the battle. Roger told him he fought like a man and shot him in the head to end the pain.

Other pirates were celebrating. Manzanares had a silk scarf on his neck and was sipping wine. Some were watching a fight and cheering enthusiastically. Many had gotten their hands on some booze. Ortega, the *Doom*'s surgeon, was helping the captain make his way back to the ship. Wright was rambling some nonsense.

Thatcher came up to them as soon as they reached the ship.

"All right, how much did you have to drink?"

"A lot," Clarke said.

"I never took you for a fucking snitch, Clarke," Hammond said.

"Just go back to the ship and sleep it off," Thatcher said. "Is this the loot?"

"Yeah."

"May I have it?"

"Oh. Sure." The pirate handed over the bedsheet with the valuables. Thatcher glanced at the contents and threw it over his shoulder.

"Go sleep it off. You fought well. Get some rest."

James found his way to his hammock, clumsily climbed in, and fell asleep.

CHAPTER VII

Williamsburg, Colony of Virginia

"And if I get shot, what then?" Rob asked.

"Try not to die."

"Are you playing with me?"

"No."

"So what am I supposed to do if I get hit by a musket ball?"

"Pray. If you get hit, you'll be lucky if you end up with a peg leg."

"So there's no trick to surviving battles, I take it."

"If you're in a fight, you already failed. Best way to survive a battle is to not get into one."

"And what did you do when you were in battle?"

"I took cover behind something. Preferably something hard enough to stop a musket ball."

"That's it? Hiding?"

"What do you want from me? I'm not made of steel. I did what I needed to do to stay alive."

"So your victories came through hiding."

"Pretty much. I got my share of the loot, those who didn't make it got a burial. Not a fancy one. Some were just thrown overboard to the sharks."

"How big was your share?"

"I was a simple sailor. I got one share."

"No, I meant how much money you got?"

"We divided everything amongst ourselves. The more money we looted, the more we received."

"Give me an estimate."

"I never cared to count. I trusted the people who did the counting."

"What if they made a mistake?"

"There was no room for mistakes. Just imagine: a crew of angry drunk pirates don't get their hard-stolen money. Whoever did the accounting would've ended up in Davy Jones' locker."

"What's that?"

"Bottom of the sea."

"All right. But your share – how long would it last?"

"Not long. We wasted that money quickly. And I mean, we *wasted* it. We made the kind of money people make in a year on one raid, spent it all in a month or two."

"Really?"

"Yeah."

"I mean, you made a year's salary in one raid?"

"Sure. Sometimes more. Depends on the target. Sometimes we came away with nothing."

"That's a lot of money that went through your hands."

"Yes. A lot of other people's money."

"Isn't all money someone else's at some point?"

"What?"

"I mean, money changes hands all the time. Whose is it, really?"

"That's an interesting way to look at it."

"What about Heartless Harry? How much money did he make?"

"The captain gets two shares."

"What I meant was, how many pounds was that?"

"Again, it depended on the prize."

"What's the biggest prize your crew ever took?"

"I don't know. I was given my share and I was happy with it."

"So you've never seen exactly how much you took?"

"There weren't any heaps of gold, if that's what you're asking. Lots of it was in the shape of other things. Rum, sugar, spices, lots of other good stuff that we would sell and divide the money. Once, near Puerto Rico, we took a ship and we figured that it was in good condition, so we forced the crew overboard and sailed it to San Juan and sold it. Didn't even need to move the cargo from the hold. Sold the cargo, then sold the ship."

"And somebody bought it?"

"Sure. You can always find a buyer if you know where to look."

"Sounds like you've made easy money."

"We did. The crew surrendered peacefully. Doesn't happen very often, but it's nice not being fired at."

"And what did you do with the crew?"

"I just told you. Threw all of them overboard and left them to drown, miles away from the shore. We didn't even give them a boat. Some of our men loaded their muskets and had a shooting match, picking off those who tried to swim."

"That's…"

"Cruel?"

"Yes."

Two cats were fighting outside. The fight ended quickly.

"What does the captain do?"

"On the ship?"

"No. In battle."

"I don't know. Never really got the chance to see him fight. He would be in there with the rest of us, but I don't remember seeing him there. When you're in a battle, things like that don't matter."

"Does he give commands or something?"

"He mostly gave commands before and after the battle. During the battle, there's not much you can hear. Gunshots and screaming everywhere."

"So no one was in charge?"

"The captain was in charge."

"But you said he didn't give any commands."

"What would he tell us? 'Kill harder'? We killed whoever wasn't us. That's it. There's not much finesse there."

"What about swords?"

"What about them?"

"I'm pretty sure there's a lot of finesse in sword-fighting."

"We didn't do any sword-fighting."

"Really? Did you even have swords?"

"I mean, we didn't do any of the stuff you're thinking of. We did have cutlasses. Those were for stabbing. If you get into a sword fight with some Spanish officer who's actually trained in fencing, your guts will end up on the deck. I don't know anything about sword-fighting. I just know that offense is better than defense, so I went right at them and killed them before they had a chance to kill me."

"And you killed them all."

"What are you talking about?"

"You lived to tell about it. Your enemies didn't. So you won."

"That's about to change."

"But you're still here. There's still plenty of time until tomorrow. Anything could happen."

"But nothing will happen. Before you know it, I'll be sun-dried and stay there until they catch someone more important to use as a warning."

"Maybe your friends have a plan."

"What friends? I don't have any friends."

"What about your crew?"

"They wouldn't bother. I'm just a regular sailor. I'm replaceable. Go to any tavern in Nassau, you'll find dozens willing to take my place. I'm not sure if any pirate crew would bother breaking out the captain, why would they waste ball and powder on little old me? Let's face it, I have nothing. Not a single person out there wants me to live."

"All right. Let's not talk about tomorrow. Let's talk about something else."

"Fine. What do you want to talk about?"

CHAPTER VIII
San Juan, Puerto Rico

After the raid on Port Bello, the crew of the *Howling Doom* spent a couple of days on the beach before setting off towards Hispaniola.

One night, they had encountered a storm that lasted several hours, and once it was over they had to fix the rigging and replace the main topgallant, which was torn off and carried away by the wind. After that, they had a moment of silence for Solomon Atkinson, who fell overboard during the storm and was never seen again.

After a good breakfast but still feeling the lack of sleep, James stood on the deck and watched the sea. The day was sunny and hot with decent wind, and the *Doom* was making good progress. They would soon pass the Windward Passage and head to Nassau.

James overheard Scott and Keeling chatting with Phillips. He went there to join them.

"Have there ever been two brothers on the same crew?" Scott asked. "I mean, real blood brothers?"

"We had two brothers at one point, David and Samuel Wyndham. I can't remember where it happened, but at some point we found Sam among the bodies. His brother took it really hard. I think he killed himself. One morning he just wasn't on the ship. Just disappeared. We were a hundred miles from the nearest shore, so he probably jumped into the water."

"Maybe he fell off the ship?" Keeling said.

"I don't think so. Maybe. It was a long time ago. Back in the early days."

"Early days? How long have you been on this crew?"

"Since the beginning."

"When was that?"

"A really long time ago. Back when we had a different ship."

"Are you serious?"Scott said.

"Before the *Doom,* we had another ship. It was a sloop. She was called *Horror*. Nice little ship, when the wind was good she was just flying. You wouldn't believe how fast she was. But then we got a chance to upgrade to a brig. We snuck on a Portuguese ship, I think it was called *São Salvador,* and made it ours."

"So you're saying that the *Doom* is actually Portuguese?" James said.

"No, she *used to be* Portuguese until we liberated her. Now she's ours."

"It's weird," Keeling said.

"You didn't think the captain built her with his own hands, did you?"

"No, I just… If it was an English ship, I'd have no problem with it, but *Portuguese?*"

"It's a ship. It takes us from one place to another. What's the big deal?"

"What was the *Doom*'s first battle?" James asked.

"Cartagena."

"*Cartagena?* You're saying this crew sacked Cartagena?"

Phillips chuckled.

"You kids have no idea what kind of things she's been through."

"Tell us!"

"Maybe some other time. Get back to work."

There wasn't much work to do, and James went back to watching the sea and enjoying the cool breeze.

"Sail! Larboard bow!" came the call.

Everyone rushed to larboard gunwale to see it. The captain came out of his quarters and everyone made way for him. Wright took out a spyglass and watched the ship for a while.

"Must be coming from Santo Domingo," he said.

"Are we taking it?" Thatcher asked.

"Get everyone ready."

"Battle stations, gentlemen! Ready your weapons! Man the guns!"

James ran to the same cannon he had crewed in the last battle. He was once again teamed up with Nicholas Scott.

"We meet again, Mr. Scott."

"Pleasure to have you here, Mr. McDougall."

"Ready to blast some Spaniards to hell?"

"I'm still an Englishman at heart."

They cleaned out the cannon and loaded it with a heavy ball. Scott gave a thumbs up to Phillips, who nodded.

The Spanish ship was getting closer and through a spyglass Thatcher identified it as a brig.

"This will be either a big prize or a big battle," Scott said.

"Or both," James added.

"Or both."

Roger stopped by. He was carrying two muskets.

"How do you lads feel about this one?"

"Pretty good,"Scott said.

"You're going on the yard again?"

"Yes. The helmsman won't know what hit him. I got the last one on my first shot."

"I remember," James said.

"And you told me I couldn't. I'm calling it now—two in a row."

"Bold move."

"The sea is calm, it should be no problem."

"Davies, stop chattering!" Thatcher yelled. "Get on the fucking yard, come on."

Roger started climbing the shrouds. James looked out the gun port at the brig. It seemed like a decent ship, a little smaller than the *Howling Doom*.

"Larboard guns ready," Phillips reported.

Thatcher waved to Roger, who had already made himself comfortable on the mainsail yard. He responded with a thumbs up.

"Shooter in position," Thatcher said.

Other pirates were getting ready for battle. Most of them were kneeling or sitting behind the larboard bulwark, occasionally sticking their heads out just a little bit to see where the brig was. Keeling was clutching his pistol so hard that his knuckles turned white.

"The first Spaniard I see will have his fucking head blown off," he whispered. "I'm about to go on a fucking rampage."

"Mr. Keene," Thatcher said, "I need you to go to the hold and get us Spanish colors. I know we had at least two."

Keene ran down to the hold and came back a minute later with a flag over his shoulder.

"Fly Spanish colors," Wright said. Keene and Johnson raised the flag at the stern.

Thatcher was on his spyglass, inspecting the brig.

"It seems to be properly armed," he said. "It may not go down easily."

Scott looked at James. He wasn't smiling.

"Ready?"

James nodded.

"Let's do this."

There was silence on the deck. The only sounds were the splashing of waves and the pirates' breathing. The Spanish brig was now well within the range of the *Doom*'s cannons.

Wright looked at Keene andJohnson.

"Raise the black."

They replaced the Spanish flag with a black one as fast as they could, but the process was much too slow to have the intended impact.

"All crews, get ready!"

The cannon crews prepared their slow matches and listened for an order to shoot. James took a deep breath. He had the swab, ready to reload the cannon.

But seconds ticked away and there was no order. James began looking around. Everyone else was just as baffled as he was. The captain just stood there and stared at the ship through a spyglass.

"Hold! Do *NOT* fire!" Wright commanded. "They surrender!"

James stood up and looked at the Spanish ship. Two sailors were holding a white piece of cloth, most likely someone's shirt.

"Didn't think it would be that easy,"Scott said.

"They're up to something," Keeling said. "This is some kind of trick. Everyone, don't let your guard down. The Spanish wouldn't give up so easily."

"Shut the fuck up, Mr. Keeling," Thatcher said. "Mr. Manzanares, you're up. Mr. Pereira, you too. Everyone else, prepare to board."

The current gently brought the two ships closer and closer to one another. The Spanish crew calmly watched the pirates. The pirates started lowering launches into the water. Once the first one made it to the other ship, the Spaniards dropped nets over the side and helped the pirates climb aboard.

Manzanares was one of the first to get across. He went to talk to the captain. James followed the stream of pirates crossing over. Aboard the Spanish ship, he noticed that the crew were scared. Some of them tried to look tough, but they couldn't hide the fear.

Wright made it to the ship and told his crew to secure the lower deck and bring anyone they found topside.

"Captain," Manzanares said. "I've talked to their captain. He said the ship is called *El Santo Crucifijo*, out of Cádiz. The cargo is ours to take, and they're offering to help us move it, so long as nobody dies. The logs are available if you want to see them. The captain really emphasized that he wants his crew to stay alive."

"Good. We can work with that."

Manzanares turned to the Spanish captain and nodded. It seemed to give him a little relief. The rest of the crew were still uneasy.

"Mr. Manzanares, ask the captain when this ship was built," Wright said.

"He said it's her maiden voyage."

"That's a mighty fine ship, captain," Thatcher said.

"And she's brand new. It's not shot up, no bloodstains, and no shipworm damage. I want to see the captain's log."

Manzanares said it in Spanish, and the first mate went to get it.

"I want to see how fast she is." Wright said.

The first mate returned, carrying the log.

"*Gracias*."

Wright flipped through the log.

"Captain, do you want us to start moving the cargo?" Hammond said.

"Not yet. Get me Ashborne."

"Right here, captain."

"Look at these numbers. This boat is pretty fast when the wind is good."

"And that's with a full hold."

"Here, you can take it back. This is a really great ship."

"Are we taking it?" Thatcher asked.

"Mr. Manzanares, tell them that we accept any volunteers. Fair wages and all that good stuff."

Carlos said a long speech, and a sailor stepped forward, followed by another one. The others looked at them with disdain.

"Antonio Maldonado," the first one introduced himself.

"Miguel Ruiz de Toledo," the second one said.

"*Bienvenidos, señores*."

Two more men, Portillo and Villalobos, worked up the courage to join.

"Tell them to haul ass to the *Doom*," Thatcher said.

The sailors shook hands with Wright, then made it across.

"All right, everyone listen up," Wright said. "This is a really nice ship, so we're taking her. Don't let this turn into a battle. Gently move every crewman out of the ship and into the sea."

Manzanares and Pereira commanded the crew to jump. Most of them were terrified, others were angry, and the captain was furious. He started yelling in rapid Spanish, but Manzanares kept telling him to jump overboard. Finally, he had enough and punched the captain in the face, knocking him down, then grabbed him by the hair, led him to the side of the ship and forced him overboard. James was the closest to the whole thing, and ran up to help. They got the captain on the other side, but he was holding on to the gunwale, so they drew their knives and started slicing his hands until he let go and fell in the water.

A few sailors calmly climbed the bulwark and jumped into the waves.

"Come on, keep it going," Thatcher said. "Pereira, tell them to hurry up!"

Pereira drew his pistol. More and more sailors realized there was nowhere else to go and jumped.

"Good, keep it going. Don't get any blood on the ship or you will have to clean it yourselves."

Finally, the last Spaniard ended up in the water – Thatcher gave him a helpful push – and the ship was theirs.

"Mr. Ashborne."

"Captain?"

"Set course for Puerto Rico. We'll sell her in San Juan and continue to Nassau."

"Do you want me here or on the *Doom*?"

"Here. The *Doom* will follow."

"I'll need to get my instruments then."

"Send someone to get them for you. Mr. Thatcher, you'll be in charge of this ship. Think of a name for her, because I already forgot what the Spaniards called her."

"*Poseidon*," Thatcher said.

"Good. Keep whatever crew you want. When we get to Puerto Rico, it will be your job to sell her."

"All right. I'll need Manzanares and Pereira then. I don't trust the new men."

"Phillips, Clarke, I'll need you back on the *Doom*. Manzanares, Pereira, you're staying, Mr. Thatcher is the captain of this ship. I'll see you all in San Juan."

Some of the pirates returned to the *Howling Doom*. James was among those who elected to stay. The *Poseidon* ended up with a crew of about thirty. Its original crew were still floating in the water nearby, some tried to catch on to the ship but were chased away by gunshots.

"Mr. Johnson, you are now the temporary bosun," Thatcher said. "Mr. Manzanares, you're the quartermaster. Pereira, first mate. Time to go, gentlemen. Unfurl the sails, set course for northeast."

On the *Howling Doom*, pirates were chasing off stowaways with musket fire, and it turned into target practice.

"Wait, let the new recruits fire a few shots," Wright said. "I want them to prove their loyalty."

"You, over here. Come on," Roger said. He gave his musket to Miguel de Toledo.

He gently rested the barrel on the stern and slowly aimed at somebody in the water below.

"What's taking him so long?" Hammond said.

Miguel fired, and the ball hit his old captain.

"He hit the captain!" Roger said. "That son of a bitch actually hit his own captain! Bravo, *señor*, bravo."

Miguel gave the musket back to Roger as everyone within reach patted him on the back.

"You'll fit right in," Hammond said. "We like overachievers in here."

Another new guy, Antonio Maldonado, took a shot but it went over the first mate's head.

"On firm ground that would've been a headshot," Roger said. "Good job. *Bueno*."

On the *Poseidon,* Keeling wagered Johnson that he could take out the furthest sailor in three shots or less. Thatcher told them to get back to work. Before long, the heads of the floating sailors were out of sight.

James, Pereira, and a few others climbed the mainmast and cut the gaskets to let the sails fly. Once the sails were unfurled and trimmed, James went to the helm to speak with Ashborne.

"How are we doing?"

"The Mona Passage is a fucking mess, with sand banks and unpredictable currents, and on top of that we'll be sailing into the trade winds."

"How long is it going to take?"

"If we were going the opposite way, about one day, give or take. So I'd say two days, no less."

"Why couldn't we go through the Windward Passage?"

"Because captain didn't want it. Then again, we got a free ship, that's extra money on top of the Porto Bello prize. I'm not complaining about that."

The rest of the day was busy. Every hour or so they had to change direction to keep the *Poseidon* moving towards Puerto Rico. They could reach no more than half of the ship's top speed. They worked until the evening, then raided the galley and ate most of what they found. After dinner, half of the crew went to sleep while the other half stood watch and kept the ship going northeast.

In the morning, James found out that Ashborne had not had any sleep.

"I think we're almost past the sand banks now, the rest should be easier. I'll get some sleep when we're out of the passage."

At noon, they had successfully navigated the *Poseidon* out of the Mona Passage and Thatcher finally convinced Ashborne to get some sleep. The crew spent the whole day working on the sails, and by dusk there were still miles to go.

The next morning Johnson woke the whole crew early.

"Let's get moving, gents. We're about to reach San Juan."

"Why did you need to wake us so fucking early?" James said, getting out of the hammock.

"We need everyone off the ship if we're going to sell it."

It was a nice sunny morning. The shores of Puerto Rico were visible in the distance.

"What's for breakfast?"

"No breakfast," Thatcher said. "You can eat in a tavern somewhere. I want to sell this ship as quickly as I can."

The pirates worked the sails and rigging on empty stomachs, complaining the whole way. After a while, they saw the city.

"Everyone, listen up," Thatcher started. "When you get to the city, get something to eat, don't drink any rum, and certainly *do not* get yourselves in trouble. Don't talk to anyone, don't go the whorehouse—save it all for when we reach Nassau. Remember, these people don't like you. The *Doom* will be here at dusk. If you're not at the port at dusk, you'll be left behind. Are there any questions? Good. Let's get this over with."

They turned the ship one last time, and the *Poseidon* was headed for the port.

"Mr. Pereira," Thatcher said, "you're going to play the captain. Carlos doesn't have the people skills for that. Come up with a fancy name. When in doubt…" He tossed Pereira a bag of coins.

"Aye, sir."

The locals cheered their arrival. A bunch of people stopped to look at the ship that had just arrived. As it approached the dock, the pirates furled the sails and let the current take the ship closer before throwing ropes to the dockers who tied the ship down. Once the ship was secured in place, the crew were finally able to go ashore.

James was the first one to get off the ship. He was stopped by a dockworker who asked him something in Spanish. The only word that James picked up was *capitán*.

"¡*Capitán*!" he yelled. Pereira showed up immediately. James pointed at the dockworker with his thumb and moved out of the way.

"¿*Eres el capitán*?"

"*Si. Capitán Bernardo Guillermo Cristóbal Alicante Menéndez de Santander*." He handed a few coins to the man to stave off further questions.

Meanwhile, James caught up with Rhodes and Manzanares.

"Hey, do you mind if I go with you? I want to be around someone who speaks Spanish."

"Sure."

Carlos approached a young woman and asked something in Spanish. She answered and quickly walked away.

"What did you tell her?"

"I asked if there was a good place to eat. She said there's a tavern just down the street."

"Do you think they know that we're pirates?" Rhodes asked.

"We sure don't look like regular sailors," Manzanares said. "Especially you, with that giant golden cross hanging from your neck. Could you at least put that thing under your shirt?"

"No. I got it in Porto Bello. It's my prize."

"Doesn't matter," James said. "They'll still notice that he's wearing a silk shirt."

"I like how it feels on my skin."

"This idiot will get us killed."

"Both of you just be quiet," Manzanares said. "Let me do all the talking. If someone tries to talk to you, pretend that you're French or something."

"We don't speak French."

"These people don't speak French either. Just make up random words. Or better yet, don't say anything."

Down the street was a small tavern. Its windows were small and it was dark inside. Carlos told James and Rhodes to sit at the corner table and went to order some food.

"Can you find out if there's a whorehouse in here?" Rhodes asked when Manzanares returned.

"You'll get in trouble. You always get in trouble."

"I'll behave. I'm sober this time."

"No you won't. You'll demand something disgusting and they'll kick you out. Whores in this town don't play with shit or blood."

"You know what, I'll find the whorehouse myself."

"I told you," James said. "This man is an idiot and he'll get us all hanged."

"Fuck you!"

"Quiet!" Manzanares whispered. "Are you *trying* to start trouble?"

A girl brought the food – three bowls of chicken stew with peas, olives, and a bunch of other stuff James didn't recognize. She also brought a jug of water.

"Why didn't you get us rum?"

"Rhodes, I swear to God, if you keep bitching about everything, I will kill you myself."

They ate in silence. A few men drinking aguardiente at the nearest table were giving them weird looks. The pirates finished their food, emptied the jug, left a few pieces of eight on the table and left.

"It's still early," James said when they went outside. "What do we do now?"

"Whores."

"Shut up, Rhodes."

"Just ask somebody where the whorehouse is."

"Fine."

Manzanares had a quick conversation with a sketchy guy.

"Second right, then left at the end of the street. Can't miss it."

"Thanks."

Rhodes split off to look for the whorehouse.

"What do we do now?" James asked.

"Go back to the dock. We'll see if we can learn something about the ships here. If there's nothing there, we'll see if this place could be sacked."

They met some of their crewmates on the way, and told them where to find the tavern and how to order food in Spanish. A couple of pirates were hanging around in the shade near the dock, just waiting it out.

There was a sloop that had just come in. Dockers were unloading the cargo. There was a schooner that was getting ready to leave in a few days, according to a man working on it. And then there was a galleon.

The ship was at least several decades old, and it showed. The sides were discolored and with a lot of paint chipped off, and some parts had been repaired or replaced to keep it afloat. It had lost its former beauty.

"Let's go talk to the crew," Carlos said.

They met a man and Manzanares politely asked if he was part of the ship's crew. They talked for several minutes, until one question made the man pause before answering. Manzanares said a few more words and they walked away.

"What did you tell him?" James asked.

"Asked a few questions about the ship. Old galleon, called *San Antonio,* on its last trip. Then I asked if they're hiring. He said no, they don't need any extra crew and they're leaving tomorrow. That last question was about cargo. He asked me why I wanted to know, so I didn't push it. I think there might be something valuable in that galleon."

"Should we ask about that frigate over there?"

"No, I think we've got our target," Manzanares said. "We just need to let the captain know."

"So what now?"

"I'd say let's go and take a look at the fort."

James and Carlos walked along the harbor, analyzing the area.

"At least a dozen guns in that bastion, six or seven pointing straight at the mouth."

"But it's unsupported from the land side," Manzanares said. "It could be taken over with a decent crew."

"I've seen maybe half a dozen soldiers so far. They're not well prepared for an attack."

"Look at the open space between us and the fortress. They're not stupid. They thought about an attack on land."

"Let's keep our distance," James said. "I don't think we're supposed to be here."

They followed the wall along the northern coast.

"They made a bunch of gun ports, but don't have any guns," James said. "Those are just holes."

"Too far from the fort to be useful. In a surprise attack, they're fucked."

They spent an hour walking along the wall and searching for good spots to land a few hundred pirates. After a while they went back to the dock to wait for their ship.

"Rhodes, did you find the whorehouse?" James asked when Rhodes returned.

"No. I went where Manzanares told me and I found a fucking graveyard."

The launches came after sunset.

"We found something interesting," James told Thatcher on the launch.

"What's that?"

"An old galleon. Leaves tomorrow."

"And?"

"Don't know what's inside, but it seems like a decent target," Manzanares said.

"Wait until we're back on the ship. Captain will be interested."

The launches quietly made their way to the *Howling Doom*, anchored just inside the harbor. As soon as the last boat reached the ship, Wright gave the order to set sail.

"How much did you get?" he asked Thatcher the moment his foot stepped on the deck.

"Plenty." Thatcher handed Wright a sack of money. "Mr. McDougall and Mr. Manzanares here claim that they found something of interest."

"Go ahead."

"There's an old galleon that's supposed to leave port tomorrow," James said.

"I talked to the crew," Manzanares said. "It's called *San Antonio.* I asked what the cargo was, and he became suspicious and didn't answer. Might be a long shot, but there could be something valuable."

"Good job, gentlemen. Whatever is in that galleon, I want it. Mr. Thatcher, inform the crew that we're going for that ship. No drinking. I want everyone rested and ready early in the morning."

"Yes, captain."

"I want every watch to keep an eye out. They'll either go west to the colonies or north back to Spain. We need to be ready to go either way."

"I'll take care of it, captain."

They sailed the *Doom* a good distance away from the harbor and anchored there.

James ate dinner and went to sleep. He woke up around dawn. Milford was shaking his hammock.

"Your watch is up."

James got out of the hammock and rubbed his eyes and went to the upper deck. Jack Hammond was watching the coast.

"You know what that galleon looks like, right?" he asked.

"Yes."

"Take the spyglass, tell everyone if you see it."

James stared at the bay, but there was nothing. San Juan was still asleep. After a while, he saw a sail and his heart started racing, only to realize that it was just a sloop. It sailed west.

When his watch ended, James went back to his hammock but couldn't fall asleep. He went to the galley to see if he could get something to eat, but it was locked, and Beasley was still asleep. James returned to the upper deck and watched the bay with de Toledo, the newest recruit. He tried to start a conversation, but the Spaniard wasn't very talkative.

One by one, the rest of the crew woke up. Some of them were loading the cannons, others were cleaning and loading their pistols and muskets. The *San Antonio* was still nowhere to be found. Keeling took over the spyglass duty from de Toledo.

"It still hasn't showed up?" Keeling asked.

"It's still early."

Half an hour later, Keeling saw a sail.

"I think that's her!"

"Let me see." James took the spyglass and looked at the ship coming out of the bay. It was the *San Antonio*. There was no doubt.

"It's her! The galleon is here!"

"WEIGH THE ANCHOR!" Thatcher shouted. "GET ON THE YARDS! MOVE IT!"

James climbed the foremast shrouds and positioned himself on the footrope of the topsail yard. Below, his crewmates were raising the anchor.

"She's headed north!" someone shouted.

"Anchor's aweigh!"

James was holding onto the gasket, waiting for the command to cut it. There were pirates on each side, each one ready to quickly unfurl the sail.

"Anchor home!"

"Unfurl all sails!"

James cut the gasket and coiled and tied it. On the deck, other pirates were bracing the yards. He made his way back to the shrouds and climbed down.

"McDougall, Milford, man the guns, starboard side!" Phillips was yelling. "You two, guns! Let's go!"

James got behind one of the starboard cannons. Scott was still on the mainmast. This time James was working with Joshua Wellington.

The *San Antonio* was heavily loaded and the *Doom* was gaining on it.

"I think they know something is up," Hammond said, looking through the spyglass. "I see a lot of movement on deck."

"Let's close the gap first, then we raise the black," Wright said. "If they want to fight, we'll fight."

The ships were just over a quarter mile apart.

The crew of the *San Antonio* raised a Spanish flag.

"Should we fly Spanish colors?" Thatcher asked.

"Don't bother. They know. We'll catch up to them soon enough anyway."

"If they weren't suspicious before, they are now," Hammond said.

They waited and watched as the *Doom* got closer, eventually reducing the distance to just under two hundred yards.

"Do it," Wright said.

"Fly the black!"

Keene and Johnson raised the black flag.

The *San Antonio* began slowly turning to larboard.

"They're trying to broadside us!" Thatcher shouted. "Helmsman, bear down, larboard!"

The Spaniards expected it. They had picked a good angle, making it difficult for the pirates to go around them and avoid the broadside. The wind was on their side.

"They aren't stupid, I'll give them that," Wright said. "Gun crews, ready! Helmsman, to larboard, as hard as we can."

"What are we doing, captain?" Thatcher said.

"They have the wind, we can't beat them. Best we can do is fight broadside to broadside."

San Antonio was bearing down more and more, and the wind pushed it faster and faster. The *Howling Doom* did the same thing, but it was at a disadvantage.

Wright watched as the ships fought for position. He seemed perfectly calm.

One of *San Antonio*'s cannons fired, then another one. The first shot fell into the water well in front of the ship, the other hit the hull just below the waterline, leaving a dent.

"Do we have guns on them?" Wright shouted.

"No, sir!" Phillips answered.

The *San Antonio* fired four more shots, two of them hitting the hull. The *Howling Doom* kept turning until finally the cannons were aimed at the galleon.

"We have it!"

"FIRE!"

James covered his ears as Wellington lit the fuse. The cannon fired, releasing a plume of white smoke and smashing a hole in the galleon's hull. Two other cannonballs hit the ship, while the rest ended up going too high or too low. The Spanish answered with more cannon fire, and this time they were more accurate. One cannonball hit the ship just to the side of James's cannon, ripping through Wellington's torso and bouncing off the deck and smashing through the bulwark on the other side.

James rammed the swab into the cannon and pulled it back out. Roger appeared seemingly out of nowhere to help out. Without saying anything, he poured the powder into the cannon. A cannonball flew right over their heads. They kept loading the cannon as if nothing happened. Roger lit the fuse and the gun fired, sending grapeshot into the galleon and killing one of the sailors.

Suddenly, there was a massive explosion on the *San Antonio*, much louder than a cannon shot. The pirates couldn't see what was going on until the wind carried away the smoke. Something had caused a fire in the ship's powder magazine, and its entire supply of powder exploded. The *San Antonio* had an enormous hole in its side that started just below the deck and ended below the waterline. It was rapidly taking water.

"What the fuck happened?" Roger said.

"Captain," Hammond said, "should we prepare the launches?"

"Don't. We won't make it in time. And you'll have to fight a bunch of desperate Spaniards trying to get into the launch. Let's just head back to Nassau."

They unfurled the sails and turned west. With the wind at its stern, the *Howling Doom* was almost gliding over water.

"I guess we'll never know what the cargo was," James said looking back at the galleon.

"Probably sugar or coffee," Roger said. "They wouldn't use a rickety old ship for anything important."

"Yeah, but still. I just want to know what was in there."

The *San Antonio* sank lower and lower. The galleon did not have enough boats to fit the entire crew. Water filled the hold and what was left of the magazine, slowly dragging the ship under. Some of the sailors couldn't swim, and they went down quickly. Others tried to hold on or climb into the launches, but the captain and the lucky ones were punching them and hitting their hands in fear that they might capsize the boat.

Forty-six members of the crew survived the sinking of the *San Antonio*. They drifted in the Atlantic for two months before encountering a British ship. By the time the boats were found, all forty-six had perished.

CHAPTER IX

Williamsburg, Colony of Virginia

"Tell me about Nassau."

"There's nothing there but pirates and whores hanging out on the beach."

"Sounds like a lot of fun."

"It stops being fun after a while."

"Why?"

"Rum and whores eventually get boring. And there is nothing else to do there."

"There is the beach, right?"

"And?"

"Are the beaches pretty?"

"Some of the most beautiful beaches you'll ever see."

"Didn't you ever go for a swim?"

"I've never seen a single person in Nassau going for a swim."

"Why not?"

"I don't know."

"It sounds nice. Going for a dip in the Caribbean, at night, with a beautiful lady by your side…"

"You mean a whore."

"All right, fine. The Caribbean, at night, with a beautiful whore. It still sounds like a good time."

"Sure, but it won't be so fun the next day, when that whore is fucking someone else."

"Are the whores at Nassau British or Spanish?"

"Both. You can also find French, Portuguese, African, mixed, even Chinese – you name it, Nassau has it. Any skin color, any hair color, hell, they'll even find you a woman with the perfect eye color, just as long as you are able to afford it."

"Wow." Rob chuckled. "Which ones were the best?"

"Everyone says the French whores are the best in the business. I don't know, I never had one. When I heard about a French brothel, I was already out of money, and those ladies charge *a lot*."

"If I ever get a chance, I'll have to try."

"Don't. They will ruin your life. Just stay away from all of them. Those women can be just as dangerous as the pirates."

"Really?"

"One man in our crew, Theodore Milford, had his throat slit by a Nassau whore."

"Damn. What happened?"

"I don't know."

They were quiet for a while.

"How many brothels are there in Nassau?" Rob asked.

"Every place in Nassau I've ever been to was either a whorehouse or a tavern. I'm not sure if there are any other kinds of buildings there."

"Where did you eat then?"

"At one of the taverns. There was more drinking than eating."

"Did you ever end up sleeping in the tavern?"

"Sometimes. Sometimes somewhere outside. Most of the time I would just wake up somewhere and couldn't remember how I got there. One time we found a crewmate on the roof."

"Must've been a fun night."

"In Nassau, when you start drinking, you drink until you drop. And then you wake up and it starts all over again."

"Sounds amazing."

"It's not amazing. It's just a bunch of pirates drinking their lives away. They're only tame because of rum. If Nassau ran out of drink, it would probably turn into a slaughterhouse."

"How many times have you been there?"

"Just once. We stayed there for several weeks. We were planning to go there when… when I got captured."

"Do you have to be a pirate to get into Nassau?"

"No. But there isn't a good reason for anyone else to go there."

"You're telling me that the whole town is a never-ending celebration on the beach with pirates, women, and booze. Why wouldn't people go there?"

"There's pirates. Trust me, a tavern full of pirates is… Let's just say there is no tavern in the world that gets so… dangerous, for starters."

"It still sounds pretty fun."

"It's pretty fun until someone knocks one of your teeth out with a tankard."

"Did that happen to you?"

"No. But I saw that happen."

"Did you have fun when you were in Nassau?"

James paused.

"A little."

"If you had a chance, would you return?"

"To Nassau?"

"Yes."

"No."

"Not even for a day?"

"Not even for an hour."

"You don't miss those days?"

"No."

"Really?"

"Really."

"What *do* you miss? From your pirate days?"

"Nothing."

"Nothing?"

"Can't think of one thing I miss."

"Don't you miss at least some of the men you sailed with?"

"All of them are dead."

"I'm sorry to hear that."

"Don't be. Even the good ones were bastards."

"Come on, there had to be a few who were decent fellows."

"Before the *Doom*, I was on the crew of a merchant ship. I'd say some of those men were good people. One of them, Mark, was my friend. Probably the only friend I had in years."

"Is he still alive?"

"He's dead."

"What happened to him?"

"We had a lot of people die. Sailing is dangerous. Some fall off the rigging and crash into the deck. Some fall overboard and can't be found, especially at night. There were a couple of suicides. And, well, many were killed by pirates when our ship was captured."

"Is that what happened to your friend?"

"Yes."

"It's sad."

"Can we go back to talking about other things?" James said.

"Sure."

"What were we just talking about?"

"Nassau."

"I hate Nassau. Can we talk about something else?"

"I think I would enjoy Nassau."

"For the first day or two. Then it starts getting ugly."

"I want to go someplace like Nassau, so I can live right on the beach, and watch the sea every day."

"You'd get tired of seeing the same thing every day."

"How can the view get boring on a beach in the Caribbean?"

"After a while, everything becomes boring. Trust me."

"I'd still rather live on a beach."

CHAPTER X
Nassau, the Bahamas

The *Howling Doom* and its crew reached the West Indies. They passed between the Inagua islands and went around the Bahamian islands from the south. The wind was good and they quickly covered a long distance.

The crew seemed more relaxed than usual. Even Thatcher started asking pirates for a job to be done rather than yelling to get to work. The journey to Nassau was like the end of a long day of work.

Some of the pirates started drinking before going to sleep, and nobody said anything about it.

"What's the occasion?" James asked one night when he found Clarke and Beasley drinking rum in the galley.

"No occasion," Beasley said. "Just helping empty the rum barrels. We'll be in Nassau in two days, we'll restock anyway."

"Nassau is wonderful," Clarke said. "It's not fun the first time, because you get one hundred lashes, but if you make it through that, it's paradise."

"What are the lashes for?"

"Don't listen to him," Beasley said. "He's just teasing you."

"Is that place really as amazing as everyone says?"

"When I die, I don't want to go to heaven, I want to go back to Nassau."

"As if you ever had a chance of going to heaven," Clarke chuckled. "You're going straight to hell with the rest of us."

"And I'll party with the devil." Beasley finished his rum and stood up to get a refill.

James asked everyone about Nassau, and everyone gave him the same answer: you'll see. The only exceptions were de Toledo, Maldonado, and a few others, who had never been there.

"I don't know what's in Nassau," de Toledo told him, "but I've heard a few people call it the Satan's den. It must be a really fun place."

The closer they got to New Providence island, the less everyone cared about work. Even the captain stopped giving commands. He would only show up on deck to enjoy the breeze and the sunlight. The *Howling Doom* was in vacation mood.

"Attention, gentlemen," Thatcher said one morning. "Tomorrow we should be in Nassau."

The pirates cheered.

"Since the journey is almost over and there's no risk of you gambling your money away on the ship, today each and every one of you will be given your share of the money you've earned."

The crew erupted. Pirates were cheering, singing, dancing, even hugging. Thatcher watched it, smiling.

"There's reason to cheer, gentlemen. You did a good job, and the shares are big. We might just be the most successful crew in the Caribbean. Now, let's get to work. Mr. Anderson, you're up."

Thatcher led Anderson to the captain's cabin, and he came out triumphantly holding a bag full of pieces of eight.

"Mr. Ashborne." Ashborne came back with a bigger bag than Anderson's. As the ship's navigator, he was paid extra.

"Mr. Beasley."

"He's in the galley."

"Go tell him to come get his money. Mr. Burbage."

One by one, the pirates received their hard-earned money. Some immediately started counting, others hid theirs. After McCaslin was called, James stood up and went to wait by the captain's cabin.

"Mr. McDougall."

James entered the cabin. The captain was lying in his cot. Byrd and Ortega were sitting at the desk, doing the accounting.

"McDougall…" Byrd said, looking at the papers. "You were on that ship we took near Jamaica, correct?"

"Yes."

"Congratulations on your first payday. I need you to sign here. If you don't know how, just mark an X."

James made a small *x* next to his name, and Ortega gave him a bag of coins.

"Don't spend it all in one place. Next."

Cartwright, who had earned extra for the bravery he had shown in Porto Bello, was showing off his cash.

"Look at all this gold. I'm a rich man now. I want to be called Sir Cartwright from now on."

He triumphantly raised the bag in the air with one hand. As he walked a victory lap, Hammond tripped him. Cartwright fell down and dropped the money. Almost half of the coins spilled from the bag. Some of it landed on deck, some of it ended up in the water. The whole crew broke into laughter.

"Nicely done, *sir*."

"You're a real aristocrat, Cartwright," Roger said. "You got your hands on some money and in five minutes you've wasted half of it. Good job, Your Royal Highness."

"Eat shit, Davies," Cartwright said, picking up coins off the deck.

James had to stand watch pretty late that night, and once it was over he went to the galley for some rum. He had a few tankards with Maldonado, who was on the same watch, and Manzanares, who was an insomniac. They left some for the next watch and went to sleep.

"Tomorrow we'll be in Nassau," Manzanares said as they were splitting up. "You boys are about to have the time of your lives."

When James woke up, he found the entire crew had gone from relaxed to excited. The ship had passed several Bahamian cays, which meant that Nassau was close.

A few pirates were cursing whoever had emptied the last rum barrel the night before. Some stood around the bow, staring in the distance. Hammond started singing an old shanty called *The Fireship*. James didn't know the lyrics, so he just stood at the bow with the others and listened. More pirates came and joined in with every verse, and near the end at least half of the crewmen were singing along.

"Hey! Enough singing!" Thatcher yelled. "I need two men in the galley helping Mr. Beasley. Come on. Warren, go. Another one. Anyone? Your Highness Sir Cartwright, would you kindly move your idiot self to the galley? Now!"

The *Doom* gently sailed along and passed the last cay in the afternoon. By then the sun was behind storm clouds. Soon it started raining.

"Fucking perfect," Hammond grumbled. "Nothing but sun the whole week, and as soon as we get close to Nassau, it's fucking pouring."

Wind picked up and Thatcher ordered the topgallants furled. James ran over to help out, and in a few seconds he was drenched. Rain still felt unpleasant, but at least he couldn't get any wetter. It was cold and James's fingers were stiff. As soon as the job was done, he went to the galley to get warm. Other pirates had the same idea, and eventually Beasley had to kick everyone out.

Hammond came down to the lower deck.

"I can see New Providence. We're almost there, boys."

In less than an hour they reached the port of Nassau and Wright gave the order to furl the sails and drop the anchor.

"The voyage is over," the captain announced. "When you get off the ship, take all your crap with you. Anything you leave behind will be mine. You were a great crew. We had a great run. Now get the fuck off my ship, shitbags."

With the rain still coming down, the pirates climbed into the launches and waded to the shore. They all had their guns, cutlasses, money, and various other stuff with them. Roger had gone to Beasley and taken a few empty potato sacks to put his belongings in. He gave one to James.

Despite the rain, New Providence Island was beautiful. The beach was full of tents inhabited by pirates, bums, and other vagrants. Many of them had fires going.

"Welcome to Nassau," Roger said. "It looks better in sunlight."

"Can we find a place to stay first?"

"I know a place. Follow me."

They ran to a house a good distance from the beach. The owner, an older man with a big belly, smiled and showed them to a shabby room with two beds. Roger paid him and he walked away happy.

"This is not a bad place," James said. "Which bed do you want?"

"They're pretty much the same. Leave your stuff, take some money, we're going to a tavern."

The rain had mostly subsided. The streets were still empty.

"The man who owns the house, he's a former pirate," Roger said. "He rents the place out because he's unable to live on a ship anymore. Says it's bad for his health."

"How many pirates are here?"

"Hundreds. We run this place. The hobos you saw near the beach—they're pirates without a ship. I don't think there's a single law-abiding citizen left here. Here we are. Watch this."

Roger opened the door and entered the tavern, James followed. They were met with cheers. Some of the *Howling Doom* crewmen were already there. James recognized several faces from the Porto Bello raid.

"Can we get something to eat here?" Roger said.

"Right away!"

Most tables were already taken, but they saw Hammond waving from across the room; there were a couple of empty seats at his table. They sat down and the tavern keeper brought them some kind of meat with vegetables and put two more tankards on the table and poured some rum from a jug.

"A toast, gentlemen," Hammond said. "Here's to us cheating death once again, and to Spanish gold."

They knocked their tankards and drank, and got a refill, and Hammond told the guy to leave the jug. Then the pirates drank to the *Howling Doom*, the captain, the quartermaster, and those that didn't make it.

"Anther toast, gentlemen," Hammond said. "To the courageous Mr. McDougall, who helped me fight off two bastards in Porto Bello. Had he not been there to watch my back, I may not be here today. Thank you, James. To you."

"Come on, Jack, you make it sound like I'm the fucking Hercules."

"To James!" Roger said.

"To James!" They drank again.

Men at another table started singing *Spanish Ladies*. Most of the tavern joined in. Some of the pirates had decent vocals, others were just making noise. James knew the song well, but wasn't drunk enough to sing. He just drank his rum and listened.

After the song was over, they toasted Spanish ladies, then English ladies. While they were drinking, a few pirates from Whitaker's crew approached the table. Among them was Moses Williams, one of the three men who scouted Porto Bello.

"Hey, Doomsmen, we haven't seen you in a while, what took you so long?" Williams asked.

"We went around Hispaniola," Hammond said. "On the way, we took a French schooner and a Spanish brig, sold that brig in San Juan, then tried to take a galleon, but the fucking thing sank."

"Sank?"

"Yeah, somehow the magazine caught fire and everything exploded. Blew a giant hole in the hull, it sank in ten minutes."

"Couldn't be a cannonball, right?"

"Don't know." Hammond took a gulp of rum. "It was in the middle of the battle. We're firing cannons, everything's going like usual, suddenly there's this loud *BANG*! Chunks of wood flying everywhere."

"Did you recover anything?"

"No. It was going down quickly. Even if we made it to the ship, there wouldn't have been enough time to get anything."

"Sea water would've ruined sugar or tobacco anyway," Williams said. "What about the brig you sold? What happened?"

"The captain was nice, he wanted us to take the cargo and leave everyone alone, but the ship was just beautiful—on her maiden voyage—so we had everyone jump in the water. A few men decided to join our ranks."

"How much did you get for her?"

"You'll have to ask the quartermaster, he did the selling. He knows how to haggle, I'm sure he got a good price."

"We just went right back to Nassau after Porto Bello."

"You boys did real well in Porto Bello," Hammond said. "It was a tough battle, but your crew fought like hell."

"Yeah. Our boys did half the work there."

"Bullshit. Us and Stafford's crew could've done it by ourselves."

"You'd be rotting in Panama sun if it wasn't for us holding your crew by the hand the whole way."

Every crewman of the *Doom* stood up. Hammond threw his rum into Williams's face, followed by a quick left hook. Roger smacked the nearest pirate with his tankard. Phillips grabbed a man half his size by the neck with both hands and started choking him. James saw a man he didn't recognize standing right next to him, and immediately socked him in the face, just like one of the many fights with other kids back in the old days in Portsmouth. The man fell to the ground and Roger, who was standing right next to James, kicked him in the head.

Roger took a punch to the jaw from one of Whitaker's men, Phillips was fighting two guys at the same time, and someone stepped in to keep Hammond from killing Williams, who was on the ground, his face and shirt covered in blood from his broken nose. Some man tried to hit James but missed, then grabbed his shirt and they started wrestling. All of a sudden, a shot rang out. The tavern immediately went quiet. Fighting stopped. Everyone was looking around. One of Whitaker's men had shot some fat guy whom James didn't recognize, a pirate of some other crew.

"OUT! ALL OF YOU!" the tavern keeper yelled. "We're closing! And take the body with you!"

Everyone who was in the tavern slowly went out the door, the gunshot still ringing in their ears. Roger was bleeding from the nose. Hammond was burning with rage and mumbled under his nose that he wanted to kill Williams, who was covered in blood and being helped by a friend. It was dark outside and the rain had stopped. Somebody dragged the corpse out of the tavern and left it in the middle of the street.

"Where are we going?" James asked Roger.

"One of the other taverns."

Just a few doors down there was a smaller tavern called *The Harpoon*. They were warmly greeted by the owner, an older guy who was missing half of of his right index finger. Phillips and a couple of others showed up too. They ordered beer and drank in peace. None of the *Marlin*'s men were there. The pirates shared memories and told jokes, but as the beers kept coming, the conversation made less and less sense. James and Roger barely made their way back to the room, then each fell on the other one's bed and they both fell asleep.

When James woke up, he had the worst headache of his life. It was almost noon. Roger was still asleep. James woke him up.

"It's late."

"So what?" Roger said. "We don't have to be anywhere. We're not on a ship. We're free to do whatever we want. Including sleeping in." He stood up and stretched.

"So what are we doing today?"

"First we're going to get ourselves something to drink. Then we'll see."

They each took a fistful of coins and went outside. The march through the sunlit street was torturous. James and Roger ended up at the *Compass*, the same tavern where the fight had broken out the previous night.

"Hey! I don't want you two in here!" the owner yelled. "I don't want any of your crew coming in here and starting fights."

Roger opened the little bag where he kept the money and took out a few coins and slammed them on the counter. James took a few pieces of eight from his own bag and casually dropped them next to Roger's.

"All right," the tavern keeper said. "What will it be? Rum?"

"Yes, please."

The owner brought a jug of rum and two tankards, and the pirates started drinking. Ashborne and Phillips showed up moments later. Phillips had a black eye. They dropped some pieces of eight on the counter and joined in.

They drank until their hangovers were gone. Phillips and Roger left. James and Ashborne talked for a while about sailing, then decided to go elsewhere.

"Hey, can we get some wine for the road?"

The owner gave them two bottles of wine and waved them goodbye.

James and Ashborne went to the beach and stood there and drank. The wine wasn't very tasty, but it was strong. The beach was gorgeous. White sand, pure and clean and soft. The sea, waves gently rolling on the beach, so clear you could see the bottom through ten feet of water. The sun beaming down from above and a slight breeze to keep the heat from becoming unbearable.

"Now I understand why everyone talks so highly of this place," James said. "This is paradise. I don't want to ever leave."

"It gets better. Let's go find some whores."

They finished off the wine and tossed the bottles into the sea and went into the town, circling around the tents of those who couldn't afford anything fancier. Drunken pirates were everywhere. Some were sleeping on the sand, and would wake up with a nasty sunburn. At least two of them had been sailing with the *Howling Doom*. One pirate was lying prone on the ground by a tavern, empty bottle in hand. When they passed him, James recognized Cartwright.

"I'm going to show you the best whorehouse in Nassau," Ashborne said.

"How many are here?"

"Pretty much every place that isn't a tavern is a whorehouse. Welcome to paradise. But the place where we're going is a level above that."

"Are the girls there goddesses or something?"

"They have the most beautiful Spanish girls you'll ever see. So yeah, pretty much."

James and Ashborne went down Nassau's unpaved streets. On the way they found a couple of smaller taverns, at least two whorehouses, and a bakery. Finally, they reached a large unkempt house.

"This part of town is mostly Spanish-speaking," Ashborne said. "Most pirates never need to go this far. Don't ask me how I found this place, because you do *not* want to know."

He opened the door and entered without bothering to knock. On the inside, the house was nice, but its age was showing. An older lady—probably the madam—was standing in the hallway. Ashborne took out several coins and gave them to her. James did the same. He decided to give the woman an extra piece of eight, just in case. She glanced at the coins, nodded, and smiled. Ashborne whispered something to her in clumsy Spanish. She nodded.

They quietly followed the madam upstairs. There was a beautiful but faded oriental rug on the floor. James was surprised how quiet the place was. Ashborne went in through one of the doors and closed it behind him.

"*Vamos,*" the madam said.

James followed her until they reached the door at the end of a hallway. The madam opened the door. She had a warm smile.

James entered the room and heard the door close behind him. The room had a large open window, a dirty carpet, a small desk with a couple of candlesticks on it, and a bed with sheets that passed for white. On that bed sat a girl.

She was about eighteen or nineteen, with flowing black hair, petite figure, gorgeous brown eyes, and a cute smile. James had never seen a girl as beautiful as her.

She stood up and slowly walked up to him.

"Hi," she said. "My name is Gabriela."

"I'm James."

Before he could figure out what else to say, she wrapped her hands around his neck and kissed him. James picked her up and carried her to the bed. They hurriedly undressed and made love. It was intense, passionate, and sweaty.

When it was done, Gabriela curled up beside him and rested her head on his shoulder. James put his arm around her. They fell asleep like that.

James woke up a couple of hours later. Gabriela was still asleep. He didn't move until she woke up.

"You're so cute when you're asleep," he said.

She smiled.

"Will you come back tomorrow?"

"Sure." James got dressed, Gabriela gave him one last kiss, and he left.

He found his way back, went to the *Compass*, and got himself another bottle of wine. James sat on the beach and slowly drank the wine as he watched the ocean. The sun was setting, and he thought how perfect it would've been if Nassau was on the western shore of the island and he could watch the sun setting over the ocean.

James threw the empty bottle into the water and went to one of the taverns and ordered some food. Manzanares was also there, passed out on the floor. When James was done eating, he joined a group of pirates at another table and together they drank a ridiculous amount of rum.

After a while, James stood up, took his tankard, and went to look for his crew. A young pirate accidentally bumped into him. Half of James's rum spilled on his hand and was dripping to the floor. Without stopping to think, he swung the tankard, spilling the rest of the rum everywhere, hitting the man in the head. He fell down, bleeding from the mouth, and spit out a tooth. James kicked him in the groin and left the tavern.

He walked slowly. His feet wouldn't move the way he wanted. Eventually, he found his way to another tavern, struggled to get coins out of the bag, and got himself more rum. Roger was there, and so was Clarke.

He woke up in the same tavern. It was morning. Other pirates were there, passed out on the tables, chairs, and floor. A couple were already awake, and they had already started drinking. James ordered a beer to help with the headache. Then another one, then a third one.

He went around drunk pirates and out of the building. It was another beautiful, sunny day. James decided to go see Gabriela again. He couldn't remember the way back to the brothel very well, but he managed to figure it out.

Inside, he handed the madam a few pieces of eight and made his way to Gabriela's room by himself. As soon as he entered, she ran up to him and gave him a kiss.

"I missed you," she said.

They made love in the blistering midday heat, and fell asleep in each other's arms.

He couldn't stop thinking about her. James came back the same night, and she was excited to see him. She was tender and loving and sweet. She made him forget everything else.

He went to see her again the next morning. James didn't even stop to eat breakfast or get a drink. None of it mattered. He just wanted to fall asleep in her embrace.

When James woke up, Gabriela was still sleeping. He looked at her face, thinking how beautiful she was, and started wondering if he should just ditch the crew and stay here in paradise. Just him and this cute angel, getting drunk on the beach and making love on the sand. He had quite a bit of money, enough to sustain them for months. And if it ran out, he could get a job. Not piracy, something else, something that wouldn't keep him away from his woman. Piracy was too dangerous anyway.

After staying there for a couple of hours, James had to leave.

"Will you be back soon?" Gabriela asked as he was getting dressed.

"I'll be here tomorrow. Maybe tonight."

"Come back tonight. I'll sneak out and we'll get drunk together."

"All right. I'll see you tonight."

James went to *The Harpoon* and got himself something to eat and a beer. He couldn't stop thinking about the upcoming date with Gabriela, and her voice with that adorable Spanish accent. And that sweet smile.

And those eyes.

James went back to his room and took most of his pieces of eight and put them in the bag on his belt. He would buy Gabriela whatever she wanted. Then he got in his bed and fell asleep.

The only window in the room faced west, and James was woken up by the evening sun shining in his face. His mind was a little hazy for a while, but he finally got his thoughts in order and went to meet Gabriela. On the way,he stopped to buy a bottle of wine.

She was waiting for him behind the corner of the brothel. She gave him a passionate kiss.

"Let's go."

He put his hand around her waist, and she rested her head on his shoulder.

"James?"

"Yeah?"

"Where are you from?"

"Portsmouth."

"What's it like?"

He told her about Portsmouth, the places he liked to go to, the friends he hadn't seen in years, the trouble that just seemed to follow him, and the decision to sail the seas. Then Gabriela started talking about her childhood in Barcelona before her family had to flee to New Spain, the difficulties they faced there,how she tried to find work but ended up in Nassau with no money. James listened, sometimes taking a sip of wine, and thought to himself that there was no good reason to ever leave Nassau.

They sat on the beach as the sun was setting, watching the ocean and drinking wine. When the sun disappeared and the wine ran out, she took him by the hand and they found a secluded spot on the beach, and he made love to her.

James took Gabriela to the *Compass*, where they joined Ashborne. He, too, was there with a Spanish girl. They ordered some rum, drank to each of the girls, then to Spanish girls in general, and then it started getting out of hand. When the four of them left the tavern, it was dark outside and both pirates were stumbling left and right. Ashborne started singing *Whiskey Johnny*, but after the first two verses he forgot the lyrics. They ended up in another tavern, drinking rum and wine. James thought to himself that life was good – he was hanging out with a friend in a company of gorgeous women, drinking good rum, with pockets full of money and absolutely no worries.

He woke up early the next morning, awakened by the sun in his eyes. His head was in awful pain. James looked around and saw that he was lying by a fence. Pigs were running around on the other side of it. Ashborne was nearby, still asleep.

"Ashborne. Ashborne, wake up."

"Fuck. Where did the women go?"

"I don't know."

"What the fuck?! Someone took my money!"

James looked at his belt and saw that the bag with money was gone. The string was still there. Somebody had cut it off with a knife.

"Shit. Mine's gone too."

"It was the whores," Ashborne said. "They got us drunk and then robbed us. We're idiots. We're such fucking idiots. I'll kill that bitch Maria."

"I think I need a drink."

"You have no money, you dolt. We'll drink when this is done."

They briskly walked to the Spanish brothel. Ashborne kicked the door open.

"Where is that bitch Maria?!" he yelled. "I want my money back!"

The madam was calmly talking in rapid Spanish. Other women showed up to see what the fusswas about. Maria was among them.

"You! I want to get my fucking money back! Now!"

"Somebody took your money?" Maria said as she came down the stairs. "Oh no."

If there were any doubts of who took the money, her sly smile erased them.

"I'll say it one last time. Give me my money back."

James saw Gabriela, watching the whole incident from the second floor, smiling. She looked him straight in the eye and waved with her cute little hand.

She took my money and now she's mocking me?!

He wanted to run upstairs and make her explain herself, and punch her in the face to teach her a lesson, and then bend that lying slut over the bed and make it hurt. He wanted to hear that bitch crying.

"I'm very sorry that someone took your money," Maria said, slowly walking towards Ashborne. "But maybe I could give you something else? On the house."

Ashborne lost it. He punched Maria in the face hard enough that she fell to the ground. She was bleeding from her nose. The madam tried to intervene, yelling in Spanish, but Ashborne slapped her and she dropped to the ground and played dead. All the other girls ran into their rooms and locked the doors. Ashborne started kicking Maria in the stomach, and her crying only made him kick with more energy. He then grabbed her hair and smacked her head into the floor, again and again and again. Ashborne stopped when his arms got tired.

For a while, both pirates just stood there, looking at the scene.

James followed Ashborne to Maria's room. They looked everywhere, but the money wasn't there.

"Let's go," Ashborne said. "They probably already divided it among themselves. How much money did you have on you?"

"Not much."

"Smart man."

They walked out into the bright sunlight and headed back towards the beach. James's headache went from throbbing to stabbing.

"Last fucking time I deal with Spanish whores. Slimy backstabbing cunts. Fuck them and fuck Spain. New and old."

Ashborne went his own way. James went to the room he rented with Roger, and took some money from his stash. They met again at the *Compass*. James got himself a tankard of rum and immediately downed all of it. He got a refill and emptied the tankard again. It wasn't so much about taking away the hangover as it was about trying to forget that he let that backstabbing Spanish whore fool him like an absolute chump.

People came and went, some of them said hi to him, but James just drank his rum and ignored the surroundings and the passing time. He snapped out of it when he heard a gunshot outside. Most of the people in the tavern rushed to see the drama. James followed along.

He made his way through the crowd to see the victim. It was Ashborne.

"Will? What happened?"

James knelt by his friend. Ashborne was bleeding from a large chest wound and coughing up blood. His hands were shaking.

"What happened? Will?"

Ashborne started choking on his own blood, and somebody helped James roll him on his side. There was a dark spot on the ground. The ball had come out the other side. Ashborne coughed up more blood, struggling to breathe. His body started shaking, and when it stopped, he wasn't breathing.

The crew of the *Howling Doom* began gathering around the body as regular bystanders got bored and went back to the tavern.

"I want to find the fucker who killed my navigator and pull his eyes out with my own two hands," Thatcher said. "Does anyone know anything about this?"

"Maybe it was an accident?" Roger said. "Will was a good lad, why would anyone want to kill him?"

"Did he get in a fight recently?"

"He's never started a fight."

"He beat up a whore this morning," James said.

"How bad?" Thatcher asked.

"Smashed her head into the floor."

"Do you know where?"

"Sure."

"Lead the way."

James led a dozen of his crewmates down the sunny unpaved streets of Nassau to the Spanish brothel. Phillips kicked the door open and went in. The rest of the crew followed.

"Which one of you whores killed my navigator?!" he roared. Manzanares repeated it in Spanish.

The madam was chattering something in Spanish.

Several whores came out to see what was going on, then went back to their rooms and locked the doors.

"Bitch is lying," Manzanares said. "Says she doesn't know."

"She didn't say they didn't do it," Thatcher said. "It was one of them."

Phillips grabbed the madam by the hair.

"Don't fuck with us, you dirty old whore. Tell us and the rest of you will be fine."

She said something in Spanish, and Manzanares slapped her in the face.

"She's still lying."

Phillips dragged her to the ground and kicked her in the stomach.

"You want to play games with us?" He and Manzanares kicked her a few more times.

"What's her name? What's the name of the bitch who killed our crewmate?"

The other pirates went upstairs, but found most of the rooms locked. One of the doors was crooked and the lock was poorly installed, and Roger got it to open with one swift kick. The whore who was hiding there, seeing the pirates, climbed out the window and jumped down.

Roger ran up to the window.

"She broke her leg," he said. "Downstairs!"

They followed him outside and found the girl rolling on the ground in severe pain. Her left leg was broken just below the knee, and the bone had pierced the skin and some of it was sticking out.

"You shouldn't have fucked with our crew," Phillips said.

They surrounded her and started kicking. It didn't matter where the kicks were landing, head, stomach, legs, even hands, they just wanted to inflict as much pain on her as they could. It lasted a couple of minutes. When the barrage was over, she wasn't moving.

"Anybody have a flint?" Thatcher asked.

"I do," Manzanares said.

"Start a fire."

"Where?"

"Inside. On the carpet."

Carlos went inside and returned a minute later.

"It's done."

Thatcher found a plank and propped it against the door handle to keep it shut.

They went back to where Ashborne's body was still lying out in the open.

"See if you can find some shovels," Thatcher said. "We need to bury him."

Scott went looking and returned five minutes later with three shovels.

"Let's go."

James, Phillips, Manzanares, Scott, Douglas, and Wayland picked up Ashborne's corpse and put it on their shoulders. They went along the beach until Nassau ended, and found a spot between trees to bury him. Thatcher, Unsworth, and Keene dug the grave. Manzanares found a pair of sticks. Wayland carved Ashborne's name into one of them. James took the piece of string that used to hold his bag with money and tied the sticks into a cross.

They gently placed the body into the grave.

"Goodbye, Will."

"You were a stand-up lad."

"I'll miss you."

"You were the best damn navigator a crew could ask for."

Unsworth and Keene shoveled the dirt and Thatcher put the makeshift cross in the ground.

"Rest in peace, Will. The *Doom* will not forget you."

They went back to the *Compass* and drank to Will Ashborne. Others from their crew joined them. A pirate from another crew tried to start a song, but Hammond beat that idea out of him.

The next day, James woke up at noon. He went to *The Harpoon* and started drinking. Hammond showed up a couple of hours later.

"What happened between you, Ashborne, and those whores?"

"Ashborne showed me that place. He said those Spanish girls were amazing."

"Were they?"

"Oh yeah."

"And then?"

"They seemed like very nice ladies, so we took them to a tavern. Got drunk. Woke up in the morning with our money missing."

"How much money did you lose?"

"I don't know how much Ashborne had. I had a bunch."

"How much?"

"Probably about half my pay. Something like that."

"And then what?"

"After that we went back to the brothel and Ashborne found the bitch and fucked her up good. We didn't get the money back."

"And then he was shot?"

"Yes."

"Why would you bring Spanish whores to a tavern? Why didn't you just fuck that girl and leave? And why did you bring that much money when you knew you were going to get drunk?"

James sipped his rum, staring at a brown stain on the table. He was sure it was blood. Someone had bled in the same spot where he was now sitting.

"You fell in love with her, didn't you?" Hammond said. "You fucking idiot…"

CHAPTER XI

Williamsburg, Colony of Virginia

"Why the beach?"

"It's my dream" Rob said. "To someday live on a beautiful sunny beach. Maybe somewhere in the Caribbean."

"Why do you like beaches so much?"

"I grew up in Massachusetts Bay. It's cold half the year, it gets windy, and rainy, and snowy. I want to live someplace warm, where there's no winter. I've heard of places like that. Jamaica. Hispaniola. Nassau. Where rain is just a slight inconvenience, and you don't risk catching a disease and maybe even dying just because you went outside in the rain."

"You'll burn your skin in the sun."

"I don't care. I love the sun."

"It gets old after a while."

"So does rain and snow."

"I get it. But there are better places to live than Nassau."

"It doesn't have to be Nassau. I just want to have a place of my own somewhere where the suns shines and waves crash."

"Sounds nice."

For a few minutes, they sat in silence and listened to a bird chirping outside.

"How did you join the *Howling Doom*?" Rob asked.

"I didn't join. The ship I served on, the *Valiant*, was captured by Wright's pirates and those of us that survived would have to either become pirates or get a musket ball through the head."

"Do all pirates join that way?"

"Some of them. Some mutinied against their captain and started robbing ships, some heard of the money we were taking in and volunteered."

"So you were captured by pirates and just became one? No initiation or anything?"

Another short pause.

"No."

"Does it make a difference?"

"What?"

"I mean, is there a difference how you join a crew? Do people treat you differently if you join a certain way?"

"No, nobody cares about that. Why do you want to know it so badly?"

"No reason."

"Rob?"

"What?"

"Are you thinking about becoming a pirate?"

This time it was Rob who went quiet.

"Rob?"

"What?"

"You don't want to be a pirate."

"Yes, I do."

"You really don't. Trust me."

"It's everything I ever wanted to be."

"Killing people and getting drunk? That's what you dream about?"

"You know what I mean."

"That's what pirate life is like. You kill and rob people, then go to the nearest port and spend it all on drink and whores, then you do it all over again until you get killed or go to prison. You don't want that life."

"Of course I do."

"Why?"

"Look at me! I'm in jail anyway. And for what? For not paying off some goddamn debts. It's humiliating! At least if I'm going to prison I want it to be deserved. I'm here for the stupidest reason there is. Debts! That's ridiculous! I feel like such a loser. I don't care if I'm going to end up in prison, because I'm already in here. At least you don't have to suffer this. You have been places and done things. I want that. I want to get to travel the seas and see beautiful islands and take gold and jewels away from some Spaniards, and have fun with some beautiful ladies. You don't know what it's like here. You don't know what kind of sad, pathetic life I've led to this point. Everyone else is getting somewhere, and I'm just rotting away, useless and forgotten by everybody. I want to be a pirate, and not just any pirate, but one that is feared by everyone. Like Heartless Harry Wright. I want to be remembered. I'm not going to discover or invent anything, but I could be the one who drove fear into men's hearts. I could be a legendary pirate. I don't want to be some lowlife that everyone is looking down on. I don't want to sweep the streets for next to nothing. I want people to fear me. I want them to respect me. I want to have the money to buy whatever I want. I want to experience everything that life has to offer. I want to see fear in the eyes of those who treated me like shit. Don't tell me you never wanted any of that."

"Rob… It's not worth it."

"Of course it's worth it. I don't care if I end up in prison. I'm already here. I have nothing to lose and everything to gain."

"You'll gain a blade between the ribs."

"So what? My life is worthless anyway."

"It's not worthless."

"You don't know what it's like being me. I'm a failure. My family probably pretends that I don't exist. They're ashamed of me."

"And becoming a pirate will make them proud of you?"

"I don't want them to be proud of me. I want to have the things I never had. Money. Women. I was told my whole life that I'm ugly. No man is ugly when he has gold."

"Rob…"

"What?"

"I've been there. You don't want any of it."

"Why not?"

"It's not like you think."

"Robbing bastards and getting drunk – I think I could get used to it. Doesn't sound very difficult."

"Rob, don't throw your life away."

"I'm throwing my life away here. I want to *live* my life."

"Piracy is no way to live it."

"Then why did you become a pirate?"

"Because I had no other choice."

"Then why didn't you quit? You could've run away as soon as you were on land. Why did you stay until you got caught?"

James was silent. He stared at the ceiling and thought about the question. Minutes went by. It was quiet in the gaol, but every once in a while the footsteps of a guard would interrupt the silence.

"James?"

"What?"

"You still there?"

"Yeah. Rob?"

"What?"

"You still think piracy is a good idea?"

"Sure."

"Listen. I was there. It seems like it's fun, but all of it gets old real quick. Take it from an actual pirate."

"James, now you listen. Nothing you say will *ever* convince me that living a life of rum, women, gold, and adventure is somehow a bad thing. Stop trying."

CHAPTER XII

Cayos de la Florida, Viceroyalty of New Spain

Nassau turned out to be an expensive place to live.

With money running low, James couldn't afford to rent a room. He would sleep in some alleyway or under a tree or even out on the beach. The beach was the worst, because every time he'd wake up with sunburnt skin and sand in his clothes.

James found a tavern that served food for cheap, and even then he only ate there once a day to make his money last.

He would sneak into other taverns and search for tankards that still had some rum in them. Sometimes he'd resort to stealing. Once, he got caught trying to leave the tavern with a bottle of wine under his shirt, and the tavern keeper gave him one hell of a beating. As if being hungry, sober, and in pain wasn't enough, he saw Gabriela walk past him. She saw him, lying on the ground by a pigsty, bleeding and bruised. And she just kept walking. He didn't have the energy to call her a filthy whore.

And then, when life could not have been any shittier, he encountered Scott.

Scott was looking just as rough as him.

"Hey, McDougall, did you hear? The *Doom* is going out again in a few days."

"Sign me up," James said. "I'll go wherever."

He made his way to the ship where he met Thatcher.

"Ready to go on another raid, Mr. McDougall?"

"Can't fucking wait."

"How's Nassau treating you?"

"Been better."

"We're going for a big one. You'll be a rich man again pretty soon. Sign your name here."

James marked an *X*.

"We're leaving the day after tomorrow, first thing in the morning. Get your stuff aboard in advance, be there early, we will wait for no one."

"Yes, sir," James said. "Hey, listen, I need to get my musket, and it's…"

"You traded it in for some extra money, didn't you?"

"Yeah."

Thatcher gave him a few pieces of eight.

"I'll take it out of your share next time we score a prize. You're not the first. If there's anything left over, buy yourself something to eat."

"Thank you, sir."

James bought back his musket and pistol. He had enough left to buy himself a shirt to replace the one he had been wearing for months and never washed.

The day before leaving, pirates started to show up one by one. Most of the old crew was there. Seeing Roger, Hammond, Phillips, Beasley, Clarke, and Manzanares reminded James that Ashborne was gone. He had drunk a lot of booze trying to forget it, but it was back.

There were a few new faces. One of them went around introducing himself to everyone.

"My name is Jean-Bernard Barbeau, but people call me J.B.," he told James.

"Nice to meet you, J.B. Are you French?"

"Yes, I'm from Toulon. Very beautiful city, more beautiful than Paris."

James excused himself to get out of the conversation. He saw J.B. introducing himself to Hammond, who responded with "Fuck off".

By nighttime, almost the entire crew was aboard. Most of them stayed up late, playing cards and telling stories.

"Did you hear about Milford?" Douglas said. "He shacked up with some whore. They lived in a tent on the beach. I met him a couple times, he loved to brag how good she was in the sack. Then one day somebody found his body. The whore slit his throat, took his money, and ran away."

"Goddamn. I liked him," Scott said. "He wasn't very smart, but he fought like hell."

Someone asked J.B. how he ended up on the *Doom*.

"I was on the ship *Avenant*, and we were sailing to Cap Français. We were very close, we could see coast of Hispaniola. Then we saw a pirate ship coming to us, and the captain said he will surrender. He said his men are more important than the cargo. Captain Smith and his men took the cargo, I helped move it, and I asked to join. They said "Sure, welcome aboard!", and now I'm a pirate!"

He laughed.

"And I never had to do anything, we went straight to Nassau. And before Nassau, they were giving each man his money. They call some man Bilton. The crew say he is dead. I want to be a good sailor, so I say I will go tell them Bilton is dead. I go in, they say, "Here is your money, Bilton," and I just took it. I hid it under my shirt, I go out, nobody knows. So now I'm in Nassau, I have a lot of money, and I didn't do anything!"

The other crewmates laughed.

"I spent all my money in Nassau, I need to go work on a ship. But now, if I go with Captain Smith, I will be in trouble. So I came here. People say this is a very good crew."

"Just call yourself Jean-Bilton and you'll be fine," Boyd said. The crew laughed.

The conversations slowly died down.

James fell asleep thinking how nice it was to not have to worry about money. For all the joys of Nassau, he was happy to be back.

After what seemed like a few seconds, Thatcher's voice woke him up.

"Good morning, shitbags, time to get to work!"

James was groggy, but so were the others.

"I forgot how much it sucks to wake up early," Scott grumbled. "I wanna go back to Nassau."

"We haven't even left yet," James said.

"Yeah, I know. I still want to go back."

Work went slower than usual. Thatcher constantly yelled at men to pick up the pace. They weighed the anchor and unfurled the sails.

The *Howling Doom* left Nassau. No one was there to see it off.

The sky was gray but the wind was strong. The *Doom* was headed east towards Florida. New Providence disappeared in the distance.

As soon as there was some free time, J.B. started asking others to teach him to shoot a pistol. He had an old blunderbuss with a few spots of rust here and there.

"I bought it from a pirate when I came to Nassau," he explained. "I wanted to have a real pistol. I have never shot it, but it looks good on my belt."

Roger volunteered to be his teacher. He slowly demonstrated each step of loading and shooting a pistol.

"All right, J.B., now do it yourself. Powder… Shot… Good, now ram it… Very good, now aim… Fire!"

J.B. carefully aimed at the horizon and pulled the trigger. A shot rang out. J.B. smiled.

"Very nice," Roger said. "Now do it all by yourself, with no help."

J.B. reloaded the pistol and looked around for something to shoot.

"I want to shoot a bird." He aimed the pistol at a seagull flying past and fired. It missed. J.B. started reloading again.

"Wait for it to land on water," Roger said.

"I want to shoot it in the sky."

"You should wait for an easier target. Shooting birds out of a sky is really hard even for great shooters."

J.B. fired again, and again missed.

"All right then," Roger said. "You need to aim ahead of the bird. And I mean *way* ahead. If you shoot when the bird is in your sights, you will miss every time. You have to shoot early, because it takes a little bit of time for you to react and for the powder to ignite. You have to shoot where the bird *will be,* understand?"

J.B. nodded. He aimed again and fired.

"That was closer. Three more shots, all right? We can't waste all the ball and powder on birds."

The seagull flew away, but another one showed up after a while. J.B. fired at it three times but couldn't hit it.

"Frenchie's a natural," Roger said as he and others watched J.B. shoot. "Just need to teach him to shoot a musket and he'll be good to go."

J.B. went down to the lower deck to put away the pistol and came back with a cutlass. He went to the stern of the ship and started practicing his swings. He kept stabbing and slashing and occasionally blocking until he got winded.

"How did I do?" he asked James.

"I think you'll be fine. Good work."

"Thank you." J.B. sheathed the cutlass. "Are you excited?"

"About the upcoming job?"

"Yes."

"I'm excited to get paid."

"Me too," J.B. said. "I want to have money, but I don't want to have another pirate's money. I want to earn it. And then I will go to Nassau again. And I will be a real pirate."

"What do you mean?"

"When I was in Nassau, I was afraid someone will ask me how I got the money. All the time, I was afraid. It was not my money, I did not do anything, I took some man Bilton's money and I act like a pirate. I was afraid there will be trouble. I see someone from Captain Smith's crew, I hide. They know I am not a real pirate. But next time will be different. I will make money, I will go to Nassau, and I will buy drink and women with *my* money. And if someone asks about money, I will say I made my money as a pirate. If they ask where, I will say I was with Captain Wright's crew, you can ask them, they will say I was fighting with them. And I will not be afraid of anything."

James smiled.

"I think you're going to make a lot of money with us."

J.B. smiled and went to put away his cutlass.

The following morning was just as rough as the previous one. Through sheer force of will, James got out of the hammock and went topside.

Being on deck again and seeing the endless blue water in the morning sunlight made James happy for a moment. Something about it felt like coming home.

About an hour after breakfast, they heard Boyd shouting from the crow's nest.

"Sail! Starboard bow!"

Everyone on deck immediately ran to the bow to see it.

"Looks like a sloop," Thatcher said, watching the ship through a spyglass. "Hold on, I'm trying to make out the colors… Dutch. We have a Dutch sloop."

The captain came to the bow and everyone moved to make space for him. Wright watched the ship for a while.

"Should be an easy job," he said. "We're taking it."

"Battle stations!" Thatcher yelled. "Load the starboard guns!"

The crew rushed to the cannons on the starboard side. Every single one was crewed, so James ran to the lower deck to grab his pistols. He encountered J.B. down there.

"We're taking a ship," James said. "Grab your pistol and let's go!"

He ran upstairs and hid behind the mainmast. J.B. was standing next to him, loading his pistol and smiling from ear to ear. In the excitement he loaded the shot before the powder and had to start over.

Pirates were gathering on deck. Some loaded their pistols, a couple sharpened their cutlasses. Cannon crews reported they were ready to fire.

James felt that rush again.

The crew was quiet. Everyone was focused on the goal.

At the stern, Keene raised an English flag. He had the black flag nearby.

The sloop's crew noticed them and furled their sails. The *Doom* was getting closer.

James looked at J.B.

"Are you ready?"

J.B. nodded, still smiling from ear to ear.

Wright was focused on the Dutch sloop, waiting. When he felt that the distance was right, he gave the order.

"Raise the black!"

Keene and Douglas quickly took down the Red Ensign and flew the black.

"Here we go," James whispered. "Get ready."

He saw sailors running about on the deck of the sloop. As the ships drew closer, one of the Dutch sailors ran over to the stern and raised a stick with a white handkerchief tied to the end.

"White flag," Thatcher said. "Get the launches ready, we're crossing over. Furl the sails!"

James put his pistol under his belt.

"They surrendered," he told J.B. "There won't be a fight."

"That's good."

"It won't be so easy next time. Don't get used to it."

"What do we do now?"

"We'll try to get on that ship."

The crew lowered two launches into the water.

James made his way through a crowd of pirates to get a spot.

"Sir, we need to get on that launch," he told Thatcher.

"Why?"

"The Frenchman's new here, he should see what it's like to take another ship."

"All right, get in."

James and J.B. quickly climbed down.

"Careful, you jackass!" Hammond yelled when J.B. casually jumped into the launch. "You'll capsize the fucking boat!"

"Sorry."

They rowed the two launches towards the sloop. The name of the ship was *Sint Pieter*.

The sailors helped the pirates get aboard. Some of them were terrified but tried to hide it. Others were more confused than scared, and a few seemed somewhat curious.

One man stepped forward.

"I am the captain," he said in surprisingly good English. "We will give you the cargo, but don't kill any of my men."

"Fine," Wright said. "But if anyone wants to join our crew, they are welcome."

"Fair wages and easy work," Thatcher said. "And you'll be free men. You will no longer be slaves to your captain. And there is a lot of money to be made where we're going."

Two men volunteered to join. They introduced themselves as Marten Visser and Hendrik Dijkman.

Douglas came back from the lower deck.

"What do we have?" Thatcher asked.

"Salt."

"Just salt?"

"And some other stuff, like beans."

"Shit. We're not gonna get much for it, no reason to have it take up space in the hold. Ask Beasley how much we need, leave the rest."

"Will do."

Meanwhile, the new guys were being initiated.

"Who's the biggest bastard in this crew?" Hammond asked. "Which man do you hate the most?"

"Boatswain." Dijkman pointed him out.

Hammond gave him a loaded pistol.

"You know what to do."

The captain stepped forward to protest, but Hammond punched him in the gut.

Dijkman took the pistol and walked over to the boatswain. The man immediately started pleading in Dutch. Dijkman hesitated for a second. Then he cocked the pistol, put the muzzle against the boatswain's chest, took a deep breath, and pulled the trigger.

Dijkman turned around and handed the pistol back to Hammond.

"Very good," Hammond said.

Thatcher drew his own pistol.

"Mr. Visser, you're next."

Visser was more reluctant, but he took the pistol.

"Anyone you want. Your choice."

The captain called Visser by name and stepped forward. He said something in Dutch. Visser protested, but the captain wouldn't hear it. He said something to the crew, and they all saluted him.

The captain stood straight and looked off into the distance. Visser put the pistol against his temple and pulled the trigger.

"Good job, Mr. Visser," Thatcher said. "I'd like to have my pistol back. Thank you."

Some of the sailors were trying their best to look stoic, others were outright weeping. A few of them picked up the bodies of the captain and the boatswain and carefully moved them aside.

"We're pretty much done here," James told J.B. "Let's just ask if they need any help moving the cargo."

"Wait," Hammond said. "Take one more Dutchman, I want French Boy to prove himself."

"Got it. Let's go, J.B."

James looked around and noticed a skinny kid of about sixteen.

"You, come with me," he said. The kid wasn't moving. "Come on, let's go." James grabbed him by the arm and pulled him away. Another sailor tried to intervene, but James drew his pistol.

"Stay the fuck away. Understand?"

He pushed the kid to the very back of the ship.

"J.B., is your pistol still loaded? All right. I need you to shoot this one."

"Why?"

"Just do it."

"But why?"

"To show the crew that you can be trusted in battle. We need to know that you are willing to do what needs to be done."

J.B. did not move. He was looking at the young sailor.

"Draw your pistol," James said.

"But I don't understand–"

"Draw your pistol."

"Why do I have to shoot this man? He is innocent. He did nothing."

"I don't care. Just shoot him."

"He is young. He is a good man. I don't want to shoot him."

"Goddammit, J.B., stop fucking around! Just shoot this fucker so we can all move on to something else. I'm not asking you to give him a full fucking burial with all the ceremonies, just pull the trigger and it's done."

"But he is innocent. What did he do? I don't want to kill him."

"It's not about him, it's about you. Show the crew that you are able to kill a man."

"I will not kill this man. If you have a bad man, a criminal, I will kill him, but this young man did nothing bad."

"If you don't shoot him, I will shoot *you*. It's either him, or you. Now draw your pistol."

J.B. stared at James for a couple of seconds, then slowly drew the pistol from under his belt.

"Hurry it up," James said. "Cock the hammer. You practiced this. Aim at either head or chest, it's up to you."

J.B. slowly raised the pistol and put it against the Dutchman's chest.

"Don't close your eyes," James said. "Look at him. I want you to look him in the eyes. Now pull the trigger."

J.B. slowly placed his index finger on the trigger. He did not pull it.

"Do it, you coward. Pull the trigger. *Pull the fucking trigger.* Do it."

The Dutch sailor was weeping. J.B. was breathing heavily. He was gripping the pistol so tight his knuckles turned white.

"Enough stalling," James said. "Just end this right now. Pull the trigger. Just get this over with. Come on. Do it. NOW!"

There was a clack, then a tiny puff of smoke.

J.B. lowered the pistol. Both he and the kid were relieved.

"I guess the powder got damp," James said. He drew his own pistol. "Take mine."

"I pulled the trigger."

"But he's not dead."

"But I pulled the trigger. I showed you, I can do it."

"Not good enough. Take my pistol, try again. We're not going anywhere until this shitbird is dead. Now take it."

J.B. put his pistol under his belt.

"But I did it. He lived. Why is this not good enough?"

"I don't wanna hear that shit. Take my pistol and do this properly."

J.B. took the pistol. His hand was shaky.

"You're a goddamn embarrassment," James said. "At least try not to cry when you do this, you don't want everyone on the ship to think you're soft. Don't be soft. Show us you have the balls."

Once again, J.B. slowly pointed the pistol at the kid's chest.

"Do it quickly this time. Or do you need somebody to hold your hand? Your mommy's not here, she can't help you. But I bet your mom would make a better pirate than you, I bet *she* would have the balls to pull the trigger."

"Shut up!"

"Or what? What are you gonna do? You're definitely not gonna shoot me, I know that. You should've gone back to France. You don't have the balls to be on this crew. If I gave that pistol to a little girl, all of this would've been done five minutes ago. If you can't even kill one unarmed man, maybe just shoot yourself, then we won't have to deal with you, you fucking coward."

There was a clack, followed immediately by a loud bang. The Dutch sailor fell over with a bleeding wound in his chest.

"Shut up."

"Finally!" James said. "Took you long enough. Let's go back to our ship. And give me my pistol back."

J.B. did not speak. When they got back to the *Doom*, a few pirates patted him on the back and congratulated him on his first kill. Even Hammond told him he did a good job. The whole time, J.B. didn't say a word. He was quiet the rest of the day.

With the *Sint Pieter* sent off on its way, the *Howling Doom* continued southwest along the small islands off the coast of Florida. The winds weren't strong, but they were making progress.

That night, James had to stand watch. He decided not to try to sleep, because he would get woken up in a couple of hours anyway. He stayed on deck, every once in a while checking if everything was working fine, and listened to his crewmates' stories.

"I don't remember what happened that first night in Nassau," Johnson said. "I remember leaving the ship and going to a tavern, after that it's all black, and then I woke up in a goat pen, all covered in goat shit."

"Happens to the best of us," Wayland said.

"The next day, exact same thing happened. Woke up in the same corner of the same goat pen. Ruined a brand new set of clothes."

"On the bright side, I'm sure the parts you don't remember were *really* fun."

"Someone later told me I was kicked out of a brothel. He said that I tried to fuck a whore in the ear."

"That was you?"

"That's what they tell me."

James left those two and just walked around the deck. There just wasn't anything to do. He checked the compass one more time, and saw they were still going in the right direction, just as they were five minutes ago. He went to the bow and leaned against the gunwale and looked at the moon.

He heard steps behind him. James turned around. It was J.B.

"James."

"What do you want?"

"You are a bastard."

"I know."

"You made me kill that poor man."

"So?"

"He was innocent. He did not deserve to die. And you made me kill him."

"You wanted to be a pirate, remember? All you ever talked about was how you were going to make a lot of money and be a *real* pirate. What did you think was going to happen? You thought there would be a chest full of diamonds and gold just lying on the beach?"

"That man was innocent. He did not have money. You could let him live."

"*You* could've let him live. I told you, it was either him or you. If you wanted him to live, you could've taken his place."

"That is not true."

"Oh really?"

"You told me to do it."

"And you listened."

"I said "no" many times."

"But in the end, you pulled the trigger."

"Because you shouted at me to do it."

"So what?"

"You made me become a killer. You made me take an innocent life."

"He was just some scrawny kid, probably would've died soon anyway. Who cares?"

"I care! Because he looked like my younger brother."

"That's what this is all about? Come on."

"My brother was always thin and weak. I cared for him. I helped him. I had to become a sailor, and he is in Toulon, alone, without his brother. I worry what is going to happen to him. I am strong, I will be safe, but he… What if he is like that Dutch man? He meets some bad men, criminals, and somebody shoots him in the chest, for no reason? Show that you can, shoot him, and bam, my brother is dead. This could happen to him."

"And you crying about it is somehow going to stop it?"

J.B. drew his pistol and pointed it directly at James.

"What the fuck are you doing?" James said.

"You are a bastard."

"You didn't even know that Dutch kid. And besides, he's dead now. You can stop worrying about him."

"I'm a killer now. Because of you."

"You are a pirate. That's what you said, you wanted to be a *real* pirate. You wanted to *earn* your money. There you go. You did it. You're a real pirate, and you earned your share. Congratulations."

"No."

"This is what you wanted."

"No. I am not like you!"

A gunshot rang out.

J.B. collapsed to the ground, a chunk of his skull blown off. Blood pooled around his head.

Wayland lowered his pistol.

"What the fuck happened?" he asked.

"French Boy couldn't take it. Pirate life just wasn't for him."

"I overheard you two arguing, then I saw him point a pistol at you. I'm glad I had mine under my belt. Looks like I was just in time."

"Not really. He didn't have the balls to pull the trigger."

CHAPTER XIII
Williamsburg, Colony of Virginia

"Goddammit, Rob…"

"What?"

"It's not about money or women or adventures. It's about the pirates. Stay away from them. Living among them is nothing like what you imagine."

"All right then, tell me. What's it like to live aboard the *Howling Doom*?"

"Always looking over your shoulder because you could get stabbed in the back at any moment. That's what it's like."

"It can't be that bad."

"It is that bad."

"How many people in your crew were the types you cannot trust?"

"All of them."

"All of them?"

"Sure."

"Not even your friends?"

"What friends?"

"Come on."

"What?"

"How could you not make any friends on the crew?"

"Nobody really wants to be friends with others."

"Is that a pirate thing?"

"I don't know."

"Why wouldn't you make any friends?"

"You never know how many will be left after a battle. On pirate ships, people die young and get replaced by newcomers. But more importantly, nobody needs a friend. What's the point?"

"Tough question. I guess, you can spend time with friends? Doing things. Having a fun time."

"On a ship, you're already stuck with the same people for months. What difference does it make if you label one a friend?"

"But you eventually get to the shore. What happens then?"

"Drinking."

"Did you drink alone?"

"No, usually with whores."

"You're making a really strong case for not having friends."

"No. Have friends. Friends are good. Just don't become a sailor and don't have pirates as friends. You can't be friends with people who are ready and willing to stab you in the back."

"But you fought with these people. In Vera Cruz, in Porto Bello…"

"We didn't fight together, we fought the same enemy. None of my crewmates would've had any problem killing me if I stood between them and money."

"Would you do the same?"

"I really don't know what I would've done. One thing I learned on that ship is that I'm capable of much more than I thought."

"Such as?"

"Killing."

"How many people have you killed?"

"I already told you, I don't want to talk about it."

"More than ten?"

"Shut up, Rob."

They heard a guard's steps going down the hallway, then going back a few seconds later. Then it was all silent again for a while.

"What's it like being surrounded by the sea in every direction?"

"I never really paid attention to it."

"Really?"

"Really."

"You never just stopped and looked at the water and just… just admired it?"

"Most of the time I was too busy. Besides, when you're on the water all the time, it quickly loses the charm. Then it's just water."

"If you don't like being out in the open sea, why would you sign up to be a sailor?"

"Because I was young and really stupid."

"I mean it. Why did you become a sailor?"

James sighed.

"Some old man on the street started telling me about all the great times he had at sea. How he visited Africa and all the amazing things he saw, how beautiful the Caribbean was, all while enjoying a sailor's life and earning good money. Then he suggested I sign up, and I did, because I believed that old bastard. When I found out that he was lying about everything, it was too late."

"He lied about all of it?"

"Every little thing. He probably had never even been to sea. He was one of those people paid to recruit sailors. And I was an idiot. I believed all of it. I thought I'd travel around the world. Ever since that moment, my life has been shit."

"You know what I think? I think it's the sadness talking. If you were free, you'd be telling a different story."

"No. Becoming a sailor was the worst decision I ever made. I wish I never stepped on the deck of that ship."

"The *Doom*?"

"*Valiant*. The one I signed up for. But I wish I was never on the other one either."

"Don't you miss anything from the time you were on that first ship?"

"Not one thing."

"Who was the captain?"

"Jonathan Spencer. He was eaten by sharks long ago. Can't say I'm sad about that."

"How was the crew?"

"I got along with most of them, but I wouldn't die for them nor would any of them die for me. When you're tricked into a godawful job with low pay, and you're constantly cold and overworked and hungry, you tend to put yourself first and others second."

"I imagine."

"Especially when you've been promised that you'll get to see lions in Africa and the wonderful islands in the Caribbean, but instead end up shivering on the deck during a storm, and then you just want to die because there's no way to get out of it. Except maybe mutiny. There was talk on the *Valiant* about that, but the captain found out and everyone involved disappeared."

"What do you mean?"

"One day we all woke up and those men weren't anywhere on the ship."

"Your captain did that?"

"Who else could it be?"

"I can see why you wouldn't like him. That's a horrible thing to do."

"I would've done the same thing."

CHAPTER XIV

Havana, Captaincy General of Cuba

After they saw the coasts of Cuba, the *Howling Doom* made a hard right and sailed west. They passed Havana and could see ships coming in and out of Havana harbor. Wright ordered the crew to fly Spanish colors, and they passed a couple of frigates and a man-of-war without raising any suspicion.

"Just imagine the kind of money they have in that town," Manzanares said, longingly staring at the city in the distance. "If only it wasn't guarded so well…"

"It might be doable," James said. "Really hard, would take a lot of planning, and leave a lot of good men dead, but doable. A well-planned assault from land. Lots of men moving very fast, taking over the critical parts. Taking the forts before they even realize they're under attack. It's possible."

"Might be doable, but it would be the toughest raid ever done."

"What if there were a dozen of our people inside the city?"

"You've got something there, McDougall. Maybe someday."

"Maybe someday."

Douglas walked up to them.

"Hey. What's going on?"

"We're planning a raid on Havana," James said.

"That is the dumbest thing I've ever heard. So, what's the plan?"

"Ground assault," Manzanares said. "A really big crew, moving fast, take over important buildings before they can prepare defense. Put a dozen or so people inside to prepare for the attack."

"If we put even more men in the city, it could make the raid easier," James said. "We don't know what the place looks like, it's hard to figure out the weak points."

"We need someone who knows the city. Until then, it's not really a plan."

"When we return to Nassau, I'll pitch this to the captain," Douglas said. "If there's a crew that could take Havana, it's us."

At that moment, Wright came out of his quarters.

"What's our speed?" he yelled.

Everyone on deck was looking at each other.

"Do any of you shitheads know our speed?"

"Last time it was eight knots," Clarke said.

"I don't care what it *was*, I want to know what it is *right fucking now*. Get on it, shit-for-brains!"

"Oh fuck," Manzanares whispered. "He's in bad mood again. Until it goes away, do what you're told, don't fuck up, and try to stay out of sight."

"Got it," James said.

"You three!" Wright yelled, pointing at James, Manzanares, and Douglas. "How about you stop admiring the water and get the fuck back to work. Move it!"

As soon as James was out of the captain's sight, he went down to the lower deck. He found Roger playing cards with a few others.

"Captain's pissed."

"Again?" Roger said.

"Shouting orders all day while everyone else does the heavy lifting," Keene mumbled to himself. "Must be taking a toll on the poor old cap."

"Want to join the game?"

"No. I'm good."

James watched his crewmates play. Roger was doing well for a while, but then lost all the money to Wayland.

One more game later, Manzanares came down.

"Sail!"

The pirates dropped the cards and ran to the main deck.

"Where is it?"

"Dead ahead."

There was already a group of pirates at the bow. Wright watched it through his spyglass.

"What's our speed?"

"Ten," Thatcher said.

"Good. Get ready, we'll catch up in no time."

"BATTLE STATIONS!"

James took up a starboard cannon. Beside him was Isaiah Summers, a veteran from Angry Mark Smith's crew who had stayed behind in Nassau and signed up to be on the *Doom*.

The wind was strong and it carried the *Doom* so fast that it seemed to be flying. The distance between her and the other ship was shrinking.

James and Summers loaded the cannon and prepared the swab, powder, and other gear for reloading. They worked without talking.

"I think that's a brig or a snow," Wright said. "A bit smaller than the *Doom*."

"Colors?" Thatcher asked.

"Don't see any."

"What's our approach?"

"The usual."

James sat on the deck, leaning against the cannon.

"We've been talking about what we're going to do after we return to Nassau."

"Who?" Summers said.

"Me, Manzanares, and Douglas."

"All right, tell me."

"Havana."

"No way."

"Why not?"

"It's too well guarded."

"I didn't say it would be easy."

"Havana is a suicide mission, kid."

"If there's one place where the guards will be lazy, it's Havana. They're so used to feeling safe, they won't expect it."

"They feel safe for a reason."

"It's not impossible."

"No, it's impossible. If the target was Cartagena, then I'd consider it. Havana? Forget it."

"What if we had people on the inside?"

"Nope."

"I mean at least a dozen."

"Nope."

"Havana can't be that strong."

"It's strong enough. Raiding it will cost so much time and men that it won't be worth it in the end."

Little by little, the ship was getting closer. Pirates were loading their muskets, a few were passing around a whetstone and sharpening their cutlasses and knives.

"Summers?" James said.

"What?"

"If you could sack any city, what would it be?"

"Either Paris or Madrid."

"Why?"

"Because fuck the French and fuck the Spanish."

"Fair enough."

Cartwright was sitting nearby and sharpening his knife.

"I'd sack London," he said.

"Why London?"

"Imagine the money in there."

At the bow, the captain was watching their target.

"They're flying the White Ensign. Royal Navy."

"Are we still going for it?" Thatcher said.

"Yes we are."

James looked at Summers.

"Royal Navy? Sounds like there might be trouble."

"It makes no sense," Summers said. "What are they doing here? A single ship sailing into Spanish territory. Something is not right."

"They won't have much money."

"They'll have a good crew that doesn't get paid," Cartwright said. "And that ship could sell for decent money if we don't end up destroying it."

Meanwhile, the *Howling Doom* was inching closer to the target.

"I think I see the name," Wright said. "Mr. Thatcher, ask Phillips and others who were in the Royal Navy if they know anything about His Majesty's Ship *Westminster* and why it's sailing in Spanish waters."

"Yes, captain."

James stood up and leaned over the side to look at the *Westminster*. It was still pretty far away.

"We have time," he said. "We're not nearly close enough."

"When we take that ship, I'm taking the flag," Summers said.

"Why?"

"I'll wipe my arse with it. Been wanting to do that since the day I joined up."

"You were in the Royal Navy?"

"Yeah. I was at Cádiz. The Spanish beat the living shit out of us. Later, I was moved to a different ship, the *Vigo*, it was wrecked during a storm and I ended up on a Dutch ship headed for Aruba."

"Damn, Summers, you've been through some shit."

"Tell me about it."

"How hard do you think this will be?"

"Their entire crew is undermanned, underpaid, and overworked. Then again, they'll be fighting for their lives. We'll see when it starts."

"Mr. Thatcher," Wright said, "fly English colors."

"Yes, captain. Get me English colors!"

After a few minutes, a large Red Ensign was flying at the *Doom*'s stern. The captain kept observing the ship. After a while, the crew of the *Westminster* started furling the sails.

"They're stopping," Wright said. "Get ready! Prepare to fly the black!"

"Yes, captain."

As soon as the ships were within two hundred yards, Scott raised the black. James looked at *Westminster* and he saw there was movement on deck. Sailors were preparing for a fight.

"FIRE CHASERS!" Wright roared.

The bow chasers fired, hitting the hull of the *Westminster*. As the *Doom* drew closer, they fired again and smashed two more holes in the ship. The crews then loaded them with grapeshot and fired high and took out the boatswain. Another ball hit a sailor's shoulder, leaving his left arm limp.

The *Westminster*'s crew unfurled main and fore sails to try to get moving and face the pirates broadside. Seeing that, Wright ordered the helmsman to make a hard turn to larboard. Both ships slowly turned left, and the *Doom*'s chaser fired again, hitting no one. They were eventually at an angle where the *Westminster*'s aft-most cannon was aimed at the *Doom*. It fired, and the cannonball flew over the bow. As soon as the ship was in their sights, the cannon crew at the *Doom*'s bow fired and the cannonball went through the wall of captain's cabin and destroyed some of the furniture inside.

James looked over the gunwale and he could see the *Westminster*'s stern. Summers had the slow match ready, they just needed to get in position. The English fired another shot, and it punched a hole in the bow. Summers was carefully watching the *Westminster*, and he lit the fuse and the cannon fired. The cannonball smashed the rudder.

"YEAH!"

"Great shot, Summers!" someone shouted.

Summers adjusted the height of the cannon as James swabbed it.

On the *Westminster*, the helmsman noticed that he had no control over the rudder and ran over to the captain to inform him, but grapeshot hit him in the spine, ribs, and head, and he fell on the deck. His blood ran on the boards and a few pieces of his flesh fell on the first mate's clothes.

A cannonball injured two pirates and bounced off the deck and hit Antonio Maldonado in the groin, destroying his pelvis. He screamed in pain as Michaels dragged him to the lower deck, leaving a trail of blood with some urine. Ortega ran up the stairs and helped carry him.

"Put him here," Ortega said. "I cannot do anything for him."

Michaels ran back up to the main deck but at the top of the stairs he was hit by grapeshot. His body tumbled back down. Ortega looked at the cadaver for a while, then grabbed his arms and dragged him out of the way.

The *Doom* was getting close, and the pirates were preparing to board. Most of those who weren't on the cannons were firing their muskets. Roger took out the quartermaster and a crewman who stuck his head out too high. The English tried to return fire, but the pirates just waited for anyone to stand up. Nobody could get off a shot without getting three right back.

The distance between the ships got small enough to where cannon crews on the *Westminster* had to grab muskets and pistols and prepare for the inevitable boarding. The pirates were throwing ropes to get the ships together, while at the same time their crewmates were firing at the English sailors. One sailor managed to cut a couple of ropes with a hatchet without getting shot.

There was panic among the *Westminster*. They couldn't hold the pirates back with their guns, which meant that now they would have to fight on the deck with swords and pistols, where pirates had an advantage.

Musket balls were flying in both directions, most of them hitting either wood or nothing at all. Pirates pulled the ships closer and closer together until the gap became small enough to cross.

James and Summers abandoned their cannon and drew their pistols. Pirates were placing boards between the ships. Summers climbed onto the gunwale, trying to be the first one to cross over, but a musket ball hit him in the side of the neck and he fell to the deck bleeding. A few others made it across. Roger was among them. As he was about to jump down to the deck of the other ship, one of the English sailors stood up and hacked him in the head with a hatchet. Roger's entire body shuddered and he fell off the ship into the water.

For a few moments, James stood there trying to comprehend what had just happened. Then he climbed on the gunwale and ran across with just three big steps. His mind was telling him one thing: *KILL*. James jumped off the gunwale and landed on the man who had just killed Roger. He shoved the muzzle of his pistol into the sailor's mouth and pulled the trigger. The man's brain ended up splattered on the deck. James flipped the pistol in his hand and attacked the next sailor, knocking him out with one good strike. But it wasn't enough, and James knelt beside him and swung the gun over and over until the man's skull was deformed on that side.

James stood up, breathing heavily, dropped his pistol, and drew his knife. He attacked the *Westminster*'s first mate, a tall, muscular man. The man managed to grab his hand, and they fell on the deck wrestling for the knife. James was on top of his opponent, trying to stab him, but the first mate was holding his wrist and not letting go. He was too strong.

Someone stepped on James's hand and pushed down, slowly driving the knife into the first mate's neck. James pulled out the knife and stabbed the man several more times and left him to bleed out on the deck. When he looked up, he saw Hammond standing beside him.

"I'd say we're even now," Hammond said.

James nodded.

He looked around for the next bastard to kill, but what was left of the crew had stopped fighting. The *Westminster* was theirs.

With no rush, Wright crossed over to the captured ship.

"Where's the captain?"

Two pirates brought the captain forward and one of them kicked him in the back of the knee to make him kneel.

"What's your name?" Wright said.

"Captain Steven Matthews." He tried to look calm, but the tone of his voice showed fear.

"What's your cargo?"

"I do not have the authority to give that information away."

"Don't fuck with me, what is the cargo?"

"I cannot tell you."

"Either tell us what you have in there, or choose which one of your men will die."

Matthews looked at his remaining crew.

"It's… It's the envoy."

"The what?"

"British envoy to Spain."

"The fuck does that mean?"

"A diplomat," one of the officers said. "We had to take him to New Spain, he was supposed to meet the viceroy in Mexico City."

"So you're just transporting some old fart with a wig?" Thatcher said. "Why didn't you say so? We have no use for him, we just want money."

"I'll give you all the money we have," Matthews said.

"There we go. Manzanares, take him and get the money."

Carlos took the captain to his cabin. A few minutes later there was a shot. Manzanares came out alone.

"All right, that's taken care of," Thatcher said. "Now, which of you fine gentlemen would like to join our crew?"

Three able-bodied sailors volunteered: Bill Martin, Rudy Mason, and Jack Flowers.

"I think we could squeeze more out of this," Thatcher said, "Mr. Flowers, what can you tell me about the rest of your crew?"

"That's Leonard, he complains a lot. Hardy, you probably don't want him either. That's O'Keefe, the navigator…"

"Navigator? We just lost ours. Get this man over here. What was your name again?"

"Paul O'Keefe. But I…"

"Mr. O'Keefe, welcome to the *Howling Doom*. You will be our new navigator."

"But I…"

"You will be paid more than your captain was. You like money, don't you?"

Manzanares took some coins he got from the captain and started demonstratively playing with them.

O'Keefe glanced at Thatcher's cutlass and pistol.

"All right. I'm in." He shook Thatcher's hand to the cheers of the *Doom*'s crew.

"McDougall, Pereira, go check up on that politician they have down there," Wright said.

"He has jewelry," Mason said. "A couple of gold rings."

Hammond walked up to him.

"Mason, isn't it? I think you'll fit in just fine." He laughed and patted Mason on the shoulder.

James, Pereira, and Manzanares went down to the lower deck as the remaining sailors were being executed.

"You know, I'm still thinking about the plan," Manzanares said.

"What?"

"To take Havana."

"Oh. Yeah."

"I think with at least a dozen Spanish on our side, our chances would be good. I mean, it's still Havana, but it would be possible."

Below they found Clarke, de Toledo, and a few others.

"We have a locked door here," Clarke said. "Something valuable must be inside."

"It's just some politician," Pereira said.

"What?"

"They were taking him to New Spain to do some politics shit, that's what they've been doing in these waters."

"Shit."

"I hear the old bastard has some gold rings, so that's something."

"We can't open the door," de Toledo said. "We'll need to destroy it completely."

"Wait," Manzanares said. "McDougall, knock on the door, tell him we just want money and we won't kill him."

"Why me?"

"Because you're English. You think he'll open the door for a Spaniard?"

James knocked on the door.

"Open the door, sir. Please. We just want to take your money. We're not looking to hurt you. We don't care if you have some important documents or something, you can keep them. Just open the door so we don't have to blow it up."

"Are you an Englishman?" said a voice from inside.

"Yes, sir. I'm from Portsmouth. My name is James."

"James, can you give me your word that I won't be hurt and none of my documents taken?"

"You have my word, sir."

A few seconds passed in silence. Then they heard a key in the lock and the door opened. Clarke immediately shot the man between the eyes and went in. Others followed.

The envoy was in his sixties. He wore fancy clothes and a powdered wig that flew off when the ball came out through the back of his head.

"Pereira, check the desk," Manzanares said. He and James started rummaging through the man's pockets. They took his rings, pocket watch, and wallet.

"I found some money," Pereira said. "And some other fancy stuff."

"Good. Take all those things to the captain."

They handed the loot over to Thatcher and went back to the *Doom*. The others were just about done cleaning out everything of value, including barrels of powder. Once the *Westminster* had no more use to them, Flowers volunteered to start a fire in the hold.

When asked why, he said, "Fuck that boat and fuck the Royal Navy."

Flowers did a good job. The whole ship was ablaze in minutes. As James watched the fire, Manzanares and Pereira came up to watch it.

"Roger died," James said. "Those fuckers killed him."

"Yeah, that's awful," Manzanares said.

"Overall, not a bad score," Pereira said. "We got several barrels of powder, some pistols, and some gold. We definitely had worse."

"Can we talk about Havana?"

"Can we talk about it another time?" James said.

"Fine."

The *Howling Doom* made its way west. O'Keefe turned out to be just as good as Ashborne, if not better.

James stood at the stern of the ship and looked at the water. Miguel de Toledo stopped by.

"Do you know where Pereira is?"

"Nope."

"I can't find him."

"Then go look for him. He has to be on the ship somewhere, there's only so many places to hide."

He walked away. James once again stared into the sea. Nothing made sense.

He lost track of how long he stood there.

Hammond yelled at him for loitering, and James decided to go somewhere else.

Pereira walked past him.

"Hey," James said. "Toledo was looking for you."

"Just now?"

"Not too long ago."

"Did he say why?"

"No. Is there something going on?"

"No. Everything's normal."

"It sure looks like something's going on. You two planning something?"

"There is nothing going on, McDougall. And by the way, you should stay out of other people's business."

"Yeah, well, fuck you too."

Pereira walked away.

"I need a fucking drink," James whispered. He went down to the galley and poured himself a tankard of rum. Beasley started yelling at him, but James told him to fuck off and leave him alone.

That night, James lay awake in his hammock. Even after quite a bit of rum he couldn't fall asleep. He stared at the ceiling, listening to the sounds of waves crashing into the hull, pirates snoring, and rats chewing on some hardtack.

Then he heard someone climbing out of a hammock. When the man walked past, James recognized de Toledo. He didn't go to the upper deck but disappeared somewhere in the darkness. He returned to his bed a few minutes later.

In the morning, Pereira cautiously walked up to him.

"McDougall, I need to ask you something."

"Go ahead."

"Miguel de Toledo. Do you see him acting suspicious?"

"No. Not really. Why?"

"If you see him doing something unusual, you tell me, all right? And no one else."

"Now that you mention it, I did see Toledo get up in the middle of the night."

"What was he doing?"

"I don't know, I didn't follow him."

"Maybe he was going through my things?"

"I don't know. It's possible. You think he took something from you?"

"Yes. There was something that is now missing."

"And you think it was Toledo?"

"No one else would take it."

"What is it that he took?"

"Doesn't matter, it is mine. I want it back."

"All right. Is the item big or small?"

"Small. You could almost hide it in your fist."

"Is it valuable?"

"Yes."

"All right… Did you ask Toledo if he took it?"

"He will just lie."

"So what do you want me to do?"

"Watch him. He expects me to follow him, he won't expect you."

"Wait, I have a better idea," James said. "Carlos! Come over here!"

Manzanares had just climbed down from the foremast. He wiped the sweat off his forehead as he joined James and Pereira.

"What's going on?"

"Pereira wanted to tell you something."

"No, it's… it's no big deal."

"What is it?"

"Never mind, it's nothing, really."

"Come on," James said. "Tell him about Toledo."

"What about him?"

"It's… it's not important," Pereira said.

"Tell me anyway."

"It's really nothing. James should not have said anything, I didn't mean to waste your time."

"Well, too fucking late for that. Don't bother me unless it's important."

Manzanares went back to his duties.

"What the hell is going on?" James asked.

"I told you, I don't want to tell anyone else about this. It's between me and him."

"You got me involved in this."

"You're fine. Just don't talk to Manzanares about this."

"Why?"

"I think he's covering for de Toledo."

"Why would he do that?"

"Miguel's name isn't Toledo, it's *de* Toledo. You know what that means?"

"*De* means *from*. I know that much."

"Most people don't have names like that. That's an aristocrat name. He comes from money. Why do you think he speaks English so good? Rich family. He had time to learn languages because he didn't need to learn a trade. He probably has so much money that he will never need to work for it. And he knows a lot of other rich and powerful people in Spain, and I bet Manzanares wants to be a part of that."

"So what are we supposed to do now?"

"We need to find it."

"Find what?"

"That thing he stole."

"What if he didn't steal anything?"

"Oh, he did. That rich bastard definitely took something for himself."

"How do you know?"

"I just know."

"So what are you going to do now?"

"I wanted to search his stuff, but there are others in there. They'll think I'm stealing from him."

"Pereira…"

"What?"

"Are you sure he took something of yours?"

"Of course I'm sure!"

"Maybe you just misplaced it."

"So you're on his side?"

"I'm not on anyone's side."

"You're either on my side or you're on that rich bastard's side. Which is it?"

"All right, I'm on your side."

"You swear?"

"Sure, I swear."

"Good. We need a plan. I need to search his things. I'll need five minutes, nothing more. Can you get me five minutes?"

"How?"

"I don't know. Create a distraction or something."

"There has to be a better way. Wait. It should be empty when everyone goes to eat."

"Perfect."

"If you find something, leave it there."

"Why?"

"So you can prove you didn't take it yourself."

"No."

"Why not?"

"He could hide it somewhere else. If I find something, I'll just take it."

"Suit yourself."

Later that day, Pereira was a few minutes late for dinner. He sat down at the table and started eating without saying anything to anyone.

"Did you find anything?" James asked later.

"Nothing. He probably carries it on himself."

"Or he doesn't have it."

"Are you calling me a liar?"

"No." James sighed. "So what now?"

"I'll need to search his pockets."

"How are you going to do that?"

"I'll wait until he's asleep. It shouldn't be very difficult."

"I'm starting to think he wasn't lying."

"Are you on his side now?"

"I'm just saying that maybe he really didn't take anything. Are you sure you didn't misplace whatever that thing was? Or maybe someone else took it."

"I thought I could trust you, McDougall. I thought you cared about justice. I guess I'm alone now. Don't tell anyone about any of this, understood? If anyone, *anyone* finds out, I'll kill you. Understood?"

"Fine. I'm tired of this nonsense anyway. Good luck."

"Don't talk to me."

Pereira walked away.

For a while James pondered if he should tell anyone about this. Probably not Wright or Thatcher, but maybe Hammond? He could end the whole feud in under a minute. Or maybe tell de Toledo that he's being accused and let the two sort it out themselves? He finally brushed it off and told himself to ignore it. It was none of his business and there was no need for him to lose sleep over it.

Pereira spent most of his day watching de Toledo. Everywhere Miguel went, Pereira would follow from a distance.

That night, James and the rest of the crew were suddenly woken up by a blast. As everyone jumped out of their hammocks, someone lit a lantern and they saw Pereira standing next to the body of de Toledo. Several pirates came down from the upper deck.

"What the fuck happened?"

"Shit."

"The fuck did you do, Pereira?"

"Fucking Spaniards."

"Mr. Pereira," Clarke said, "give me your pistol."

Pereira handed over the gun.

"Topside. Move it."

The pirates moved out of the way as Pereira and Clarke went upstairs.

Thatcher showed up.

"What happened?"

"Pereira killed another man."

"Fuck."

Somebody lit a lantern and gave it to Thatcher. He inspected the body.

"What was his name?"

"Miguel de Toledo," James said. "He joined from that ship that we ended up selling in San Juan. Pereira thought Miguel had stolen something from him."

"Come with me, McDougall. Anyone else who knows anything about this, you come too. And bring the body. Everyone else, stay here."

James and Manzanares picked up de Toledo's body and carried it upstairs. Wright was already there, wearing only pants. With no shirt or coat, the captain couldn't hide his fat hairy stomach.

"Apparently Mr. Pereira shot Mr. de Toledo. Mr. Manzanares, what do you know about this?"

"Pereira and McDougall spoke to me yesterday, but Pereira suddenly changed his mind and said there was nothing. I don't know, you'll have to ask McDougall."

"McDougall is a dirty rat," Pereira said. Clarke punched him in the face.

"You'll speak when you're spoken to."

"Thank you, Mr. Clarke. Mr. McDougall, what do you know about this?"

"Pereira says some item of his has gone missing and that Toledo probably stole it from him."

"Did he?"

"Yes," Pereira said.

Thatcher looked at Pereira.

"So you're saying that you knew there was a thief on this ship, and you didn't tell anyone?"

Pereira was silent.

"I asked you a question, shit-for-brains. Why didn't you say anything?"

"I wanted to keep it for myself."

"What was the item?"

Pereira was quiet.

"Hand it over."

Pereira sighed and took a small purple velvet bag out of his pocket. Thatcher untied it and turned it over. Several rubies fell into his palm.

"Where did you get these?"

"From the last ship we took," Pereira said. "The one that had the politician."

"Keep talking."

"Miguel and I checked the desk, we found money and other stuff, and I grabbed this bag and put it in my pocket. I forgot about it. Then later, Miguel asked me what was in it, and we found a bunch of rubies, so we decided not to give it to you, and instead just split it between me and him."

"And then you tried to fleece him, you stingy bastard."

"Yes. I only gave him two. He was furious."

"I thought so. What happened then?"

"He found where I was hiding the rest of them and stole it."

"Is that why you shot him?"

"When he was asleep, I checked his pockets and took the rubies back. He woke up. We fought."

No one said anything for a long time.

"So," Wright started. "You kept the loot that belonged to the entire crew, then you decided to stiff your friend, and when he realized it, you shot him. Pereira, you are a worthless turd and this whole time, ever since we picked you up, you've been a massive pain in the neck. You knew the rules – never steal from a shipmate. We rob and pillage elsewhere, but never on the ship. You broke that trust, and then to top it off,you killed a member of the crew. We can't have you on the *Doom* anymore. Mr. Thatcher, I'll leave the rest to you. I'm going back to sleep."

Wright went back to his cabin and Thatcher went down to the lower deck to inform the crew. He returned with a length of rope. Other pirates showed up to witness the execution.

Clarke held Pereira while Mason and O'Keefe held up de Toledo's body and tied them together. Pereira looked stunned. He didn't say a word.

"José Manuel Pereira," Thatcher said, "for your crimes of theft and murder, you will be rewarded with the opportunity to spend the rest of your short life in the embrace of your partner in crime. Throw them overboard."

Clarke, Mason, and O'Keefe pushed the two men into the sea through the gangway.

"Everyone who's not on watch, back to sleep."

The two bodies floated away with the current. Pereira did not make a sound.

CHAPTER XV
Williamsburg, Colony of Virginia

"Really?"

"Sure. The only other option would be to get killed and thrown overboard or be left at sea in a boat without paddles. Mutineers don't show mercy."

"Do these things happen often?"

"All the time. Sailors get tired of the captain and the constant misery, take over the ship, and head for home. Or turn to piracy. A lot of crews become pirates that way."

"Was that how Heartless Harry started pirating?"

"I don't know. Maybe."

"Nobody ever told you how it all started?"

"No. Then again, I never asked."

"It's hard for me to imagine Heartless Harry as a young sailor."

"You've never even seen him."

"You're right. But still, a legendary pirate captain, being told to scrub the deck… Just feels weird imagining it."

"We all started somewhere."

"I know, but it's… How do you imagine Harry before he became a pirate?"

"I don't think about that. He wasn't always the captain, obviously."

"Did he… never mind. Tell me about something else."

"What kind of ships did you attack the most? I mean, what flag?"

"When I was there it was mostly Spanish. We spent a lot of time in Spanish waters."

"I bet the Spanish were afraid of you."

"I wouldn't know. Although we did encounter some Spanish pirate hunters, so I guess they weren't too fond of us."

"Pirate hunters?"

"Yup."

"And how dangerous were those pirate hunters?"

"I can't tell you, because we avoided them. None of us wanted to take any chances."

"So you never actually fought them?"

"Not face to face. I remember only one encounter. We evaded them."

"You should've just fought them and gotten rid of them for good. You fought crews of other ships, right?"

"Those other ships had gold. Why fight when you can, you know, not fight?"

"To get them off your tail, so they never bother you again."

"We got away. We got rid of them without any effort."

"But there was still the chance those same Spaniards would show up later."

"Do you really think we cared about what's going to happen later?"

"I don't know."

"The sea is big. The chances of finding the same ship again are pretty slim, unless you know where it's going. And we never really had a long-term plan, we were just going to wherever we saw a good opportunity. Hell, we hardly ever planned attacking ships. Most of the time we just saw a ship and said, here's a ship, let's take it."

"Sounds nice."

"What?"

"No worries, no plans, just the job at hand. Going where life takes you. Not knowing where you're going to end up."

"We all knew where we were going to end up. Floating face-down in the sea or swinging in the noose. I remember seeing one sun-dried lad hanging from a rope in Kingston, to scare people away from piracy. They put a sign on the corpse that just said, *Pyrate*."

"Didn't scare you away."

"I guess not."

"How many of your crew ended up in the noose?"

"We called it *dancing the hempen jig*. As far as I know, most of those we lost went out in battle. Only a few of us, me included, got caught alive."

"What happened?"

"Doesn't matter."

"Don't start that again. How did you get caught?"

"Let's just say we bit off more than we could chew."

"Was it a Spanish ship?"

"No."

"British?"

"Leave it be, Rob."

"Why?"

"Just ask me something else."

"All right. Did you have a favorite type of target?"

"Sure. Easy and with lots of gold."

"No, I meant like Spanish, British, and so on."

"I just said it. Easy to take, lots of gold to be stolen. Everything else is not important."

"How do you know if a ship has gold?"

"You don't. And in most ships it's not gold but the cargo. We'd take everything that's worth anything and sell it."

"And how much money would you make?"

"Let's just say I made more money when we sacked Porto Bello than my father would've made in a couple of years."

"What does your father do?"

"He was a chandler."

"Where are you from?"

"Portsmouth."

"I'm from Massachusetts."

"Does your family still live there?"

"I don't know. I haven't been there in years. There's probably my cousin, if he hasn't moved somewhere else. Other than that, I don't think there are other living Blakewells out there. What about you? Your family's still in Portsmouth?"

"I know most of them are still there. But they wouldn't want to talk to me now that I'm a pirate."

"When was the last time you were home?"

"A long time ago. Years."

"At least you have someone to go home to. My parents' shack is probably completely gone."

"I can't go home." James sighed heavily. "How long have you been here?"

"A few weeks now. It's hard to count. What day of the month is it?"

"I don't know. Wasn't keeping track of time recently."

"How did you get here?"

"I was transported here on a boat. It was dark there the whole time. No idea how long I was there."

"James?"

"What?"

"Are you scared? About tomorrow?"

"A little bit."

"You'll be fine."

"All right."

CHAPTER XVI

Isla Contoy, Captaincy General of Yucatán

The sky had been cloudy since the early morning, and now the first drops started to fall. A minute later it was pouring. Wind picked up, and James along with others had to help furl the studding sails.

He carried one of the sails to the storage and stopped to take a break. O'Keefe passed him by.

"You're going back out there?" he asked.

"Yeah."

"Tell the captain we should be at the destination tomorrow evening, maybe sooner."

"What are you talking about? We haven't even reached the Bay."

"We're not going there yet."

"Where are we going then?"

"Captain will tell you tomorrow. Maybe even tonight." O'Keefe smiled and was about to walk away.

"Can you give me a hint?"

"Sure. You're not going to like it."

"We're going to hunt giant sea monsters?"

"Worse. Much worse."

James went back out into the rain and found Wright talking to Manzanares.

"Captain, O'Keefe says we should be at the destination tomorrow evening, possibly sooner."

"Good. Thank you."

James went to the stern where Hammond was checking the spanker.

"Jack, do you know anything about a change of plans?"

"What?"

"I talked to O'Keefe, he said we'll reach the destination by tomorrow evening."

"We haven't even entered the Bay yet!"

"I asked him what *is* the destination,he just said we're not going to like it."

"What the fuck? I'm going to talk to the captain."

"Don't tell him you got it from me."

Hammond ran over to the bow and spoke with Wright. He returned visibly angry.

"Son of a bitch," he said.

"What is it?"

"We're stopping at some random beach to careen the ship."

"Fuck. Now I know what O'Keefe meant."

"We could've careened the ship back in Nassau, before we left."

"Most of the crew would've been drunk or not showed up altogether."

"I know." Hammond spat into the water. "I would've been one of those who didn't show up."

"I would've been one of those who showed up drunk."

"I already miss Nassau."

"Me too. But on the bright side, this job should get us enough money to stay in Nassau for months. We'll just have to tough it out."

"Manzanares told me about the idea to sack Havana."

"And?"

"If done right, it's entirely possible. We could end up with so much money we'd never have to sail again."

"It would take a much bigger crew to do it," James said.

"So?"

"More people to split the money."

"It's Havana, half the crew would die in the raid. The survivors will be rich men."

"Convincing enough men to risk their lives will be tough."

"McDougall, haven't you learned anything? The job itself doesn't matter, it's how much it pays. And I'm thinking that we should drop one of our Spanish lads in Cuba with a bunch of cash. He goes to Havana by land, gets a small place, watches ships coming in and out, and then we know when to strike so we make the most money. A few days before the raid we send some people to stay there, they help us get inside the city and take down Spanish soldiers."

"We'll need a lot of Spaniards we can trust. We have what, four? Five? That's including the second mate."

"We need one spy right now. Then we return to Nassau, get every trusted man who speaks Spanish, and come back."

"I think this could work."

"It *will* work, and when that happens, we'll be known as the most dangerous sons of bitches that ever sailed the seas. I hear that after Porto Bello the Spanish became afraid of Captain Wright and the *Howling Doom*. We could be even bigger. We could have the entire *world* afraid of us."

"The entire world… But you said we'd never have to sail again. We would be the scariest men out there and we'd be drinking in Nassau all day."

"We could go on more raids if we wanted to."

"Where would we go after Havana?"

"First to Cartagena, then to Tripoli," Hammond said. "Then Naples, then Barcelona. If we can take Havana, we can take any city we want."

"Even London?"

"Even London."

"You're going crazy."

"Not at all. Give me enough men, and I'll take London. Hell, give me even more men and I'll become the king of England. But I think I'll rename it Hammondland."

"You're definitely crazy."

"If you want to be feared, you have to be crazy. Sane is too predictable."

"All right…"

They said nothing for a few minutes. The rain kept pouring.

"Did you tell the captain or the quartermaster about the Havana plan?" James asked.

"Not yet. First we need a good victory. Nobody will agree to it unless they feel invincible. Let's get this raid over with, then we can plan for Havana."

"What if this one fails?"

"This is the surest thing in all my years as a pirate. But if for some reason it doesn't end in triumphant victory, we'll go for another one. There is another plan."

"Really? What's the target?"

"I don't know. I do know that the captain always has a backup plan. There's no way we'll return to Nassau without a good prize."

"What do you think it could be? Campeche?"

"Maybe Campeche. It's a good target. Maybe it's Villahermosa or one of a few others. Who knows. We'll probably do good. I don't think we'll be using that backup plan."

"All right," James said. "Now we need to convince the captain and Thatcher that this is going to work. If those two are on board, everyone else will join."

"I talked to Clarke, he says he's in if there is a good plan. He doesn't want to just show up in Havana and charge."

"Good. Neither do we."

"That's what I told him. He's pretty much on board."

"So now we wait for this one to be over?"

"Yes. Once we sober up after the victory, we'll tell the captain. He never passes up a challenge, especially when it means we could become the most feared crew on the seven seas."

"Can we go somewhere with a roof or something? I hate this rain."

"No. I need to keep an eye on the sails and rigging, now that the wind's picking up."

"Can *I* go somewhere else?"

"No. Stay here and keep me company."

"Go fuck yourself."

The wind wasn't as strong as it was when the *Doom* sailed past Havana, but they were making decent progress. The rain ended after a few hours and after that it was sunshine the whole way.

In a couple of days they saw land in the distance. It was a small island about four miles long and half a mile wide.

"O'Keefe, where exactly are we?" Hammond asked.

"Just to the east of the very tip of Yucatán peninsula. After we clean up the hull we'll go straight to the Bay of Mexico."

"How much time will it take?"

"We should be right on schedule for the raid if we don't waste any time."

When the *Howling Doom* was about a hundred yards away from the shore, they dropped the anchor and lowered the launches and paddled to the island. The sea was so clear they could see through several feet of water. A manta ray swam under one of the launches.

The shore they landed on was rocky, and two pirates were sent in opposite directions along the coast to find a good beach to careen the ship.

James followed Phillips, Hammond and others into the forest. The pirates slowly made their way through the woods, constantly looking around and listening to every sound. There were no animals around except for a black-and-yellow bird with a massive colorful beak. The bird observed the humans with calm curiosity, knowing he was too high for them to reach.

Suddenly, Phillips motioned the crew to stop.

"What?" Hammond whispered so quietly it was barely audible.

"Deer," Phillips answered just as softly. He pointed to a spot between trees.

Hammond nodded upward, telling Phillips to lead the way. He carefully placed one foot in front of the other, trying not to cause any noise. Everyone else followed, looking at the ground to avoid stepping on a twig or causing some other noise.

Phillips got to the spot where he had seen the deer and stopped and looked around for a while.

"It's gone," he said.

"Shit."

"Are you sure you saw a deer?" Hammond asked.

"I'm pretty sure it was a deer."

"Pretty sure? So you're saying it could've been a tree or something?"

"I saw a deer."

"I think you saw something else and there was no deer."

"Go fuck yourself."

The bird lost interest and flew away.

The pirates returned to the shore. Anderson returned with good news.

"I found a perfect beach," he said. "And I caught a sea turtle!"

He led the crew north and after a mile and a half the rocks ended and they were on a beautiful sandy beach. There was indeed a sea turtle there. Anderson had flipped it on its back.

"That's a big one," Phillips said. "Did you find any eggs?"

"No."

"Damn it. Turtle eggs taste amazing."

Clarke took off his boots and walked into the sea until he was waist deep in water.

"The bottom is good," he said. "Soft sand, not too deep, not too shallow. We'll see how the tide moves, but it should be good."

"I'll go find Thatcher," Anderson said.

He paddled back to the ship and relayed the location of the beach to the quartermaster. The rest of the crew, except for half a dozen men staying on the ship, took to launches and joined the others on the shore.

Beasley drew his knife and immediately went to work on the turtle.

"That won't feed the crew," he said. "You boys will have to find more turtles."

"I saw a deer in the forest."

"Shut the fuck up, Phillips," Hammond said. "There was no fucking deer in there."

"Look, I really don't care what you saw," Beasley said. "I care what you bring for me to cook."

"You know what?" Phillips said. "I'm going to find that deer, I'm going to kill it, and I'm going to eat it. And I'm not going to share it with you."

"Fine," Hammond said. "I'll have some of that turtle."

"Fuck you."

Phillips went into the woods.

Meanwhile, Thatcher and O'Keefe were putting sticks into the sand to mark where the water level was. O'Keefe then had to wade chest-deep into the water to put a few more markers in.

"Mr. Martin, did you bring the axes?" Thatcher asked.

"They're in the launch."

"Get them. All of you," he pointed at a group of pirates, "take an axe and go get me some timber. We'll need it to secure the ship."

They got axes from the launch and went looking for wood. James didn't have an axe so he just followed the others. They found some tall, straight palms and started chopping. Johnson felled one first and then chopped off the canopy.

"Can you help me carry this?"

"Just cut it in half," Martin said. "We don't need logs that big."

"Fine."

Johnson started chopping right in the middle. Once he got tired, he gave the axe to James who continued the work. After a while, the log was finally halved and it took three pirates to carry one of them to the beach. Then they came back and brought the other one. When they dropped it on the sand, James noticed that everyone was looking at something in the distance.

"What's going on?"

"Ship. Over there."

A ship was coming from the northwest. It was a sloop flying a Spanish flag.

The half-dozen men remaining on the *Doom* flew the black flag at the stern.

The sloop immediately changed direction. The Spaniards knew they had no chance against a pirate brig.

"That's right," Manzanares said. "Go back to mama."

"I wish I could've seen their faces when they saw the black," Hammond said.

The sloop kept going and then disappeared over the horizon. The men remaining on the ship lowered the black flag.

James and a few others went back to the woods and brought back more lumber. They finished the job before dusk. Other pirates were in the longboat, moving things from the hold to the shore. The ship had to be as light as possible to make the whole process easier.

Beasley finished cooking dinner. James didn't get to try turtle, but others said it wasn't that good. Midway through the meal, Phillips returned.

"Hey, Phillips, where's the deer?"

"Go fuck yourself, Hammond."

Wright allowed the crew to have some rum, but they got carried away and emptied almost half of their supply. Talking and singing continued well into the night. Eventually,the pirates fell asleep all over the beach. The only ones awake were two men standing security and another one watching the tide.

Wright woke up first and went around kicking his crewmen in the ribs to wake them up. Some went for a quick dip in the sea to help relieve the hangover. James was among them. He waded chest-deep into the water, took a deep breath,and dunked his head. The cold water made him feel a little better.

The breakfast was decent. After eating, Thatcher informed them that they had missed the morning high tide and the next one would be in the evening. Until then, they had to move the remaining things from the ship to the beach.

They started with the cargo they had taken from the last ship they captured. Then they moved the rest of their supplies, and then it was time for cannons. The cannons had to be lifted out of their carriages and moved to the longboat. The boat could only handle three at a time. Then they would have to be carried further inland to avoid any saltwater damage, and then the process started all over again.

By afternoon, the *Howling Doom* was mostly empty. The last items were placed in a longboat and several crewmen started tying lines to the beak of the ship. Thatcher wanted to sail the *Doom* as close to the shore as possible, but the wind was too weak, and thus the sails were all furled.

As the tide started rising, the entire crew picked up the ropes and started pulling the ship in. The progress was good until the keel hit the sand. Captain Wright announced a short break, just until the tide rose higher. Then it was back to pulling.

The entire keel was dragging through the sand, and there was less and less water under the ship. The pirates kept pulling it onto the beach, occasionally getting a really short break to rest their muscles. *Howling Doom* was beginning to tilt toward larboard.

The ship kept getting harder and harder to pull, and breaks were taken more and more often. The *Doom* leaned larboard until it was resting on the keel and hull. It still wasn't out of water. The masts made a forty-five degree angle with the ground.

"This is hell," Cartwright said during the next break. "How much more?"

"Until she's out of the water," Manzanares said.

"When is that?"

"When the stern is past that marker." He pointed at a stick directly to the right of them.

"I hate my life."

After more labor, the rudder finally reached the marker for high tide. *Howling Doom* was completely out of the water. The pirates started placing logs and tying lines to secure the ship in place. James stepped into the sea and dipped his hands into cold water to soothe the pain in his palms.

"One of the shrouds is ripped," Hammond said. "We'll need to replace that."

"Jesus Christ, Jack, one job at a time," James said.

"We'll have to fix that sooner or later."

"Fine. We'll do it later."

It was getting dark, so the pirates ate and went to sleep. In the morning, the work began. The hull was covered in barnacles that needed to be removed. Over a dozen pirates were scraping them off with knives. The barnacles had securely attached themselves to the ship, and the process went slowly.

James's hands were still aching from rope burn, and removing sharp shells was agony. An hour into the job, he found a hole.

"Did you see Jim?" he asked Mason.

"I think he's talking with the quartermaster."

James went looking and found the carpenter on the other side of the ship.

"I think I found something."

They ran back to the spot and James pointed out the hole.

"Shit. It's shipworm."

"Is it bad?"

"Shipworm is never good. We'll stay afloat though."

Jim walked away and James returned to work. After a few minutes, the carpenter returned. He shaved the bark off a stick, put some glue on it and stuck it in the hole.

"Right now this is all I can do. I'll cut off the end later. Let me know if you find more shipworm damage."

The pirates worked in rotation. Every once in a while somebody would take a break and someone else would take over. In one day, they managed to clean most of the starboard side. When James went to sleep, his hands were tired and aching and full of small cuts.

The next morning,they went back to scraping barnacles. The job was finished in the afternoon. Then they started making boat soup, a mix of pine tar, linseed oil, turpentine, and some other materials. The entire hull had to be coated to protect the wood from rot, shipworm, and a whole list of other things. The pirates only had small brushes, and the stench of the tar was unbearable. They took turns standing upwind from the ship.

"This must be what hell smells like," O'Keefe said during one break.

They worked well into the night, as Thatcher wanted to apply another layer of tar. They finished the job around midnight.

The next day, they loosened the lines holding the ship and carefully pulled her until the starboard side was on the sand. They tied it to some palm trees and placed support beams under it, and went to work cleaning barnacles.

"Days like this make me want to quit sailing," Manzanares grumbled.

"A big prize is waiting," Clarke said.

"Yeah, that's the only reason why I'm still here."

As the ship's surgeon, Ortega was excused from manual labor, so he volunteered to take one of the boats and go fishing. A lot of men volunteered to go with him, but Flowers won, being the only one who had worked on a fishing vessel.

Cleaning went slower than before, but the pirates were making good progress. At dusk, work was over and the fishermen returned. They caught several really large yellow-and-green fish with stubby, round heads.

"What the fuck did you idiots bring me?" Beasley said when he saw them. "Those things look inbred. Couldn't you find something decent?"

"Shut up and start cooking," Thatcher said.

The weird colorful fish turned out to have a very nice taste, especially when washed down with some rum. After dinner, several pirates went to Ortega and told him that the fish was great and that he should go fishing again tomorrow.

"Take a bigger boat and start early. Just bring us more fish."

Ortega and Flowers recruited Mason and left in the longboat early in the morning. The rest of the crew went back to cleaning barnacles off the hull. Shortly before dusk, the hull was cleaned and a layer of boat soup was being applied. That's when the fishermen returned.

The longboat was at full sail. Its arrival was met with cheers. When they got close to the shore, Mason jumped out and ran to the beach.

"Captain! Where's the captain?!"

"What is it?"

"Captain, we saw a Spanish man-of-war."

"Where?"

"By the shore a few miles to the south. We came back as fast as we could."

"Shit."

"Did you see fires on the shore?" Thatcher asked.

"No. Definitely no fires."

"They're not staying there. They're preparing to attack, either at dawn or at midnight."

"Do they know we're here?" Manzanares asked. "Maybe they're just sailing by."

"Remember that sloop that we saw a few days ago?" Thatcher said. "It could be they encountered a man-of-war and told them where they could find some pirates."

"So what now?"

"Here's what we can do. We get all the guns, line them on the beach, and hide. Let them think the *Doom* is a shipwreck. Then we wait for them to come ashore to investigate, and when they do, we attack. We can't get on water, so we make them go on land."

"Thank you, Mr. Thatcher," the captain said, "but if they already know there's pirates here, they won't fall for such tricks. They'll just open fire on the *Doom* and smash it to pieces, and we'll be stuck here with no means to get out. We'll be at their mercy."

"If we bring the guns to the beach, they'll be within range themselves. We could just show them that we're ready, and it might scare them away."

"They have a fucking man-of-war, they're not afraid of a few guns. That could work with a smaller ship, but not a big one. They can sit and wait for reinforcements to arrive. Our position is terrible. We have no advantage. We need to get the *Doom* out into the water and get out of here before we get cornered."

"I have a suggestion," James spoke up.

"Let's hear it," Thatcher said. Wright nodded.

"The Spanish don't know that we expect them. We could build bonfires on the other side of the island. Make them think it's our camp. We could lead them the wrong way, maybe even get them stuck on a shoal."

"Thank you, Mr. McDougall," Wright said. "How about you stay out of this from now on?"

"We could attack them now, when they least expect it," Flowers said.

"Mr. Flowers, how did you live this long being this stupid? Of all the things I've ever heard, this one makes the least sense. Now, does anyone else have useless ideas, or can we get moving?"

"I still think we should make a stand," Thatcher said. "Only the stern is exposed. If we remove the rudder, they can't do much damage. We have all of our guns. If we position them on the beach, we can cover a wide area."

"We'll still be sitting ducks, goddammit! We'll be stuck here with nowhere to go. If we don't go now, we stay here forever. The Spanish won't let us get away."

"We can't launch the ship. There's not enough time."

"There's plenty of time if we start right now. High tide just started, it's now or never."

"They're already prepared to attack."

"They'll attack at dawn, maybe midnight," Wright said. "The surprise will be lost if they attack now. We have time to make it out of here."

"You mean run away."

"It's a retreat."

"You don't want to fight."

"I don't want to fight a battle I cannot win. Even if we win and sink the man-of-war, what do we get out of it? Nothing. We'll just waste ammunition and good men. Better retreat now and fight another day, when we at least stand to get some money from it."

"I guess we've run out of options, captain," Thatcher said. "We put this to vote. Let the crew make the call."

"No."

"You can't deny the crew's vote."

"In battle, the captain's word is the law."

"We're not in battle."

"You just said that we don't have time to launch the ship and the Spaniards are already prepared to attack. Doesn't that mean that a battle is imminent?"

"But it hasn't started yet."

"When does it start? When the first shot is fired?"

"Yes."

"So if that man-of-war was right here, two hundred yards from us, it would still not be combat, because nobody fired a shot?"

"But it isn't there, it's a few miles away."

"For all we know, the Spanish are on the way. Either way, a battle is imminent, and right now everything we're doing is focused on that battle."

"Fine! You win. Happy now? You win. We're in a battle. What will our orders be, captain?"

"Launch the ship!"

Some of the pirates ran over to the palm trees and untied the lines, others kicked support beams from under the *Doom*. They started moving the ship. Some pushed at the keel and the hull, the rest grabbed the ropes still tied to the beak and pulled it. They were sweating and their hands were burning, but they managed to move the ship faster than a few days ago.

"Tide is moving out!" Hammond shouted. "We need to hurry up!"

James held the rope and pulled with everything he had, and he couldn't see the markers in the ground, he just knew the ship was slowly inching towards the sea. He kept pulling, and heard Hammond telling everyone to move it, but it seemed that the ship was barely moving, not enough to be in the water in time for them to escape.

And then he took another step back, and felt water touch his foot. James couldn't pause to take a look around, but now he knew they had reached the water. From there it would get easier.

Soon both of his feet were in water, then it was up to his knees, and before he knew it, he was waist deep. *Howling Doom* was touching water.

James had a hard time pulling the line once the water reached his chest, and he went to the others to help them push the ship. A dozen or so pirates had their hands on the ship, the rest pushed those in front of them. Several pirates climbed aboard and unfurled the sails to give them a little extra push.

It was almost night, but the *Howling Doom* was finally in the water.

"Get the guns!" Wright commanded. "Everyone, start moving the guns!"

The crew's hands were so tired most of them could hardly grip anything, but they started moving the cannons back to the ship. Each one was carried by three or four men. The longboat could carry three, but they decided to risk it and moved them four at a time.

While moving one of the cannons to its carriage, Boyd dropped it on the deck and crushed Scott's ring and pinky fingers. Clarke told Scott to go find something useful to do, smacked Boyd over the head, and helped him put the cannon in place.

After cannons came the cargo. James was on the beach, moving boxes and barrels to the boats. He didn't have the strength in his hands to hold an oar.

Manzanares came back in one of the launches and as they were loading cargo, he said that Fuller was dead.

"What?"

"I just found his body floating in the water. Probably fell in the water and nobody saw him in the dark."

"I thought he could swim."

"I guess he couldn't."

No matter how fast everyone worked, moving the cargo was painfully slow. The only upside was that the Spanish man-of-war wasn't anywhere nearby.

The never-ending pile of random stuff began to shrink and eventually there were just a few more trips to the ship. James climbed into one of the boats and sat there holding onto boxes. When he got to the *Doom*, he went to Thatcher.

"I want to take the very next watch."

"Done. You've done well today, McDougall."

"Thank you."

The job was done. They raised the anchor and unfurled the sails and were off to the Bay of Mexico.

James sat amidships leaning against the mainmast while others went to sleep. He was exhausted.

Phillips and Hammond stopped by.

"Hey, McDougall," Phillips said. "Just wanted to say it was actually a good idea."

"What?"

"Your suggestion to light bonfires and get the Spanish on a shoal. That was brilliant. I honestly wish *I* came up with that."

"Thanks."

"I wish we would've done it. We could've had that ship. I think the *Doom* could hold its own against a bigger ship; if it was stuck it would've been easy."

"We could've taken a fucking man-of-war," Hammond said. "If it wasn't for the captain's idea to retreat."

"You retreat from *battle*, when it's already decided and you don't want to waste men and ammunition," Phillips said. "This wasn't a retreat from battle, this was running away to *avoid* battle. We should've fought them on the ground. We should've just lit bonfires to get them to the opposite side of the island, and then slaughtered them in the forest."

"When we get to Mexico, you can kill all the Spaniards you want."

"We could've been the first crew to take down a man-of-war. It would've been historic."

"Nothing we can do about it now. Just go to bed. Goodnight, McDougall."

"Goodnight. Sweet dreams."

There was a scream. Ortega couldn't fix Scott's fingers that got crushed by a cannon. He had to amputate them. Jim did it for him with one good swing of a hatchet.

Once his watch was over, James went to bed. He stopped by to check on Scott, whose left hand was missing the ring finger and the pinky. The bandage was soaked with blood, and the blood was slowly dripping on the floor. Scott was asleep, or maybe passed out. James climbed into his hammock wondering if Scott will get paid for getting maimed, or if it was only for injuries suffered in battle.

CHAPTER XVII
Williamsburg, Colony of Virginia

A dog was barking somewhere outside the walls of the gaol.

"James?"

"What now?"

"Do you think I would fit in with the crew of *Howling Doom*?"

"No."

"Why not?"

"You're not a complete degenerate."

"Come on, your crew can't be that bad."

"It can, and it was."

"I think you're just trying to scare me out of it."

"I am, because I've seen some really disgusting things during that time. Let's just say that the life of a pirate is much worse than what you imagine."

"If you didn't like it, you would've quit the first chance you had."

"Shut up."

"Seriously, if it was so bad, why didn't you just quit?"

"I said shut up!"

"Fine. I'll shut up."

The dog stopped barking.

James and Rob both tried to fall asleep, but both of them had too much on their minds. They just lay in the dark listening to each other's breathing. Their eyes had adjusted to the dark just enough to be able to see silhouettes of objects.

"How hard is it being on a ship's crew?" Rob asked.

"Depends on the ship and on your job."

"Can you elaborate a little?"

"On the *Valiant*, the merchant ship I was on before piracy, we were short on crew, and whenever there's a job that needs to be done and it's not assigned to anybody, everyone has to pick up the slack. Whatever job you have, you'll have to do extra because every single ship is always short on manpower. I have never even *heard* of a merchant ship that had enough crew."

"And on the *Howling Doom*?"

"On the *Doom* we had plenty of crew. Almost twice than what the ship required. There was plenty of time off. Occasionally I had to help out with something, but most of the time there wasn't much to do. Unless we went into a battle."

"What was your job on that merchant ship?"

"I was listed as able-bodied sailor. It simply meant that I didn't have a specific job and did whatever the quartermaster or captain or whoever else told me to do."

"Like scrubbing the deck?"

"And a bunch of other stuff. There was always something to clean. A couple of times I helped out the cook. Worked on rigging and sails a lot. And there was a lot of time in the fucking crow's nest."

"What's so bad about the crow's nest?"

"You have to stand for hours until you don't feel your legs, you're holding to a thin strip of metal, can't move because there's no space to move, and most of the time there's nothing there, just water in every direction. And it seems like whenever there's something to spot, like land or a sail, it's always someone else, and when it's your turn again, it's just water."

"Did you have to do that on the *Howling Doom*?"

"Of course I did. And it was equally terrible. But at least with more crew I had to do it less often."

"So it's better to be a crewman on a pirate ship?"

"Rob, don't be a pirate."

"Maybe I want to join the merchant navy now."

"Don't do that either. I joined because I was stupid. I thought there would be adventure, and faraway lands, and I'll be standing on the deck in the sunlight, watching the blue sea, and it all will be so great and exciting, and I'll be paid to do what I'd do for free. Boy was I wrong."

"I think that's why most kids want to be sailors."

"And then they get to scrub the deck, and eat terrible food, and do hard work out in a thunderstorm in the middle of the night, and the quartermaster's yelling, and the ship is rocking every which way, and suddenly being on land seems so nice that you forget why you ever wanted to be on a ship in the first place."

"Don't tell me there are no good moments."

"There are. Every once in a while you actually have one of those moments where you're just standing on the deck in the sunlight, there's a cool breeze, and you pass by beautiful tropical islands. But those moments don't happen very often."

"How long have you done this?"

"I don't even know anymore. A few years. I lost track long ago. Not that I care right now."

"Do you miss it?"

"I don't know. I mean… a lot of it was bad, some of it was horrible and I want to forget it, some of it was really good. I do miss the good parts. But the good parts come with the bad parts."

"What do you miss?"

"I've met some people who are now dead. I miss the time I spent with them."

"Those friends, were some of them pirates?"

"You're not going to stop pushing this topic, are you?"

"No."

"Look, some of the pirates were fun to be around, especially when drunk. But those same men were killers. I've watched some of them doing horrible things to innocent people. I want to say that they were good people, but I can't. They were decent people some of the time."

"I still don't think it was as bad as you say."

"It was worse than you think."

"Sounds to me like they were regular folks, and piracy was their job."

"Not sure if I would put it that way."

"I think you're being a little harsh on them."

"Anyone who has ever encountered a pirate crew would tell you that I'm not being harsh enough. Especially a crew like ours."

CHAPTER XVIII

Campeche, Captaincy General of Yucatán

The *Howling Doom* sailed into the Great Bay of Mexico, following the coasts of New Spain. Captain Wright wanted to stay near the shore and avoid going too far into open waters. In a few days, they were in the Bay of Campeche.

Nicholas Scott spent three days fighting gangrene. In the end, the disease won. Scott's body was put in a bag that was then sewn shut. They threw him into the sea with no ceremony.

After the funeral, Hammond assigned James and two others to replace one of the foremast starboard shrouds. The pirates brought a few coils of line and started working.

As they were running a lanyard between deadeyes, Hammond showed up and decided that the other three lanyards were due for replacement too.

"We'll get to it when we're done with this one," Johnson promised.

They measured a length of rope for the shroud and cut it to length and started worming it – wrapping the rope with a thin string in between the strands. Once that was done, they took some canvas and cut it to strips and wrapped them around the rope. Then they covered the whole thing in tar. Finally, they tightly wrapped it in twine and gave it another coat of tar and left it to dry.

While the shroud was drying, they cut the lanyards of the other shrouds one by one and replaced them with new ones.

The tar dried quickly, and soon they were able to tie one end of the new shroud to a deadeye and the other to the foremast top. With the job done, they reported to Hammond, who insisted on checking it.

"Not bad. It'll hold."

"*Not bad*?" Johnson said. "That's it?"

"What do you want, a fucking medal? If you want to get a compliment, feel free to take it down and start over."

"Get fucked, Jack."

That same afternoon, they saw the city of Campeche in the distance, but were too far away to make out anything more than some dots of various colors peeking out from behind foliage.

James found the ship's new navigator, Paul O'Keefe, leaving the captain's cabin.

"Hey, O'Keefe, how much more to go?"

"Two days if we change course."

"Wait, why are we changing course?"

"I just talked to the captain about it. He wanted to sail along the coast, but if we cut straight to the target we'll save about sixty miles. Winds aren't very strong here, so it would cost us an entire day, maybe more."

"And we wouldn't be there on time."

"Unless we suddenly get really favorable wind, we won't be on time."

"Shit. That doesn't sound very good."

"Tell me about it."

The *Howling Doom* sailed directly west, leaving the coast behind. Once again there was nothing but water as far as the eye could see.

As evening approached, somebody spotted a sail in the distance. Wright commanded that they follow it.

"Captain, it could take us off course. We'll waste hours."

"I'm not going to pass up a good target, Mr. O'Keefe. If there's nothing promising about that ship, we'll ignore it and pick up where we left off."

"Sail, starboard side!"

Everyone immediately turned their attention to the other ship. Wright pulled out his trusty spyglass.

"I think it's coming towards us," he said. "I think we'll be taking a ship today, I just don't know which one."

He moved the spyglass from the bow to the starboard and back to the bow, observing both ships.

"Which one will be our target, captain?" Phillips asked.

"One of those ships. Whichever one is easier to take."

The ship in front of them was a brigantine. It was slow, and the distance shrank quickly. The one on their starboard was fast, and seemed to be chasing the brigantine too. It was still too far away to make out its shape.

As the *Doom* drew closer to its target, they could make out the colors of the brigantine. It was flying a Spanish flag.

"I think this one will be it," Wright said. "Keep an eye out for the other one. We don't want them to interrupt us when the fight starts."

"Captain, I think that's a galleon," Thatcher said, watching the ship through a spyglass.

"What?!"

He ran over to the starboard and watched the ship for a couple of minutes.

"Well I'll be damned. It's the *Merciless*. And here I thought old Charlie wasn't sailing anymore. Turn a couple degrees to starboard, let's get closer and say hello."

The ship drew closer and closer, and the distinct shape showed that it was indeed an old galleon.

"Raise the black, then lower it again," Wright said. "I don't want the Spaniards to see it."

Cartwright and Richardson did exactly that.

The galleon was close enough for them to make out that there were people on deck. Two men on the galleon raised their own flag. It was black with white figures, and it showed a skeleton, representing Death, and a man wearing sailor's clothes, representing the ship's captain. He was punching Death in the face.

"That's Bedford all right," Phillips said.

"What's the plan, captain?" Thatcher asked.

"Let the old bastard have it. We have a better prize waiting for us anyway. Round in the main sail!"

James untied the nearest buntline and started pulling. The sail quickly furled. It was a signal to the *Merciless* that the *Doom* was not going to pursue the brigantine.

"Let's watch," Wright said. "I want to see if the old man still has it."

The *Merciless* pulled ahead. It was getting close to the brigantine. Bedford's black flag was still flying at the stern. The Spanish crew saw it, and they saw a brig coming after them from behind. There was movement on the brigantine.

"Prepare pistols and muskets," Wright said. "If Charlie gets himself into trouble, we might have to go in. Unfurl the main sail."

James followed others down to the lower deck to pick up his weapons. He checked the sharpness of his cutlass, then loaded both of his pistols. One was a heavy blunderbuss he had since the beginning, the other was very fancy and had the previous owner's name engraved on the barrel. He had picked it up off a dead body when they took a ship not far from Havana.

James went back up to the main deck and climbed the foremast shrouds to be able to see over the mass of pirates at the bow. The brigantine had not fired its guns. The Spaniards had decided it would be better to just surrender and give up the cargo to avoid unnecessary bloodshed.

The *Merciless* slowed down as it got side-by-side with the brigantine. Its name, written on the stern, was *Santa Cruz*. Bedford's crew began throwing ropes with hooks and pulling the two ships together.

On the *Doom*, the crew furled the sails and watched the two ships.

"Should we load the guns, captain?" Phillips asked.

"No. If we end up fighting, it will be on the deck. Have your pistols ready."

The sun inched closer to the horizon. Evening was fast approaching.

Aboard the *Merciless,* Captain Charlie Bedford watched as his men were preparing to board the *Santa Cruz.* The Spaniards surrendered without firing a single shot, which meant less work for them. It also meant that the captain didn't value the cargo enough to fight for it, either because he was a coward or because the crap in the hold wasn't worth much.

Bedford glanced at the *Howling Doom* floating nearby. Wright was nice enough to let him have the brigantine, and it wasn't a good sign. If he expected the ship to have something valuable, he wouldn't have given it up so easily. More importantly, Wright never did any favors to anyone unless he was sure he would get something in return.

We'll probably find the hold full of salt or olive oil, Bedford thought.

The two ships were finally close enough for the pirates to put a gangplank between them. The pirates began climbing aboard the *Santa Cruz.* Sterling, the quartermaster, went first. The Spanish captain shook his hand and said something to him.

"I have no idea what that means. We'll just take your cargo and go."

The captain drew his pistol and fired. The ball went through Sterling's heart and then lodged itself in the foot of a pirate who was climbing over the gunwale. He fell down on the deck, screaming in pain.

Other Spaniards drew their own pistols and fired on the pirates. One shot destroyed the second mate's skull and flew inches above Bedford's head. A young Spanish sailor fired too fast in the excitement, and the ball smashed his friend's jaw before getting lodged in the mainmast of the *Merciless.* A couple of pistols misfired. Two pirates were hit and fell overboard. Several others were lying on the deck, a few of them dead, some seriously injured.

Aboard the *Howling Doom,* the crew watched with interest.

"They played dead," Thatcher said, watching through a spyglass. "Sneaky bastards."

James could only distinguish small clouds of white smoke and some movement. He couldn't make out what exactly was going on. He just knew both sides were firing shots.

Bedford's crew reacted immediately, drawing their own guns and firing back at the Spaniards. In a couple of seconds, there were six dead Spanish sailors on the deck, and their captain was one of them. Several shots hit nothing and landed in the sea, one sailor was grazed on the arm, a couple of others barely avoided getting hit.

The Spanish dropped their empty pistols and attacked the pirates with knives and swords, one of them yelled,"*¡Viva España! ¡Viva el Rey!*" and was immediately taken down by a shot to the chest. Several pirates couldn't draw their blades fast enough and were stabbed or hacked and fell as more of their crewmates climbed aboard the brigantine, firing their pistols and drawing their cutlasses. The deck of the *Santa Cruz* was covered in bodies and blood, and the living were fighting with everything they had so they wouldn't join them.

"They're not doing well," Thatcher said.

"It's a bloodbath over there," Wright said. He put his spyglass back in his pocket. "We're going in!"

The *Doom*'s crewmen quickly untied the buntlines and let the sails fall.

"What's our course, captain?"

"Get us to the starboard of the *Merciless,*" Wright said. "Prepare to board!"

The wind was picking up and the *Doom* quickly glided towards the two ships. Once they were side by side with Bedford's galleon, they threw hooks and pulled the ships together while others furled the sails.

The three ships were now linked together. It seemed like no one on the *Merciless* or the *Santa Cruz* paid much attention.

"Go in and kill everyone!" Wright shouted. "No mercy! Anyone who isn't on this crew doesn't see tomorrow! LET'S GO!"

They placed planks between the ships and crossed over to the *Merciless* and drew their swords and started hacking everyone. Most of the galleon's crew died without realizing something was up. A couple of pirates figured out what was going on, but their captain couldn't hear them and the shots that killed them blended in with the carnage and went unheard.

With the *Merciless* empty, they started shooting the pirates and Spaniards sword fighting on the deck of *Santa Cruz*. Their shots took out several men, including a pirate and the Spanish quartermaster, who were killed by the same ball. When their guns were empty, the *Doom*'s men drew their cutlasses and jumped into the fight. Most of Bedford's men didn't realize those were not reinforcements, and were quickly slaughtered. A few others were distracted by the new enemy and got killed by the Spanish.

When James landed on the deck of the *Santa Cruz*, he saw Bedford get pinned against the mainmast by a brawny Spaniard wielding a knife. The captain drew his pistol and shot the man in the face. As the body fell to the ground, James ran over and drew his second pistol and shot Bedford in the forehead. For a brief moment before he pulled the trigger,

James saw the surprise in the captain's face. The ball punched a hole just above Bedford's left eyebrow and came out the back of his head with a pink cloud.

James looked around and saw that the battle was almost over. His crewmates outnumbered everyone else three or four to one. He ran over to one Spaniard who was valiantly fighting two pirates with a sword and struck him with his pistol and knocked him down. The two pirates immediately stabbed the sailor several times. James then attacked another sailor, who successfully parried the strike, but James kicked him in the groin and hacked him in the neck with the cutlass, unleashing a stream of blood.

One Spaniard saw that the battle was lost, so he dropped his sword and put his hands up. Cartwright immediately sank his cutlass into the sailor's chest. He was the last member of the brigantine's crew. The only ones still defending the ship were five pirates from the *Merciless*. They were badly outnumbered, standing in a tight circle with their backs to each other, wildly swinging their cutlasses. Hammond reloaded his pistol and shot one of them. It caused momentary confusion, and seconds later the remaining men were overwhelmed. It was done.

The *Santa Cruz* and Charlie Bedford's *Merciless* were theirs.

The deck was covered in bodies. A few were still moving. Bill Martin was among the dead, shot through the neck. Davenport was coughing up blood and shaking, waiting for death to come and rescue him from the pain.

"Grab the bodies and start throwing them overboard," Wright said. "There's not enough space to even place your foot."

James and Cartwright grabbed the nearest body. It was still breathing. They lifted it over the gunwale and let it fall. All over the deck of the ship bodies were being thrown out, loud splashes coming nonstop.

"Wait, let's play a game," Douglas said. "We throw them at the same time and try to get them to hit each other in the air."

"You're on," Cartwright said. He and James picked up a pirate, while Boyd and Douglas chose the body of a Spaniard.

"This one is skinny, he should fly better," Boyd said.

They tossed the bodies as high as they could, but Boyd and Douglas were a little late and the corpses fell into the water one after the other.

"Damn it. Let's try this again."

They tossed two more bodies, but the result was the same.

"All right, this time I'll count to three," Douglas said. "Ready? One… Two… Three!"

The bodies of two Spanish sailors hit one another in the air with a quiet thud and fell into the water with a loud splash.

They managed to get two more mid-air collisions before they ran out of bodies.

"Go search the hold," Wright said. "Has anyone searched the *Merciless* yet? Then go. Let me know what you find."

The hold of the *Santa Cruz* held boxes and barrels full of cinnamon, sugar, tobacco, and avocados.

"Don't take any of it," Wright said. "We're looking for gold and silver, not cargo."

Half a dozen pirates went to search the *Merciless* and reported finding boxes of cochineal in the hold and a good bit of money in the captain's quarters.

"Take the money, ignore the cargo. We'll need that space in the hold for our next raid."

The valuables were quickly moved to the *Howling Doom.* It took only three men to do the job.

James went back to the *Doom.* On the deck, Cartwright was talking to Flowers.

"You think we were wrong for attacking them?" Flowers said.

"Why? No rule says we can't take whatever prize we want. Bedford should've done a better job and got it sorted out quickly. Maybe he would've stayed alive."

"Bedford was a sucker," Phillips interrupted. "He actually thought we were giving the prize to him. He got what he deserved. Old Charlie should've known better than to trust us."

Once the job was done, Wright gave the order to set both ships on fire. Two volunteers went over to the brigantine.

"I feel bad for the *Merciless,*" Hammond said. "It's a nice ship. You don't see those old Spanish galleons anymore."

"It's because they're not very good," Phillips said.

"Who cares. Look at the shapes. It's a beautiful ship. It's a shame we have to burn it."

The two pirates crossed over from the *Santa Cruz* and cut off the ropes holding it and the brigantine began to drift away. They went down to the hold of the Merciless and came back out a minute later.

Once the two men were back on the *Doom*, James, Hammond, and other crewmates drew their knives and cut off the ropes.

"Unfurl all sails!" Thatcher yelled.

"We did something fun with that Spanish ship," one of the pirates said. "Just watch."

They watched the *Santa Cruz* for a few minutes. All of a sudden, there was a massive explosion. The crew cheered.

"We found the powder magazine, decided to have some fun with it."

"Good job, boys," Hammond said. "I couldn't have done it better myself."

A few minutes later the main deck of the *Merciless* was in flames. As they sailed away from it, they could see smoke climbing up into the orange sky.

The pirates had taken a couple of barrels of rum from the *Merciless*, and they quietly gathered in the lower deck to have a few drinks before bed. James drank a couple of tankards and went to sleep.

Around midnight, Johnson woke him up. It was James's turn to stand watch. He climbed out of his hammock and went up to the main deck.

The night was cool but there was little wind, and the *Doom* moved slowly. James stood at the bow, looking out into the sea. It was just a wide mass of black, meeting the dark blue of the sky at the horizon. He could hear the waves crashing into the ship's hull.

Wayland was at the helm. With the ship moving so slowly, there wasn't much for him to do.

James overheard two voices talking. He thought one of them sounded familiar, but he couldn't put a face on it. The other was so indistinct it could've been anyone's.

"We're pretty much becalmed here," the second voice said. "You think we'll make it in time?"

"We were supposed to be there already."

"Shit. I hope they don't start without us."

"Why? They would do all the fighting and dying, and we'll show up for the looting."

"Sort of like what we did yesterday."

"Yeah."

"You think someone's going to miss him?"

"Who?"

"Bedford. You think there will be questions?"

"Bedford was a son of a bitch. I could enter any tavern in Nassau and announce that I killed Charlie Bedford, and there would be at least three men who would shake my hand and buy me a drink."

"Didn't he have any friends?"

"Of course he did. But he fucked most of them. Then again, who hasn't? Our captain used to be friends with Bedford. Not just friends, but very good friends. You saw how that ended."

"Yeah."

"Whitaker was a friend, then something happened in Nassau, so he's not invited to join us for this job."

"Wait, really?"

"Yeah. Grant and his crew will be going with us."

"Who the hell is Grant?"

"Who cares? He has good men and his men can fight. That's pretty much all I care about."

"What about Stafford and Angry Mark?"

"They're coming. They're probably already there, waiting for us to show up."

One of the men spat into the water. For a while, there was no sound but the waves hitting the hull.

"What do you think the loot is going to be?" the second man said. "Like Porto Bello? More than that?"

"I'd say about twice as much as Porto Bello, maybe even three times."

"Are you serious?"

"Of course. It's a good fat target that hasn't been sacked in decades. And it's one of their most important ports. Do you know what comes through there?"

"What?"

"Silver. All the silver mined in New Spain has to be taken back to the king. We're going to snatch us one of those ships with boxes full of silver, maybe even two ships. We're going to be rich men after that."

There was a long silence. Then the manwith the indistinctvoice spoke again, but this time quietly, almost whispering.

"Hey, I was thinking… What if… What if there was a way we could make even more money on that job?"

"I'm listening."

"What if… what if we did the same thing as yesterday?"

"What do you mean?"

James could've sworn that he knew that voice, but just couldn't figure out whose it was.

"I mean… If we thinned down some of the other crews, that means there's more money for us."

"They outnumber us pretty heavily."

"I know. But what if we got rid of just a part of them, like just one crew. The smallest one. Just take them out quietly."

"There's no way it would go down quietly."

"But in the middle of a battle, there's chaos, guns being fired everywhere, a couple dozen men could be taken out and no one would notice. Or maybe their ship sinks."

"While the silver is in there?"

"No, not like that. Maybe the silver is stored in another ship. Somebody sneaks on their ship, starts a fire in the magazine, quietly jumps out and swims back to his own ship, and then oh no, an explosion."

"These are pirate crews we're talking about. Everyone would *immediately* suspect foul play. How about we just take our fair share and be done with it. It will be plenty. And those other crews, you don't want them to be your enemies. They'll see you in Nassau, you're dead. They find you in Tortuga, you're dead. They spot your ship, they'll sink it. You go all the way to Madagascar, they'll find you even there. We're already enemies with the British, the Spanish, the French, the Dutch, the Portuguese, and who knows what else. There's enough enemies as is."

"But imagine the kind of money we could make."

"Yeah, I can imagine. I'm not saying the idea is bad, I'm saying it won't work. Maybe some other time it would work great, but not this time. Not when there's four crews on one job."

"Unless we side with one crew and kill everyone else."

"And then they get greedy and decide to kill us too."

"We kill them first."

"They'll be expecting it. Give it up. It's a plan for the future. You'd have to set up the entire job around this, you can't just start killing your fellow brethren and expect to get away with it. But keep that plan in mind. I like your plan. You have the right brains for this kind of work."

James heard footsteps as one of the men left. The other one spat in the water and walked off. The *Doom* was quiet again.

The sky was starting to get brighter in the east. James sat in the same spot, watching the sea. After some time, Hammond showed up.

"Your watch is over," he said. "I already woke up Boyd."

"Thanks. See you in the morning."

"Wait." Hammond looked around. "Listen, there's no plan or anything, I just wanted to ask… Just out of curiosity… If I started my own crew, would you join it? I'd make you first or second mate."

"Sure."

"Good to know."

"Why? Something going on?"

"No, there's nothing… nothing is actually happening. I was just wondering."

"All right."

James went down to the lower deck and climbed into his hammock and closed his eyes. He fell asleep trying to figure out what would be the name of Hammond's ship. Probably something that had to do with blood. He seemed like the kind of man that liked the word *blood*.

CHAPTER XIX
Williamsburg, Colony of Virginia

Rob went quiet.

"Ask me about something else," James said.

"Tell me more about the treasures you stole from the Spanish."

"Why do you keep asking about money?"

"I just like money," Rob said. "Who *doesn't* like money?"

"All right."

"Fine. I want to hear about money because I never had any. Happy now? I grew up in a tiny shack in Medford. We were dirt poor. I wore my brother's old clothes my entire childhood. Do you know what it's like to only eat bread with some water, because father stopped for a drink and wasted half of his pay? Hell, sometimes we didn't even have that. There were times when we ate once a day."

"Rob, you don't have to tell me about that. I know what it's like to try and fall asleep on an empty stomach. And my father was a drinking man too."

"And you got yourself into a spot where you could make the kind of money others can only imagine. Sailing the seven seas and taking money away in the company of legendary men."

"And look where I ended up. Locked up here with every pickpocket and… thug, and… thief. And they're going to hang me tomorrow. I have none of that money, I'm never sailing the seas again, and all those men I sailed with are either dead or in prison."

"At least you've done something."

"What do you mean?"

"We're both in here. I'm in here because I don't have money, you're in here because you were a pirate, sailed with Heartless Harry and fought in battles. You've done things, I've done nothing. I have nothing to show."

"You can still make something of yourself. I can't."

"I want to do what you did. I want to be on the crew of *Howling Doom*."

"Do something else. I mean, do *anything* else."

"Why?"

"You'll end up here. Again. But next time, there will be no leaving."

"I think I understand the risk."

"Do you?"

"Yes."

"You've never been shot at."

"So what?"

"You've never seen anyone getting hit. It's… One moment a person is right there next to you, the next one he's gone. And it makes you think. You could be next. Any moment you could get hit and drop dead. And there's nothing you can do about it."

"I get it. But still, there's those who survive. Like you."

"There's still tomorrow."

"I thought you didn't want to talk about tomorrow."

"Still don't."

"Let's talk about those who survived."

"If you survive a battle, pretty soon you'll be going into another one. And then another one after that. And another. Your luck is going to run out eventually."

"Unless you get out of there at the right time."

"When is it the right time?"

"When you have enough money."

"There's no such thing. You'll just keep going for more. Everyone does. Once you're in, you don't leave."

"Andrews did."

"Who's Andrews?"

"You don't know him?"

"Can't recall anyone who went by that name."

"He was a pirate."

"I don't think I've ever encountered an Andrews."

"Maybe he was on another crew."

"Maybe. What was his first name?"

"I don't know. I only know that others called him Andrews."

"All right. So who was this Andrews?"

"I encountered him at a bar in some small town not twenty miles from here. He was some kind of adventurer. He had been in all kinds of places, and for some time he was on pirate ships. Sailed with several of the great pirate captains, and fought the Spanish in more than a dozen battles."

"He could've been just a regular storyteller."

"I don't think so."

"Why?"

"He didn't seem like the lying kind."

"All right. What did he tell you?"

"Well, he didn't tell anything to me, he was talking to other people, I just happened to listen in."

"So what did he say?"

"That he was on the crews of Whitaker, Bedford, and others. Sailed all over the Caribbean and made a lot of money."

"Go on."

"He said one time they attacked a big Spanish ship, and he was given the job to take out the helmsman with a musket."

"Possible."

"Did your crew have someone like that?"

"We did. His name was Roger Davies."

"Anyway, he also said that he took out the helmsman with one shot, loaded the musket again and hit the Spanish captain in the chest."

"I can believe that. Takes a talented shooter and a good musket, but it's possible."

"Then they took everything of value and sank the ship."

"Did he tell you anything else?"

"He talked all night without taking a break, there's plenty."

"Let's hear it."

"There was a long story of how he and others sacked a city."

"Which city?"

"Vera Cruz."

"What did he say?"

"He said that he and four others were selected to be the scouts because they were the best swimmers. They swam for two miles to reach the Vera Cruz harbor. Then they quietly climbed out of the water onto the pier. One of the other men was climbing out of the water and was about to be spotted by a guard, but Andrews threw his knife and killed the guard. Then the other man caught the body and gently lowered it into the water so no one would hear the splash."

"Good job."

"Then they signaled their ship to sail into the harbor, and when it came in the whole crew quietly got off the ship. So they moved as quickly as they could, barely making a sound, until they had men in all the important positions, and then they charged. Andrews shot ten Spaniards, one after another."

"Impressive."

"Yeah, he said the Spanish were dropping like flies."

"Then what happened?"

"They killed most of the soldiers, and kept pushing them further, until they had nowhere to retreat. Eventually the Spanish had enough and surrendered. Andrews and others took away their muskets and then they led the soldiers into the prison and locked all of them up. In their own prison. Can you believe it?"

"And then?"

"Then they took all the money, all the diamonds, the gold, anything that was worth any money. It took them an entire day just to move all of it into the ship. Then they left for Tortuga, where they sold everything and divided all the money. Andrews said his share alone was… I'm not entirely sure, but I think he said one thousand pieces of eight."

"That's a ton of money."

"I bet it was."

"I mean, it's a ridiculous amount of gold. That can't be one share."

"I don't know. Maybe it wasn't a thousand."

"Did he have any other adventures?"

"Sure. Andrews also told how they attacked a Spanish ship off the coast of Florida and found it full of silver. The captain was killed in the battle, so the crew asked Andrews to be the new captain, but he refused."

"Why?"

"I don't know. He has also traveled a lot. Once, in Havana, he pretended to be a famous playwright, and it worked so well that he was invited to dinner with Governor Cervantes, then seduced his daughter, but the governor walked in on them making love, and Andrews had to run away."

"That story is definitely made up."

"Could be. I don't know. But all those stories about piracy sound true. There was actually a raid on Vera Cruz not that long ago. I think he was actually there."

"He wasn't."

"You think so?"

"I was on that raid in Vera Cruz. There was no surrender."

CHAPTER XX

Vera Cruz, Viceroyalty of New Spain

Crossing the Great Bay of Mexico took longer than expected, as the winds were weak and unpredictable. The pirates cheered when they saw the land in the distance.

"This calls for a celebration!" Clarke said. "Let's go get us some rum!"

"No!" Thatcher yelled. "No drinking, not until the job is done."

"Come on, we just want to have a little fun."

"We're several days behind, there's no time for fun. When the job is done and we go back to Nassau, you can do whatever the fuck you want. Right now all of you need to focus on the task."

Thatcher handed his spyglass to Mason.

"Go to the bow and look for the other ships. When you see them, immediately report to me or the helmsman. Understood?"

"Yes, sir."

Captain Wright was leaning on the starboard gunwale and looking down into the water. He was oblivious to everything that was going on.

"Mr. O'Keefe," Thatcher said, "what is our speed?"

"Six knots."

"Shit. I'm never sailing into this bay again. Mr. Mason, are you seeing anything yet?"

"No, sir."

Thatcher looked up to see if there was anything they could do to add a little speed, but the *Doom* was at full sail. The studding sails had been out since the previous day. There was nothing left to do but hope for a stronger wind.

"Quartermaster!" Mason yelled.

"Where are they?"

"Starboard bow."

He gave the quartermaster his spyglass back. He easily found three ships anchored just off the coast.

"Good job, Mr. Mason. Helmsman, head north-northwest."

The *Howling Doom* slowly made its way towards the other ships. The pirates were getting excited. Some were cleaning their weapons, a few discussed how much money they expected to make and what they were going to do with it.

It took longer than it should have to reach the ships. They recognized Stafford's *Sea Dragon*, Smith's *Devil's Reject*, and Clifford

Grant's schooner *Pale Horse*. They anchored the *Doom* just far enough from the others to avoid any issues once it was time to leave.

The crew lowered the launches and paddled to the shore. The other crews were waiting for them on the beach. Angry Mark and Stafford came up to greet Wright, whose launch was the first to reach land.

"You were supposed to be here days ago!" Smith started. "Where the fuck have you been?"

"The winds here are painfully weak," Wright said.

"Yeah, we know. We sailed here the same way. And we did it on time!"

"Seriously now, what happened?" Stafford said.

"All kinds of things. We took several ships, we had to careen…"

"Wait, you careened the ship?"

"Sure. The *Doom* was getting slow, besides, we had shipworm damage. My navigator said we should make it on time."

"Just fucking great," Smith said. "You were busy cleaning the fucking hull while we waited."

"We encountered a Spanish man-of-war and barely made it out, while you were here, drinking on the beaches and having a swell time."

"Sure you did. The man-of-war sounds like another one of your stories."

"It's already afternoon, and we still need to sack the city tonight," Stafford said. "I'm going to need you both to shut the fuck up and get to work. And where the fuck is Grant?"

Grant showed up a couple of minutes later. He was a very tall and equally wide man, with long, unkempt black hair and a beard that extended down to his belly button.

"You're finally here?" he said. "We were already considering attacking Vera Cruz without you."

"He's not lying," Stafford said. "We have wasted too much time as it is, we need to attack tonight. I have scouts watching the city."

"How far is it?" Wright asked.

"About four hours walking."

"What did the scouts say?"

"Low walls, we can easily climb over them," Stafford said. "The main fort is a good distance away from the city, its artillery can't do much damage. If we don't fuck up, this won't be particularly difficult."

"Is the treasure fleet there?"

"We think so. We couldn't get our scouts close to the harbor to check. We didn't see any big ships leaving, so they should still be in the dock. Just in case, we plan to have all four ships set sail after we leave.

Sea Dragon and *Howling Doom* will attack the fort, the other two will block the harbor."

"Good."

As the captains discussed strategy, the *Doom*'s crew were given some cold meat and fresh fruit.

"Is that true? The man-of-war stuff?" one pirate from the *Devil's Reject* asked.

"Yeah, we were careening off the coast of Yucatan and we had two men fishing," Phillips started. "They saw a Spanish man-of-war, returned to us, and the captain made the call to pack up and leave. One of our men lost a couple of fingers when a cannon fell, another one fell out of the longboat and drowned. It was a fucking mess."

"I'm really glad you boys showed up, we were about to do this without you," another pirate said. "We anchored a week ago, haven't had any rum for the past three days, and have nothing to do all day. Everyone was getting really pissed."

"You can let them know they'll be rich men after tonight," Hammond said. "I want to lay my hands on some of that Potosí silver."

"You boys ready to kill some Spanish?"

"We're ready to burn Vera Cruz to the ground."

James had not eaten since breakfast, so he ate as much as he could and stuffed some extra food into his pockets. He had overheard that the city was four hours away, and he knew he would need a lot of energy. If the raid on Porto Bello taught him anything, it was that marching through the jungle for hours was even tougher than it sounded.

Once he was stuffed, James cleaned his musket. It didn't need cleaning, but he figured it wouldn't hurt. Then he cleaned and loaded both of his pistols and borrowed a whetstone to make sure his cutlass and knife were razor sharp.

He returned the whetstone to its owner, the *Sea Dragon*'s second mate.

"What do you know about Captain Grant and his crew?" James asked.

"They certainly know how to have a good time, I can tell you that. Don't know what they'll be like in battle, but from what I've seen so far, they don't fuck around."

"Good to know."

"They sacked Villahermosa not too long ago," said another pirate, who had overheard the conversation. "Anchored on the bay, marched thirty miles, razed the city. Those are some tough men. Be careful around them."

"Why?"

"They'll drink you under the table," he said and laughed.

James sat down among a group of pirates. The master gunner of the *Devil's Reject* was telling a story about seeing the Kraken while taking a ship near Florida.

Captain Stafford used his hand to estimate the time until sundown.

"One to two hours until dark. Let's get moving."

"All crews, time to go!" Angry Mark yelled.

James stood up and went to his crewmates. He felt more comfortable being around men he knew.

One of the scouts from Stafford's crew led the way. The crew of the *Doom* was near the tail end of the group. The jungle was quiet, except for a few birds somewhere in the distance. The silence amplified the pirates' footsteps, and it always seemed like they were making a ton of noise.

The canopy didn't allow much sunlight, and as the sun set, the jungle became darker and darker, until eventually it was pitch black. The pirates had to rely on their own eyes adjusting to the darkness. The terrain wasn't doing them any favors. Men were constantly hitting their toes on rocks and logs. In several spots the trail got so narrow they could only squeeze through one or two men at a time. One pirate stepped into some kind of puddle and immediately sank deep into the stuff. His right leg up to the knee was covered in mud and smelled like a combination of rotten meat and fresh shit. The other pirates whispered to those behind them to watch their step.

James tripped on a fallen tree and fell on his face. A few other pirates ended up doing the same. James inspected his musket and pistols as best as he could in the low light. There seemed to be no damage and they didn't get wet. The march continued.

A loud cry came from somewhere further down the trail.

"Somebody needs a surgeon," James heard someone say.

"Ours is back on the ship," Hammond said. He turned to the men behind him. "Somebody needs a surgeon, pass it on."

As they went on, they saw a pirate lying on the ground. He was blocking a part of the trail and they had to pass one at a time. A tall man with bushy eyebrows knelt beside him.

"What happened?"

"Snakebite."

"Did you see the snake?"

"No."

"If it wasn't venomous, it wouldn't be so quick to bite." The surgeon wrapped a bandage tightly around the man's wrist.

"You, hold his arm. Don't let him move it an inch."

He took a branch off the ground, broke off a piece, and put it in the patient's mouth.

"Bite on it. You, cover his eyes."

The surgeon took a hatchet off his belt and calmly swung it, almost chopping through the entire wrist. As the patient tried to scream, he swung it again, separating the hand completely, and threw it away, then started bandaging the wound.

James took some of the meat and fruit out of his pocket and started eating it. As he chewed, he realized he should've brought some water. The last time he drank was right after they came ashore. James told himself that he'd be just fine.

The group suddenly stopped. They were still deep in the jungle.

"What's going on?"

"We stopped."

"I swear, one day I'll shoot you myself."

"What's happening there?"

"The captains found a watermelon, so they cut a hole in it and now they're taking turns giving it a good time."

"Shut up."

"Quartermasters, go see your captain," somebody half-said, half-whispered. "Quartermasters, to the captain."

Thatcher made his way to the front of the pack. He came back after what seemed like fifteen minutes. Wright was with him.

"*Doom* crew, listen up," Thatcher said. "One of the scouts will take us around, we'll sit there until we hear shooting, meaning that the attack has started. Don't start shooting until you hear shooting, pass it to the others. All right, *Howling Doom* goes with us."

"*Howling Doom*, with us," several others repeated. A couple of pirates from the other crews walked away.

They followed a scout down another trail. They had to walk single file because the path was so narrow, but it was firm and even and slightly easier to hike. James's knees and feet were aching, he was tired and his throat was dry. He had stopped sweating, but his shirt was uncomfortably moist.

The group stopped. James looked around but could see only the jungle. Then he saw the scout walking towards them.

"What's going on?"

"I've only seen this place in daylight. We need to go back a little."

"Are you fucking serious?!" Boyd yelled, and Keene smacked him on the head.

"We're almost there."

The scout managed to find the right way and they were walking towards Vera Cruz again.

Not too long after, they heard a shot.

"What the hell?"

"Shit. It started."

"Let's go!" Thatcher yelled. "The battle is on, RUN!"

They ran down the trail and a minute later saw the walls surrounding the city. More shots rang out. The pirates emerged from the tree line and were in a mad dash to make it to the wall, the only cover in sight. Between it and the trees there were over two hundred yards of open space.

The crew made it to the wall without a shot fired in their direction, and climbed over to the other side without much difficulty. Once inside the city, they had to wait for the captain and the quartermaster to cross over, as nobody else knew what to do or where to go.

Wright made it first.

"Orders, captain?"

"Go and kill!"

"Go where?"

"Wherever you hear shooting, you shit-for-brains!"

They ran down an empty street. James, like most of the crew, had no idea where they were going, and just followed the others. There were more and more shots in the distance, meaning that the other crews were already engaged in a serious battle.

The gunfire was getting closer, and after many turns and one dead end, they found some of the *Pale Horse* crew. They were hiding behind the houses that surrounded the main plaza. There were several injured among them.

"What's going on?" Manzanares said.

"We have a bunch of soldiers firing on us. We need you boys to go around and hit them from the side. We'll keep them occupied."

"You heard the man," Hammond said. "Come on."

He ran down the street and a couple dozen men followed. James was among them. Hammond would stop at every house to peek around the corner. Several houses later, they found the enemy.

"They're here. Have your guns loaded."

James checked if he had remembered to load his musket. He had.

"Go around the corner and blast them."

They went into the open three or four at a time, fired at the silhouettes of Spanish soldiers, and ran back to cover to reload while their crewmates went in. Five Spaniards were killed before they realized they were being flanked, and retreated to another position. The pirates advanced. The plaza was theirs.

James and the others rejoined their crew and advanced to the next street. They were immediately met with musket fire. The pirates ran back to cover. Two bodies remained. One was a pirate from the *Sea Dragon* who took a musket ball to the head. The other was Manzanares. He took a shot to the chest. He was coughing up blood and trying to breathe, but his body was giving out. The others couldn't leave cover and even if they could, there was nothing they could do for a wound like that. It was over.

Cartwright carefully stuck his head out just enough to look around.

"Shooters in the balcony. Right side."

With his musket up, James carefully leaned to the side, just enough to see the balcony, and quickly fired a shot at the figure standing there. He went right back to cover. He didn't know if he hit anyone. The soldiers responded with a shot that bounced off the ground.

"If we run fast, they'll only be able to take out one or two," Hammond said. "The rest could make it to the house and throw a grenade inside."

"Do you want to go first?"

"Sure. I don't care. But we need others, so I won't be the only target. Who else is going?"

James raised his hand, as did Cartwright, McMillan, Burbage, Flowers, and a couple of others.

"Good. Get ready."

Hammond stepped out from behind cover, fired one shot into the house, and stepped back. Two shots hit the pavement.

"Go!"

Hammond went first, followed by Flowers and Burbage. James was behind them. He could hear McMillan's heavy steps behind him.

The house was thirty or forty yards away, but as they ran it seemed more like a half mile. The soldiers fired a couple of shots, and for a brief moment James thought that Hammond's plan was stupid and that they would all be killed and that it would've been smarter to look for another way first. But then it all ended as they reached the house and leaned against the wall under the balcony.

James glanced to his left and saw Cartwright. He looked around and saw McMillan's body on the ground just a few yards away from the house.

Hammond drew his pistol, kicked the door open, and went in. Others followed. There was one soldier on the first floor, and moments later his brain was on the nearest wall. There was shouting in Spanish, probably because the soldiers realized the pirates were inside the house.

Flowers ran upstairs first. A Spanish soldier came out of one room. Both men fired at the same time. The Spaniard wasn't hit, and he retreated back to the room. The ball from his pistol hit Flowers in the left hip, destroying the joint. Cartwright ran up and grabbed his crewmate by the clothes and dragged him down the stairs. Flowers's wound was bleeding heavily, and there was no doubt that the battle was over for him.

"McDougall, aim at that door," Hammond said. "You see someone, you end that son of a bitch. Burbage, get those chairs. Pile them on the stairs. If we can't go in, they can't leave."

While James was on overwatch, Hammond and others piled chairs, a table, a bench, and other furniture on the stairs.

"McDougall, you still watching?"

"I'm watching." James slowed down his breathing, his finger on the trigger. The tiny lull in the action made him realize how thirsty he was. His throat was sore.

Hammond took several books from a nearby bookshelf and dropped them on the stairs by the furniture pile. He opened his powder horn and put some gunpowder on one open book. Then he lit it with the flint on his musket. The book immediately caught fire.

"Cartwright, get some more books in here."

One Spanish soldier came out to see what was going on, but had to go back immediately. James's shot barely missed his head.

The pirates threw more books into the fire, and it caught the furniture. The flame grew more and more. Smoke filled the room.

"We're done here," Hammond said. "Let's go."

They went outside and waved to the others. The remaining pirates advanced down the street.

"Did you take them out?" Clarke said.

"No. We blocked the stairs and set the place on fire."

"Good. It won't be long."

They saw smoke coming out through the windows. One soldier yelled something in Spanish and jumped out from the balcony. He broke his leg on the fall and was rolling on the ground in pain.

"*Señores, por favor…*" he uttered.

Cartwright grabbed him by the hair and slit his throat.

"This is for Carlos."

Several pirates were aiming at the balcony, waiting for more soldiers to come out. A couple did, and were shot.

Once the whole building was in flames, the pirates went on, and further down the street encountered over a dozen Spaniards. Both sides immediately took cover behind buildings. Clarke started assembling groups of seven or eight and told them to go around and flank the

Spanish unit. The soldiers weren't stupid. They realized what the plan was and ensured they had men covering every flank.

James was among the seven men that went for the right flank, but encountered another dozen soldiers that had just come in from somewhere else. Villalobos got killed, Burbage took some shrapnel to the arm, and the pirates retreated.

"There's a dozen more Spaniards," Crawford reported. "They came out of nowhere. We had to fall back."

They went back out there, this time thirty-five men strong. They had more firepower than the Spaniards, who had a better position. They were in a building with arches all along the façade, and they could hide behind the columns and take shots at the pirates. The *Doom*'s men couldn't find a way to move forward, so they opted for a more dangerous strategy. They moved back and lied on the ground prone, aiming their muskets at the Spaniards and waiting for one to stick his head out. The pirates were sure of two things—that their muskets were better, and that they could shoot better. It was hard making out silhouettes in low light, but they successfully killed two soldiers, one after another. The Spaniards became cautious and would quickly fire off their guns without even looking where they shoot. It wasn't very deadly, but it kept the pirates from advancing forward.

This stalemate felt like it went on for hours. Eventually, a few pirates decided to take over a nearby building and fire on the Spaniards from there. They ran over to the building and kicked down the door and made their way inside. One of them caught a musket ball and died on the street.

With shots coming from down the street and from a second floor balcony, the soldiers had no choice but to retreat before the pirates slaughtered them all. They fired a few more shots and ran.

James went into the house his crewmates had just taken over.

"I need some water," he said.

"I found something better," said one of the pirates.

He gave James an opened bottle of wine. James took a good swig. It made his throat feel better.

"We took all the valuables," the pirate said. "Let's keep going."

Soon after, they encountered pirates from the *Pale Horse*.

"Are you the *Howling Doom* boys?"

"Yeah."

"Where the fuck is your captain? We're getting slaughtered here."

"We don't know."

"Where's the quartermaster then?"

"Don't know. Probably with the captain."

"Just find your fucking captain and tell him we need him and all of his men here before we get overrun. There's way more fucking Spaniards than we expected."

"I'm on it," Hammond said. "I'll need three men."

"I'm going," Malone said.

"Me too," James added.

"Good. Finley, you in? Let's go."

They followed Hammond back the same way they had just fought their way through, jumping over an occasional corpse. The building that they had set on fire was now one massive blaze. They could feel the heat from fifty yards out. Hammond paused for a second to admire it, then they were running again, past the empty main plaza.

"Wait!" Finley shouted. Everyone stopped. He pointed at a couple of pirates not far away on a street to their right.

"Good eye, Finley," Hammond said. "Hey! Hey! Where's the captain?"

One of them pointed behind himself.

As they ran, they saw more of their crewmates. The *Doom*'s men were looting houses.

"Douglas, did you see the captain?"

"Sure, follow me."

Douglas realized the importance of whatever business Hammond had. He ran full speed. The others were barely able to keep up.

They took a left and stopped by a small house. The door was ajar.

"Here."

"Thanks." Hammond went in, James, Finley, and Malone followed. "Captain?"

Wright was on the floor, forcing himself on a teenage girl who resisted as hard as she could. Her parents were lying dead on the same floor just a few yards away. He either ignored or was oblivious to the four men.

"Captain?"

"What do you shitbirds want?" said a voice behind them. It was Thatcher. "Get out of there."

All four went outside. They could hear the girl crying.

"What the fuck do you want, Hammond?"

"What are you doing here? The battle's over there."

"We're collecting the plate. Why are you here?"

"Why aren't *you* over there?! Grant's men need reinforcements so they don't get fucking wiped out. Tell the captain that as soon as he's done fucking that girl he needs to round up all the men he's got and go help out. It's a fucking slaughter out there!"

"We'll be there, Mr. Hammond. You may return to your usual duties."

They met Douglas on the way back.

"Douglas, tell everyone to stop looting and get their asses to the battle. We need all the men we can get."

"Got it."

"We're going back there. Let's go."

Finley, Malone, and James followed Hammond back the same way they had just returned.

They saw at least three fires going on. Gunshots in the distance came nonstop. The closer to the action they got, the more corpses they had to jump over. They encountered a mixed group of about fifty pirates from every crew. The unit was regrouping to attack the Spanish from the west. James, Hammond, Finley, and Malone joined in. They ran for several blocks then turned north and found themselves on the Spanish right flank. Swafford, a crewman of the *Devil's Reject*, told them to take up firing positions and wait for his command to fire. James found himself a building corner to hide, loaded his musket, and waited.

Swafford fired the first shot, and the rest of the pirates followed. James couldn't make out soldiers, but he was pretty sure he was aiming at one of them, more or less. The Spanish unit had to retreat to a safer position. One pirate took that as an opportunity to charge them and ended up getting a musket ball through the stomach.

The pirates moved north hoping to repeat the maneuver, but there were Spanish soldiers waiting for them. As soon as they saw pirates trying to flank, they opened fire. James saw two men right in front of him get cut down by Spanish muskets. He stopped just as he was about to step out into the open, and signaled others to stop.

James carefully peeked around the corner. He saw two Spaniards about twenty yards away, loading their muskets.

"What do you see?"

"Two men. At least. They're reloading."

"Let me through," someone said. A short fat pirate came forward. He had a grenade.

"Someone light this for me."

Finley lit the fuse with the flint of his pistol. The fat man stood in front of James, quickly leaned forward, and threw the grenade. A couple of seconds later, there was an explosion. The pirates rushed into the street, shooting any soldier that still moved or didn't seem dead enough. A moment later, three men were taken out by shots fired from down the street. James quickly looked left and right, and saw others take up every good piece of cover. He dropped to the ground, lying flat on his stomach.

He saw a silhouette moving in the distance and aimed and fired, but was almost certain that he didn't hit anything.

Loading a musket while lying prone turned out to be surprisingly difficult, but James didn't want to stand up and become a target. It took twice as long to load the gun, and he fired at a running soldier but missed badly. He cursed and started reloading again.

As soon as there was a lull in the fighting, one of the pirates would run ahead and either hide behind something or lie down on the dusty ground. One by one, the pirates pushed forward. Spanish soldiers tried to hold the position, but they all saw that they were outgunned. A few of them were hit by pirate muskets, and the distance between them only kept shrinking. One soldier told his comrades to hold their fire for a few seconds. A pirate from Stafford's crew saw an opening and stood up to run closer. The Spanish soldiers fired, and hit the man in the chest. The soldiers retreated.

James and the others held the position until they rejoined the remaining pirates. The battle was not over, but the Spaniards were mostly taking inaccurate shots from long range. It slowed the pirates down, but it wasn't enough to stop them. They pushed the Spanish soldiers all the way to the water.

The soldiers took to boats and retreated into the fort of San Juan de Ulúa. The pirates followed, and the men in the fort answered with cannon fire. The cannonballs couldn't reach the pirates on the shore, but the pirates couldn't get to the fort either.

"Leave the fort alone," Smith commanded. His clothes were covered in dirt and blood. "They have nothing. We want the ships with silver."

They moved along the water towards the dock. Some pirates split off the group and started kicking in doors and looking for valuables. A few others broke into a tavern and left with all the drinks, including two barrels of beer that barely fit through the door. They placed them outside, smashed the tops open, and filled the tankards.

"Stop drinking, shitbags!" Smith yelled. "The job's not done!"

A few pirates downed their beer as quickly as they could and rejoined their crew, others ignored the captain and calmly enjoyed their drinks.

The captains and most of their crews were approaching the dock. A few pirates had already made it there. One of them came back running.

"Captain Stafford," he said. "We can't find the treasure ships, captain."

"What?!"

"There are two sloops, a beat-up old schooner, and some smaller boats, but that's it."

Stafford started running, a few others followed along, and then the entire group of over a hundred pirates ran alongside, some of them having no idea why.

The pirates got closer to the dock, and they saw it. The treasure fleet was not there.

"What the fuck?!" Stafford yelled. "Where are the fucking ships?! Where's Wright?"

"I think I saw him, captain," one pirate said. "I'll go get him."

"Hurry up!"

They stood there watching their crewmates breaking into houses, three or four fires somewhere in the distance, and the dock with none of the promised silver.

After a while, Wright showed up. He was in no rush.

"Wright!" Stafford yelled. "Look at this shit! Do you see the goddamn treasure fleet in there?!"

"What happened to the ships?" Wright said.

"I don't know, I thought you could tell me. It was *your* source who got us the fleet's schedule. What the fuck happened?"

"I don't know."

"Fuck you, Harry! Fuck you! You promised us Spanish silver. Where the fuck is it?! Where is it?!"

"Mr. Clarke, find someone who lives here and bring him to me. I have a few questions."

"Yes, captain."

Clarke and several others went looking for information. It was quiet for a short time.

"They probably left," Smith said. "The silver's gone. You promised us that ships loaded with treasure would be ours for the taking."

"I know what I promised."

"And now we won't be seeing any of it. We sacked this fucking city for nothing."

"Not for nothing. There's plenty of loot in those houses."

Clarke and others returned with a middle-aged mestizo and forced him to kneel in front of Wright.

"Someone ask him if he knows about the ships."

A Spaniard from the *Pale Horse* stepped forward and said something to the prisoner. He refused to speak.

Wright pulled out his cutlass and went around the man and stabbed him in the calf. The tip of the blade came out the other side. The prisoner was screaming in pain.

"Ask again."

This time the man answered.

"He says they left earlier today."

"*Today?*" Smith said. "You mean we could've had that silver if we attacked a day earlier? Perfect. Just fucking perfect. We lost all that treasure because you were late to your own raid."

"I wasn't late," Wright said. "The ships left early."

"Fuck you, Harry."

"It's not all lost. Let's go search the houses, take all the plate—we'll find plenty."

"We didn't come here to search house to house for an occasional piece of eight."

"What do you want me to do, Mark? I can't bring those ships back. They're gone. The only thing left to do is take what we can and move on."

"Fuck it," Stafford said. "You heard it. Go search every house and take whatever you can. We leave at noon. Somebody signal the ships to go to that bay south of here."

The sky above the sea was turning red. The pirates went into every house, looking for money, expensive items, and maybe some food and drink. Some of the residents had left once the shooting started, others had not. Some took their valuables with them, others did not.

In the very first house James and two men from the *Devil's Reject* found a terrified family. James held them at gunpoint while the others searched the house. The next one was empty; the owners took everything of value with them.

The owner of the next house greeted them warmly and poured some beer he brewed himself. It tasted great. James and the others thanked the man for the drink, said goodbye, and left. They didn't realize they forgot to take the man's money until much later.

Another resident was yelling something in Spanish while swinging a large knife. James shot him in the chest. He was tired and just wanted the whole thing to be over.

James visited over twenty other houses. He decided it was enough and he headed for the bay where the ships were anchored. Most of the pirates were already there.

Once back on the *Doom*, James turned in the goods he had stolen. He wanted to get some sleep.

"Everyone, listen up," Thatcher said. "Since Mr. Manzanares has died, we are going to need a new second mate. Any suggestions?"

"Alexander Douglas," Hammond said.

"All right, raise your hands."

James raised his hand. Almost all of the crew had their hands up.

"Good. Anyone have any other candidates? Anyone? Mr. Douglas, you are now the second mate of the *Howling Doom*. Congratulations."

The crew clapped.

"Now, about our next destination."

Everyone suddenly went quiet.

"Since this raid was a bit of a disaster, the captains have agreed to take the backup option suggested by captain Stafford. We are going to Cuba to sack Santiago."

There were no cheers. Santiago de Cuba was a difficult job. But it was also a rich target.

"Let's get underway. Weigh the anchor."

Four days later, the money from the sacking of Vera Cruz was counted and distributed. The pirates were excited to get paid. Enthusiasm died when the first man returned with his reward.

James, like other able-bodied sailors on the *Doom*, received a mere thirty pieces of eight.

CHAPTER XXI

Williamsburg, Colony of Virginia

"You were at Vera Cruz?"

"I just told you."

"And you think Andrews wasn't there?"

"There was no surrendering in Vera Cruz. Everyone fought to the death."

"So he was a liar then."

"Not even a good one."

"You think he could've actually been on Bedford's or Stafford's crew?"

"Stafford was with us in Vera Cruz. Bedford and his crew were wiped out."

"Wiped out?"

"There were no survivors."

"So he was never a pirate?"

"No way. What you just told me makes almost no sense."

"Yeah, I figured he was lying. That part about being offered to be captain but saying no. Why would he not take it?"

"How does somebody even get an offer like that? A pirate captain is chosen by a vote. I've never seen a vote, but I'm sure any captain who refused the position would be immediately labeled a coward. If there's one thing you don't want to be known for on a pirate ship, it's cowardice. You could be hated by everyone on the crew, they'll still keep you around. But cowards are dealt with quickly."

"Wow. You guys don't mess around."

"That's nothing, you should see what everyone else does to pirates. Actually, I hear you'll get to see it first thing in the morning. They'll even use me for demonstration."

"Don't talk like that."

"Why? It's what happens to pirates. Eventually there comes a point where you can't run away anymore."

"You make it sound like all is lost."

"Is it not?"

"What if we were to break out of here?"

"It requires a plan. There's just not enough time."

"Then let's start thinking right now."

"Look, don't worry about me. Worry about yourself. Do your time, get out, do something with your life. It's too late to help me."

“Come on, there’s got to be something. Are you sure your crew don’t have something planned?”

“I already told you. No pirate crew would go out of their way to help me. There’s nothing in it for them. If I had a chest full of gold, they might just break in and shoot me and take it, but now… Forget it.”

“Maybe they’ll attack in the morning, during the execution?”

“Why would they do that?”

“I don’t know. Maybe to sack this town?”

“Again, no one cares about little old me. And this town isn’t much of a target. Forget it. There will be no surprises tomorrow. There’s nothing left to do.”

“How do you do this?”

“Do what?”

“Just calmly lie here when you know you’re going to be executed tomorrow.”

“What else can I do? Even if I escaped, I’d have nowhere to go. I knew this would happen eventually. I knew all along that I was going to end up like this, but I just pushed that thought aside. I never really took the time to think about it. Now… I guess we’re all going to die anyway, right?”

“If I were you, I’d try to escape. Sure, there’s a possibility the guards would shoot me, but at least I’d go down fighting. I wouldn’t let them have the joy of watching me swinging. There would be a fight, and I’d take some of the bastards with me.”

“All right.”

“How come you didn’t do that?”

“Do what?”

“Fight to the very end. Go out fighting.”

“I wanted to, but the situation changed.”

“What do you mean?”

“Don’t underestimate a man’s will to live.”

“I feel like a true pirate should go out fighting. I’d take a glorious death over chains.”

“It probably wouldn’t be as glorious as you think. Pirates don’t die like that. A pirate gets his belly sliced open and his guts fall out all over the deck, or he gets shot in a brawl in a Nassau tavern, or you walk into a room in a whorehouse somewhere and find him dead on the floor while the whore demands that somebody pay her. These are the kind of deaths a pirate can expect.”

“Not everyone ends up like that.”

“You’re right, I forgot to mention drowning in the sea, falling off the mast while drunk, plain old gangrene… you get the idea.”

"Do you think that's how Heartless Harry will end up?"

"Definitely."

"Can't be."

"Why not?"

"A man like that cannot die like a dog."

"He's only human."

"But still…"

"What?"

"I don't think he'll end up like that," Rob said. "He's a legend. He's been sailing the seas for years, and nobody managed to kill him. Countless battles, and he survived all of them. They won't blow his head off like any random bastard. Mark my words, his death will be legendary. He will leave this world one day, and people will talk about that day for years to come."

"Yes, about how he ended up in a ditch somewhere."

"What is it with you?"

"Huh?"

"I get that you've seen all kinds of deaths when you were a pirate, but can you give your own captain a break?"

"Why should I?"

"He was your captain."

"So?"

"And he is known all over the world."

"He was just another pirate."

"Don't you think he deserves some respect?"

"Stop worshiping him. He was just a pirate."

"I'm not worshiping him."

"You are."

"No. I respect and admire him because he achieved great success."

"In the field of killing people and taking their money."

"He's no saint, but he is a living legend."

"No he's not."

"He is. He's known all over the world. Neither the Spanish nor the English could take him down."

"He was just a pirate. No different from any other pirate. Just a bad person who chose to sail a boat and rob people for a living, and did not feel bad for one moment for all those who suffered and died because of him."

"You really don't like him, do you?"

"Can't say I do."

"Even though he was your captain?"

"This goes deeper than just who was on which ship."

"All right. Tell me. What else makes you dislike him?"

"My life would've been so much better if it wasn't for him and the crew. I'm sure many others felt the same way about him."

"But you can't deny that he led men to great victories. Like Porto Bello, or Martinique."

"And you can't deny that he led men into slaughter most of the time."

"There will be losses in any battle. Some men will have to die."

"Goddammit, Rob, will you stop trying to make him into some kind of hero?"

"I'm not."

"You are. You just refuse to see it. He was no hero, no matter what stories you read. He killed people. He tortured people. He robbed them. He led his men into battle where *they* lost their lives so that *he* could get money and spend it on rum and whores. You're worshiping a man who never cared for anyone but himself, a man who would've called you his friend and then stabbed you in the back. Don't forget that in all those great battles that you heard about, he sunk ships, and good men died. I sailed with Wright, and I've never seen him do one decent thing. What is it exactly that you are worshiping him for?"

"I am not worshiping him."

"I won't hear it, Rob."

"Fine. Let's never talk about Heartless Harry again."

"Works with me."

"Just one last question?"

"Fine. Go ahead."

"Where do you think Harry is now?"

James stared at the ceiling in the darkness. He was quiet for a while.

"Loyalty is a strange thing."

CHAPTER XXII

Santiago de Cuba, Captaincy General of Cuba

The winds were very mild and constantly changing. It took the pirates five days just to get out of the Great Bay of Mexico and reach Yucatán. In the strait of Yucatán it got even worse, as they had to fight easterly winds the entire time.

There was a lot of discontent once the money was divided among the crew. Most of them received forty pieces of eight, when the captains had promised them hundreds. The Spanish treasure fleet was gone, and everyone on the *Howling Doom* knew that other crews hated them for showing up late. Captain Wright personally punched two of his crewmen for complaining about low spoils.

The next target became the main topic of conversation. Almost any time two pirates started talking about anything, eventually it would shift to Santiago.

"We fucked up in Vera Cruz, we're probably going to fuck up in Santiago even worse," Cartwright grumbled at dinner. "The biggest difference between those two is that we have fewer men. And we'll probably be going against more soldiers."

"Santiago is unprepared," Hammond said. "They haven't been attacked in decades. They don't even consider the possibility of being sacked. Soldiers get lazy, lookouts don't bother looking, guns get rusty, powder barrels sit in some damp cellar and nobody remembers where they put the key."

"Didn't somebody say that about Vera Cruz?" Douglas asked. "That they're not taking security seriously because they haven't been raided in a long time?"

"Villahermosa was sacked not too long ago," Phillips said. "They probably heard about it and decided to beef up security. The difference here is that Cuba hasn't seen attacks in decades and nobody thinks of Santiago as a target, and Vera Cruz is the place that all the silver and gold go through."

"We never took the fort," Cartwright said. "They retreated and left the town for us. If their guns could've reached us, things would've been much worse for us."

"But they retreated," James said. "We made them retreat, and they decided that giving up the town was the better option. If they had stayed in the fight, we would've killed all of them."

"We could've had more money if we took the fort. They probably had all the silver stored safely in there."

"The treasure fleet left earlier that day," Hammond said. "All the silver was there. There's no way they had another batch ready in there."

"We don't know," Douglas said. "Maybe they had too much silver. Maybe the miners worked extra hard and there was leftover silver. Maybe one of the ships wrecked and they couldn't take all of it."

"Maybe."

"If there was any silver in the fort, the Spanish are now laughing at us."

"They won't be laughing when we take Santiago," Phillips said.

"They're probably sending letters to every city that pirates are coming," Cartwright said.

"We'll be in Santiago before anyone from Vera Cruz can get there," Hammond said. "When they get the message about us, it will be too late."

"Other cities will know. They'll beef up the defenses. And then every major port will be as hard to take as Havana."

"Shut the hell up, Cartwright. You really think they'll suddenly build massive forts with hundreds of guns overnight? Most of them will ignore it. They're not going to waste money on defenses when they had no trouble in the last thirty years. The smaller towns will think they're too small to be good targets. Others will get cocky and think their defenses are good enough to stop anything. Stop shitting your pants. There will be many other targets after Santiago."

"If we can even take it," Cartwright grumbled.

"Shut the fuck up."

"Cartwright has a good point," Douglas said. "We lost a lot of men."

"Not that many. Porto Bello was worse."

"Maybe. Sure, the *Doom* did pretty well, but others? Stafford's men took big losses. Grant's crew got slaughtered."

"Grant's crew was inexperienced," Phillips said. "Too many fresh faces. Now the weak ones have been weeded out, the strong ones know what it's like to be balls-deep in shit, they'll unleash hell on Cuba. I think Vera Cruz was a slap in the face that we all needed. It was a reminder that we shouldn't get cocky. Now the men are hungry. There's a lot of anger in all the crews. When we reach Cuba, don't get in their way. They'll raze the fucking city. They'll burn the whole thing to the ground and salt the earth."

"What if we get there and find out we're outmanned and outgunned?" Cartwright asked. "Experience means nothing when there's one man against five Spanish."

"Don't underestimate these men," Hammond said. "They're angry and bloodthirsty. And they want the gold they rightfully earned.

Determination can be powerful. A group of smart, brave, and really determined men can defeat an enemy twice its size. If that enemy is terrified and unprepared, make it three times its size. The soldiers in Santiago are unprepared and they will be terrified. They have no idea what's coming and they don't believe anyone will ever attack them."

"Most of them have probably never seen any combat," Phillips added. "But I understand where you're coming from. It's not going to be an easy battle. We'll lose a lot of good men. Probably more than in any other raid. The battle could last two days, maybe even three. Maybe even longer. This is going to be the biggest challenge this crew has ever faced. Worse than Porto Bello, worse than Cartagena, worse than fucking Maracaibo."

"What happened in Cartagena?" James asked. "You still haven't told that story."

"Another time."

"Why not now?"

"I said another time."

They finished eating and the conversation ended. Everyone went back to their duties.

The *Doom* followed the *Sea Dragon* to the waters south of Cuba. The ships spent almost two days being carried by the current, as the wind was so mild it was pretty much nonexistent. It finally picked up again and they sailed around Isle of Pines and towards Jamaica. From there they would make their way to Santiago de Cuba. With strong eastern winds, there was no way to go along the coast.

The pirates anchored their ships in Grand Cayman for several hours to refill on fresh water and grab a few turtles for some fresh meat. The island was often visited by various crews, but there was no one there when the four ships arrived. As soon as the supplies were replenished, the pirates left the island and continued on towards Jamaica.

The journey to Vera Cruz had been exciting. The crew was full of hope, eager to sack the city and take its riches. Now the excitement was gone. Santiago was not a promising target. Everyone on all four ships would've preferred to take Vera Cruz and go right back to Nassau, but they couldn't return without something to show. They needed a good prize. If they came back with next to nothing, they would run out of money in a week and have to go back out again, and the talk of the town would be that they couldn't pull it off. And the meanest pirate crew in the Caribbean couldn't allow that.

After several days they reached the coast of Jamaica and turned northeast towards Santiago de Cuba. They encountered a British schooner and let it pass them by. They spent three days navigating to their destination. The pirates dropped the anchors at dusk.

All four crews took to launches and landed on the beach to the west of the city. Stafford gave them simple instructions: no bonfires, no hunting, no anything; stay on the beach and wait for orders. He met with the other captains.

"Are we attacking tonight?" Smith asked.

"No. Tonight we rest," Stafford said. "We'll attack tomorrow."

"We already lost one prize because we waited an extra day."

"The crews are tired. We can't force them to walk for miles. We don't know how far away Santiago is."

"We could still make it. It's not very late."

"Let's say we strike tonight. The men are tired, they'll be even more tired once we get there. Do you think they will fight well? We don't have anything to lose if we wait another day."

"What if we show up there tomorrow and find out they're ready for us?" Smith asked.

"What if we show up tonight, and they're ready for us? The only difference is whether or not our men will be at full strength."

"Wright, what do you say?"

"Tomorrow."

"Stafford's right," Grant said. "Waiting is the better option here. We'll need every ounce of strength for this."

"Fine," Smith said. "Tomorrow it is."

Swafford and Matthews, two sailors from the *Devil's Reject*, volunteered as scouts. The captains gave them very detailed instructions before they waved their crew goodbye and left. They walked east along the beach before disappearing in the darkness.

James thought he could sleep on the beach sand, just like in Panama, but the beach they landed on was covered in rocks. He found a nice piece of grassy dirt and made it his bed for the night. Johnson and Hammond were on his right and left, a few feet away.

"Haven't seen a beach this bad in a long time," Hammond said. "At least we'll only be here one night."

"I thought the Caribbean had great beaches everywhere," Johnson said. "And we just happen to land on one that's nothing but gravel."

"I want to go back to Nassau. I want that shiny white sand. And the best whores. Two of them. I can't understand why, but I've never done it with two at the same time."

"You haven't?"

"No. It seems like every time I think of it, I'm either surrounded by men, or I've already ran out of money. This time it will be different. McDougall?"

"What?"

"Remind me as soon as we get to Nassau that I want to fuck two whores at once."

"Leave me alone."

"Johnson, you'll have to remind me then."

"Sure. Just remind me to remind you about the whores."

"Can you two stop talking about whores?" James said. "I'm trying to sleep here."

"What, you don't like whores?"

"Why can't you sleep?" Johnson said. "Is all this talk about doing two whores at the same time making you hard?"

"I said shut up and go to sleep, cocksuckers."

They woke up early the next morning. It was windy and the sky was clouded. Ortega and two others took the longboat and went fishing. A few pirates went along the beach and managed to catch a pair of sea turtles. Several others went into the forest to hunt and returned an hour later with some kind of rodent that weighed over ten pounds. Nobody wanted to eat the mystery rodent, so Beasley threw it away.

After breakfast, there was nothing to do but wait for the scouts, the fishing crew, or lunch, whichever came first. James went for a walk in the forest and brought his musket just in case he saw a deer. He didn't see anything but a lot of plants and a few birds.

Shortly after he returned to the beach, Ortega and others came back and brought back several decent fish, including a very large tunny, and Beasley fried them. Other crews had sent their own boats, but they returned empty-handed.

A couple of hours after lunch, the scouts finally returned.

"Well, what did you see?"

"It's far," Matthews said. "Really far."

The captains immediately pushed everyone out of their way and huddled around the scouts.

"It's a really long walk. We had to go around the bay, because the city is on the far side." As Matthews spoke, Swafford drew a crude map in the gravel.

"There's no wall around it. We can just walk in."

"What about the forts?" Grant asked.

"Guarded. Every fort has soldiers standing guard. We don't know how many."

"Any ships in the harbor?"

"A few smaller ones," Swafford said. "Nothing unusual."

"How much movement is there at night?" Wright asked.

"Almost none."

"Any soldiers outside the forts?"

"Could be. We didn't see any."

"So it's pretty much what we expected," Stafford said. "I say we go. Mark?"

"No soldiers patrolling at night. No wall. Of course we're going."

"I'm with you," Grant said. "Harry?"

"Let's do this."

Stafford motioned everyone to gather round.

"We are sacking Santiago tonight. I need you all ready by dusk. No drink for the rest of the day, you can drink when the city's ours. Any questions? Good."

James cleaned his musket and pistols. His cutlass was sharp enough. He had plenty of powder in his horn. There was nothing to do but wait.

After dinner, James stuffed his pockets with food. He then found an empty wine bottle and filled it with water from a stream. He sat down and leaned against a tree and waited for the sun to go down. Other pirates were cleaning their weapons, pacing around, or staring out into the distance. A few were quietly passing around a bottle of wine.

The sun finally went down. Stafford gave the order to get ready. The raid was on.

The pirates put out the bonfires. Some of them loaded their weapons. Captains exchanged a few thoughts about the approach. For a few minutes, several hundred pirates waited on the beach, clutching their muskets, not saying a word.

"Let's go."

The mass of bodies started moving. James was uneasy, but he told himself that everything would be fine. He survived the other raids, he'd survive this one.

Matthews and Swafford, the scouts, were in the front of the pack. They led the crew along the beach, where they didn't have to fight through the foliage. The beach was rocky and easier to walk on than sand, but most of the pirates were barefoot and for them the walk soon became agonizing.

The coast got steeper and rockier. Waves smashed into the rocks, splashing loudly. Twilight was giving way to night, and it was getting harder to see. There was no talking, only breathing, grunting, and occasional cursing. Douglas was singing *Running Down to Cuba* under his breath.

After walking for miles, it was fully dark, but the pirates were still walking along the coast. They passed a small beach where the waves spilled on the gravel and cold water drenched their feet. Before long, even those wearing boots felt seawater soak through.

The coast was littered with small coves, and each time they had to go around them. Every time they changed direction it seemed they were about to head into the jungle, but the party would turn back towards the coast. At the next cove, it would happen again. After miles of walking, the city didn't seem to be any closer.

It was almost midnight, but the pirates were still walking along the coast. James was starting to get nervous. They were supposed to go through the jungle by now. Did they go the wrong way? He reminded himself that the scouts had been there once and knew where to go. But his feet were sore and he estimated they'd already been walking longer than in Vera Cruz.

An hour past midnight, they reached the mouth of a large river and turned north. James's feet were both sore and numb, his legs ached, and his back was burning. He had already eaten all the food he brought. The bottle of water was empty and lying on the ground a few miles back. James was glad that he had brought it, even though the march wasn't over yet and he had already sweated out twice as much water.

The pirates finally turned north and entered the jungle. They could only see a few feet in front of them. There was a little bit of moonlight, but it couldn't make it through thick foliage and only lit the treetops.

Suddenly, everyone stopped.

"What's going on?"

A message came down that the captains decided to take a break and rest. The pirates all sat down on the ground. James felt some of the soreness in his legs and back being relieved. He looked up and saw several stars through the canopy. It made him wonder what time it was. They had been walking in the dark for hours. There might not be much darkness left by the time they get to the city.

After a few short minutes, everyone stood up and the walk continued. James wanted to sit for a couple more hours, but he forced himself to stand up. He was hungry, thirsty, and exhausted. But everyone else was still going, and he had to keep up.

The pirates had to take another break two hours later. Word came down from Matthews that the city was just a couple of miles away. The sky was starting to get lighter. It would be morning soon.

Thatcher went to talk to the captain and returned a minute later.

"Break's over," he said. "We need to hurry up, because we're losing darkness. Let's go."

“Are you serious?”

“You want that money or not? Get going.”

James stood up. His legs were aching in several places and his back was sore. His steps were automatic. He was placing one foot in front of the other without even thinking about it.

A mile or so later, as the sky got brighter and brighter, everyone stopped.

“What’s going on?”

“Are we taking a break?”

“Shit!” someone yelled. A gunshot followed.

“Are you stupid?!” Angry Mark yelled. “Now they definitely know we’re here! Run! We don’t have time!”

The entire crew started running. Their legs were beaten to hell, but they ran.

After a half mile or so, the pirates saw the buildings on the edge of Santiago de Cuba. It was light enough to make out each house.

Then the first shot rang out.

James didn’t know who fired, but now the battle was on. He ran towards the nearest house, thinking only about getting behind something tough. One man in front of the pack tripped and fell and everyone had to jump over, a few pirates stepped on him.

They spread out into a bunch of small groups taking cover behind houses. James was in the same one as Matthews.

“What happened there?”

“Some kid spotted us,” Matthews said. “Wright tried to shoot him, but missed. He ran back to town.”

“Shit.”

A few shots came their way. Several pirates fired their muskets and started reloading. A couple dozen used the opportunity and ran forward. They took cover and fired at the soldiers in the distance, giving another group of pirates an opportunity to run ahead. James was among them. A pirate right in front of him collapsed and James had to jump over him. A musket ball had bounced off a rock in the dirt and lodged itself in the man’s ankle.

James took cover behind a large house with a bunch of other pirates. He carefully peeked around the corner, but couldn’t see the enemy.

“What do you see?” someone asked.

“Nothing.”

“Then move.”

James ran out into the open, and others followed. He quickly realized there was no cover, just a grassy field on one side and a vegetable garden surrounded by a low wooden fence on the other. James ran down the hill towards a tall building, most likely a church, and he heard three shots being fired. Three musket balls took out one pirate and injured another.

"We need to spread out," someone said when the entire group was at the church. "We make for an easy target when we move in big groups."

"Spread out! Move to the right, go! You, left!"

James ran out of the cover and towards the nearest house. He peeked around the corner and saw a large house with a stone wall around it. Several soldiers were positioned behind the wall. They could fire on the pirates and duck behind cover to reload. One musket ball flew just above James's head.

"Shit!"

One pirate quickly stuck his head out and pulled it back immediately.

"We'll need to hit them from the side," he said. "There's too many of them."

"Right," another pirate said. "We're going around. Follow me."

They ran further down and turned the corner, only to find more Spanish soldiers. A few shots were fired, and one pirate fell. They had to rush back to cover.

"How come there's so many fucking Spanish?" someone said.

"There's three or four there, we outnumber them. Fire!"

James stuck his musket out from behind cover and fired blindly in the direction of the enemy. Some pirate fired right next to James's head, and his right ear was ringing.

Both sides were sending lead towards the enemy, but nobody wanted to spend an extra second aiming and risk getting shot. Musket balls were flying everywhere and hitting no one.

"What are we doing?" one pirate said after fifteen minutes of this. "There's three of them, and more than a dozen of us! Charge!"

He ran out into the open and others followed. The Spaniards fired off a couple of last shots and ran.

They went around another corner and found themselves on the flank of the soldiers behind the stone wall.

"The gate is open," somebody said. "If we move quickly, we can get in and slaughter them."

"Let's go."

Over a dozen pirates ran as fast as they could towards the gate. The soldiers were too busy to notice they were being flanked. When the pirates entered the courtyard, a Spaniard who was reloading his musket spotted them.

"*¡Piratas!*"

Both sides opened fire on each other. The distance was so small that neither could miss. Five pirates were killed. All eight Spanish soldiers were shot, several got shot again or stabbed for good measure.

A few small groups of soldiers either retreated or were killed, and the pirates moved forward. They made it less than a hundred yards before taking fire from a unit of at least fourteen men. They had taken position in a small cemetery, a sloping grassy field with a few dozen wooden crosses.

The pirates opened fire on them. Others came in and joined the group. There were dozens of pirates, and the small Spanish force was quickly overwhelmed by their firepower. The soldiers quickly realized their situation was bad and about to get worse, and retreated behind a three-foot wall at the end of the cemetery.

"They're running! Charge!"

The pirates ran into the cemetery, hoping to hack the cowardly Spaniards to pieces and move towards the forts. Instead, a dozen soldiers rose from behind the wall and fired. Each ball killed or maimed at least one pirate. James immediately took cover behind one of the two trees growing in the cemetery. Others did the same, shoving their crewmates to make room for themselves, and James had to push back to not end up out in the open.

They scattered after the first volley of fire, but the Spanish soldiers immediately ducked and another dozen soldiers stood up and fired another volley. The pirates were in a field with no cover, and the musket balls tore through them. Most of them immediately scattered in every direction, but some were too slow or had someone get in the way. The Spaniards fired a third volley, mostly with pistols, and again almost every shot killed or injured a pirate. They were led right into a trap.

James was hiding behind a tree with four others. They watched their crewmates die. Some were dead before they hit the ground. Others bled out. Some tried to breathe as blood flowed into their injured lungs and eventually choked on it. A few were only maimed and screamed in pain. One man with a massive bleeding wound in his pelvis crawled toward them, but there was nothing to be done. The first man to leave cover would be dropped instantly.

"I have a grenade," one of the men said.

"Give it here." One man from the *Pale Horse* lit the grenade, stepped out, and tossed it behind the wall. A couple of seconds later, there was an explosion.

"NOW! CHARGE!"

James and two others left the tree and ran towards the Spaniards. Others ran from whatever cover they had and joined in. Two soldiers stood up and were immediately shot. James paused to quickly grab a couple of pistols he knew his crewmates wouldn't need anymore, and held one in each hand as he approached the Spanish position. A few shots were fired, then the shootout morphed into a sword fight. James fired one, then the other pistol, killing two men, then drew his cutlass and stabbed the nearest soldier. Within ten seconds, the fight was over.

"Cocksuckers," one of the pirates grumbled. "They planned it all along. For every man they lost they took two of ours. And the worst part is, we gave them exactly what they wanted. How could we be so stupid?"

"There's nothing we can do now." James recognized the voice. It was Stafford himself. "They outsmarted us. We need to keep going. Check the bodies, take their pistols and whatever else you can find."

James took a very nice musket from one of the bodies and a powder horn from another. One man had a beautiful emerald ring, but it was stuck on his finger. James didn't want to waste time cutting it off, so he just left it, hoping to get the ring once the raid was over.

The sun was already up. It had been almost twenty-four hours since James had last slept, but he wasn't sleepy, just tired and hungry. He told himself that the battle would be over before he knew it, he just had to hold on.

Soon after walking into a trap, the pirates encountered more Spaniards. The soldiers got them pinned down, and immediately sent teams to flank them from the left and right.

"We're surrounded!" Stafford yelled. "Fall back! Fall back!"

A musket ball hit him in the neck. Two of his crewmen dragged his body as the pirates retreated.

After going back two hundred yards, they sent out more men to secure the flanks, but the Spanish managed to find a way around them and once again the pirates were being hit from three sides. They took more casualties and once again had to fall back.

The battle ground to a halt. Both sides were exchanging blind shots. Neither side could flank the other. Half of the pirates were sitting around doing nothing, waiting for something to happen. Noon came and went, and the stalemate continued. By then it was one big lull, occasionally interrupted by a shot or two. A few men even managed to get some sleep.

Thatcher and a few others were going around explaining the new plan.

"We can't get stuck here. We're going to mount a charge, otherwise we'll never take the city."

"What's the plan?"

"Captains are still working on it."

"Come back when you have something."

Wright, Smith, and Grant discussed their options for at least half an hour and finally agreed to a plan. They would send two ten-man teams to sneak past the Spanish lines and attack them from behind. It would cause disarray, and give the remaining pirates an opportunity to attack. Twenty men were quickly selected, given extra weapons, ball, and powder, and instructed on when and where to attack. They left.

Pirates were separated into units of twenty to thirty men. Thatcher instructed James's unit to have their muskets and pistols loaded and to be ready to advance as soon as an order is given.

An hour later, the ten men that were headed west returned.

"What the fuck happened?" Wright asked.

"We couldn't find a way around without being seen. There's people watching everywhere from here to the harbor."

"Fuck! Fuck fuck fuck fuck FUCK!"

"There's still ten others," Grant said. "The plan is still on."

"Right. We'll wait for them. Tell the men to be ready, there will be no second chances."

Half an hour after the orders were passed down, there were shots in the distance. Eight of the ten pirates had successfully made their way to the roof of a large house and fired on Spanish positions, killing several soldiers.

"Wait for it," Grant said. "Let them forget about us."

Two Spanish soldiers managed to get close to the building with pirates on the roof. They lit a leafy tree branch on fire and threw it inside, then blocked the door with a large rock.

"NOW!" Wright yelled. "ATTACK!"

James watched as several men from his team ran towards the enemy.

"DIE YOU SPANISH FUCKS!"

The soldiers opened fire, and several pirates dropped. The Spaniards weren't scattered or distracted. Their shots were accurate.

The eight pirates behind Spanish lines didn't notice the smoke until most of the house was engulfed in flames. The roof was too high to jump. Five of them tried anyway and fell to their deaths. The remaining three burned with the house.

James watched as other pirates either got shot or dove for cover. Some managed to return to the same spot they were a minute ago. For the next fifteen minutes, there was intense shooting, then it diminished and both sides were back to doing nothing and firing a shot every now and then.

After an hour, Thatcher appeared again.

"We're done. We're not taking Santiago."

"What?!"

"We lost almost half of our men. The captains decided that we will hold out until dusk and then retreat."

"This is bullshit!"

"Look, we lost. There's nothing we can do. It's either retreat or die here."

For the next several hours there was nothing to do but sit around and wait, and occasionally fire a shot towards the Spanish to make them think the battle was still on.

James was exhausted. He didn't even want to take Santiago anymore. All he wanted was a warm meal and a warm bed. James paid little attention to his surroundings. He just waited for the sun to set so he could go back to his hammock on the *Doom*.

Time went by slowly. Boredom and exhaustion made it go even slower. Eventually the sun disappeared beyond the horizon.

One of Smith's men was going around giving instructions. There would be three or four men every few hundred yards firing on the Spanish. The rest would quietly move back to their ships. Then the decoys would fire the last few shots and make their retreat.

James was assigned to be one of the decoys.

"I'm not doing it."

"Look, all you have to do is stay here a little longer and fire a few shots. That's it."

"Fuck you. I'm leaving right now."

"It's not going to take long. Maybe half an hour."

"Find someone else. I'm leaving."

He stood up and joined the large mass of tired men. The march began.

James's feet, legs, and back were still sore from the march forward. The ships were probably anchored closer to Santiago, but they still had to make it through the jungle and to the coast. And they had to do it in the dark and without Swafford or Matthews to guide them. Both of them had died in the ambush at the cemetery.

James went wherever everyone else was going. He couldn't remember anything from the march forward except trees and darkness. Everyone around him looked barely alive, dragging their feet and stumbling. Many of them were limping. A few miles in, one man sat down on the ground and said he would take a quick break and then catch up. As they went on, a few more did the same. One of the *Sea Dragon*'s crewmen collapsed and was left there. Nobody even checked if he was alive.

Several miles into the march, James started feeling pain in his right knee and had to walk with a limp. Bending the leg caused a jolt of pain. He thought he would collapse at any moment, but somehow he managed to keep going.

Wright was at the front of the group, but he stopped repeatedly and then had to catch up with the others. He was blundering left and right as if he was drunk. Smith wasn't doing much better. Grant was being helped by his quartermaster. He was delirious.

James tried to ignore the dull pain in his feet and the soreness in his back, telling himself that he'd be back on the *Howling Doom* very soon. Then something amazing happened. James glanced to his left and through the trees he saw water. It was the same river they had followed when they entered the jungle. The coast was less than a mile away.

The realization that the march was pretty much over made James happy, but instead of motivating him to push forward, it made him want to sit down and rest. Walking became even harder. His body seemed to like the idea of the march being overand was preparing itself for rest.

A couple of minutes later, James heard the waves. They were almost at the coast. The ships will be waiting there. It was over. That goddamned catastrophe of a raid was over.

They walked out of the jungle onto the same beach they had walked on just a day ago, although it seemed like it had been weeks. The ships were already there. James slowly lay down on the ground. No more walking. The launches were coming. It was finally over.

The next morning, he woke up late. Most of the crew were still asleep. James went to get some breakfast. His legs and back were still sore, but at least he could walk without a limp. There was a strange mood on the ship. Everyone was depressed, irritable, and tired. Some of the crewmates wouldn't even talk to others. Some tried to pretend that the raid wasn't a big deal, but James saw in their faces. They would never be able to forget Santiago.

The *Devil's Reject*, *Sea Dragon*, and *Pale Horse* each went their own way. The *Howling Doom* was headed east-southeast towards Hispaniola. When asked why, O'Keefe just shrugged.

"I tried to ask the captain last night, but he was barely stringing words together. Quartermaster was grumpier than usual and started yelling at me. I figured we will probably head towards the Windward Passage. I'm pretty sure we were heading for Nassau after this."

"Nassau is still in question," James said.

"Why?"

"Because we didn't make much money in Vera Cruz and we got crushed in Santiago. We're in a bad place right now."

"So what's going to happen now?"

"I don't know."

Wright came out of his cabin only once, in the evening. He exchanged a few words with Thatcher, told O'Keefe the new course, and spent the rest of the time at the bow, watching the open sea. For the next two days, he was in a constant bad mood, spoke little, and ignored questions.

On the afternoon of the second day, they saw a ship.

"Sail, starboard bow!"

Wright slowly searched his pocket for the spyglass, pulled it out, and inspected the ship.

"It's a sloop," he said. "Spanish colors."

"What will the orders be, captain?" Thatcher said.

Wright paused, then looked through the spyglass again.

"I'd say let's take it."

"We're taking that sloop," Thatcher said. "Battle stations!"

James took up a larboard cannon with Wentworth, a *Pale Horse* crewman who ended up on the wrong ship after the raid. Once the cannon was loaded, James went to the lower deck to grab his pistols.

Then they waited.

Two men raised a Spanish flag at the stern. Others furled the *Doom*'s sails. The wind was strong and the sloop was quickly approaching. James loaded both of his pistols and prepared the slow match.

Wright went amidships and leaned against the mainmast. The crew was quiet. Everyone was focused on the task.

Wright found Douglas and told him to put a ball through the helmsman's head the first chance he got. Douglas nodded without saying anything.

The sloop slowly got closer. The pirates could distinguish sailors on the deck.

"Captain," Phillips said, "do we fire the chasers?"

"No. I don't think we'll need them."

"Then what are we going to do?" Thatcher said.

"Let them come to us. We'll attack from up close. Let's not give them a chance to fire their guns."

The sloop drew closer and its captain yelled something in Spanish but got no answer. It was approaching *Howling Doom*'s starboard side, and James put away the slow match and drew his pistols. Wentworth started loading his own pistol. The Spanish captain yelled again, and again he was ignored. He sounded frustrated.

The ships got even closer, but the Spanish captain had still not realized something was up. Once they were close enough, Thatcher gave the order and the pirates threw grappling hooks and started pulling the ships closer. Douglas stood up and shot the helmsman. The ball hit him in the right upper arm, ripping through bone and tissue in a cloud of blood. The helmsman collapsed. It wasn't the shot Douglas wanted, but it was enough.

The pirates started placing boards between the two ships to be able to cross over. James ran across one board and jumped down on the deck of the sloop. He shot the nearest sailor in the pelvis, then aimed the other pistol at another one. As James pulled the trigger, he saw the terrified man put his hands up, then drop with a hole in his chest. He saw his crewmates firing their pistols, killing most of the Spanish crew.

Of the twenty-two sailors onboard, twelve were dead or gravely injured. The Spaniards surrendered. The entire battle did not last a minute.

The sailors were terrified. A couple were crying. The captain was pale and his hands were shaking. One of the pirates spoke to him in Spanish and learned that the ship was called *Río Verde* and carried cinnamon and sugar. They started moving the cargo to the *Howling Doom*.

"What are we doing with the ship?" someone asked.

"Leave it," Wright said. "It's useless."

"Are we going to sink it?"

"No. Leave them be, so they can tell the tale."

The cargo was loaded in just five minutes. The pirates let the *Río Verde* sail away and continued toward the West Indies.

"Gentlemen," Wright spoke to the crew. "We had some bad luck in Cuba, but we are back. That loss is in the past. We took a ship. This is what we are good at. That's what we'll continue to do. Overwhelm ships and take their cargo. I want you to forget Santiago. We don't need to sack their cities. We'll cut them off from Spain by taking out their ships. We might even target their treasure fleet. Right now, we are headed for Tortuga. We will sell our cargo to make room for future loot and we'll spend a few days there relaxing before we go back to raiding ships."

The crew cheered at the news of stopping at Tortuga. It had been a while since they had an opportunity to get drunk. Tortuga wasn't anything close to the paradise that Nassau was, but it was good enough.

"Tell me about Tortuga," James asked Hammond one evening. "I heard it's pretty much like Nassau."

"It used to be. Back in the days of Henry Morgan and others. But then the Brits took the island back. Most pirates switched to regular jobs.

Others left and found their way to Port Royal in Jamaica. I hear it was a fun place to be. Then an earthquake hit it back in… ninety-two, something like that, and most of Port Royal ended up underwater."

"And now we have Nassau."

"Yeah."

"Ever been to Port Royal?"

"No. Ask Old Man Farnham, he'll tell you all kinds of wild stories."

"So what's in Tortuga?"

"Lots of law-abiding citizens. A few people that will gladly buy any cargo from us. And also a couple of taverns and whorehouses."

"So not much different from Nassau."

"Except in Tortuga they'll hang you if they find out you're a pirate."

For several days, they sailed east along the coast of Saint-Domingue. It wasn't far, but the wind worked against them.

Eventually they reached Tortuga. It was raining heavily. By the time they got the ship in the dock, evening had come. An old man met them on the shore.

"Good evening," the old timer said. "I need to know the name of this ship and its captain, and what cargo is in the hold."

"Captain Joseph Santiago, of the... The *Porto Bello*," Thatcher said. He dug in his pocket and handed the man several pieces of eight. "Anything else or can we go now?"

"Of course. Enjoy your stay, brethren."

The crew, led by Wright, went straight to the nearest tavern. Some split off and went to a different one. It was nice and warm inside. There were few people in the tavern, and several dozen men entering at the same time caught everyone's attention.

"You must be the crew of that ship," the keeper said. "What brings you here?"

"We just want to drink," Phillips said.

"Of course. I'll be right there."

James, Hammond, Douglas, and O'Keefe occupied a table in the corner. There weren't enough chairs in the tavern, and at least half of the pirates had to stand.

"So, where are you boys headed?" a man asked. "Jamaica?"

"Mind your own business," Hammond said.

Another man stood up and slowly approached their table.

"Jack Hammond?"

"Who the fuck… Williams? Where the hell did you come from? Sit down."

James finally recognized the man. It was Moses Williams, one of the crewmen on Whitaker's *Marlin,* the same man who started a fight when they had last met in Nassau.

Williams quickly looked around.

"Where have you been?" he said, keeping his voice down. "I mean, after we last met?"

"All over the place," James said. "Took a ship near Havana that was carrying some kind of politician, barely evaded a Spanish man-of-war, sacked Vera Cruz, attacked Santiago de Cuba…"

"That one didn't end well," Hammond said. "And then we took a tiny sloop and came here. What have you been up to? Where's your crew?"

"Dead."

"What?"

"The *Marlin* sank a few miles from Maracaibo. Three Spanish ships. We stood no chance."

"Survivors?"

"Me, Logan, and Madison. That's it. I don't know where they are now."

"Shit," Douglas said. "Oh shit. I can't believe it."

"So the entire crew is gone?" Hammond said.

"I just told you."

"To Captain Whitaker," James said. "And to the crew of the *Marlin.*"

They raised their tankards and drank, and after that nobody said anything for a while.

"How did you get here?" Hammond interrupted the silence.

"I managed to get on a French ship. They treated me like shit, so I left the first chance I got. Found work here. I've been hearing rumors lately."

"What kind of rumors?"

"That the English are angry. They don't like what's going on in the Bahamas, especially New Providence. They want law and order in there."

"So?"

"They're planning to take over the island and get rid of pirates for good. I don't know when or how."

"Shit."

"I'll go get Thatcher," Douglas said. "We're not going to leave you here. You're joining our crew."

"Thank you."

Douglas returned a minute later with the quartermaster.

"Remember Moses Williams, from Whitaker's crew? He's joining ours."

"So you finally realized that Whitaker is a pompous idiot?"

"The Spanish sunk the *Marlin*," Williams said. "Only three of us survived."

"What?! Shit. In any case, welcome aboard, Mr. Williams."

"He said there are rumors about the English cleaning out Nassau," James said.

"We moved from Tortuga to Port Royal and from Port Royal to Nassau. We'll just find a new spot. The English won't accomplish anything."

They continued erasing the tavern's supplies of rum and beer. Hours went by. Some of the pirates left the tavern and went to the whorehouse. A few ended up snoring on the floor. A couple got into a fight and were told to leave, and they went to another tavern, and some of their friends followed them there. Byrd started singing *Leave Her, Johnny*, and several crewmates sang along. Wright would empty his tankard in about five minutes, then refill and start over. Around midnight, he stood up and left.

After a while, James, Hammond, and Douglas were still sitting at the same table. Douglas was asleep.

"What do you think of the rumors? You know, about England taking back New Providence?" James asked.

"Could be just a story made up to scare the pirates. Or it could be a real threat."

"If it's not real, why would they spread it in Tortuga? Why not somewhere closer to Nassau?"

"To make it seem real. And then everyone starts believing it, packs up their stuff and leaves, and they can take Nassau without firing a shot."

"So you think it's a trick?"

"No," Hammond said. "I think it could be real. I don't know."

"What's going to happen to us?"

"We'll be fine. We've been through worse."

"How long have you been on this crew?"

"About… ten years. Almost ten years."

"Were you at Cartagena?"

"Yes."

"Tell me about it."

"Whitaker planned the whole thing. I don't know what the full plan was, but there were a lot of moving parts. These men go here, these ones go here, these ones wait for the shooting to start, that kind of thing. We lost over a third of our crew, but we took it. Without Whitaker planning it, there would've been no chance. Not with Wright. His plans are always the same. Find a poorly guarded town and just go in and kill everybody."

"How much were you paid?"

"For the Cartagena job? A lot. I was living like a king. Burned through all that money really quick, though. Next time we sailed, I was promoted to bosun. The previous bosun, Callaway, died in Cartagena. Took a blade to the ribs."

"What did we do in Santiago?"

"What do you mean?"

"I mean, how did we fuck up so badly?"

"We shouldn't have attacked a strong city with so little preparation. We didn't know they would have so many soldiers. Whoever told Stafford it's not well-guarded was a liar, or just had old information."

"How bad was it?"

"It's was a fucking disaster. Our worst loss ever. We retreated without getting anything. And to think we considered taking down Havana."

"We're not finished yet," James said. "We'll be taking ships from now on. Our crew is good at it."

"Yeah. We should stick to ships. Lone ships, not the fucking treasure fleet. Wright better not be planning that. They would sink the *Doom* in five minutes."

"And I guess we'll be staying away from Nassau. Just until we know if the rumors are true."

"Staying away would be cowardly, but risking it just for drink and women would be stupid. I say we wait and see. If New Providence is taken over, at least we won't get caught in that mess."

"Nobody in Nassau will be sober enough to fire back."

"The whores might."

"Imagine how hilarious it would be if the Royal Navy were held back by a bunch of whores."

"Nassau will fall eventually," Hammond said. "We'll just build a town somewhere else. There are a bunch of small islands off the coast of Florida. Then there's the Cayman Islands. There's plenty of places to go. We'll build our own town and we'll name it Paradise. Drink and women, more than you can handle."

"Sounds beautiful. Maybe we shouldn't wait?"

"For what?"

"For Nassau to fall. Let's start it now."

"I like you, McDougall. You have balls."

Thatcher entered the tavern. He looked around and went to James and Hammond.

"You two, can you still walk?"

"Sure." They both stood up. It wasn't very graceful, but they could hold up.

Thatcher slapped Douglas.

"Wake up, shithead. There's work to do."

"Huh? What…"

"Stand up! Come on, follow me."

They left the tavern. It had stopped raining. The sky was turning red in the east.

Douglas was still a little dizzy, but he could walk on his own.

"Where are we going?" he asked.

"The whorehouse," Thatcher said.

"Shit, why didn't you say so?"

"Shut up! All of you! You don't speak unless spoken to, understood?"

"All right, all right."

They followed the quartermaster in silence. The whorehouse was nearby.

The four pirates entered the brothel. Thatcher headed straight for the stairs to the second floor. He knew exactly where he was going.

James, Hammond, and Douglas followed Thatcher to the end of the hallway, where he opened a door without knocking. They entered the room.

Captain Wright was on the floor, completely naked. His skin was pale and his eyes wide. A small line of blood ran from his nose to his open mouth.

"FUCK!" Hammond shouted.

James and Douglas were stunned. Neither said anything.

"Can I get paid now?" said the whore. Only then they noticed she was still in the room.

Hammond took a couple of pieces of eight from his pocket and gave them to her.

"That's not enough."

"Take the fucking money and get the fuck out of here!" he yelled.

She gave him a nasty look but left the room and closed the door behind her.

"Shit," Douglas said. "What do we do now?"

"Can't leave him here," Thatcher said. "Wrap him in bedsheets."

Hammond took the body by the legs, James grabbed the arms. Wright's skin was cold.

"All right, one, two, three."

They put the body on the bed and wrapped it tightly in bedsheets, making sure to leave no skin visible.

"Grab it, let's hurry up."

The four pirates, Thatcher in front, carried the body downstairs and out the door. Thatcher guided them towards the beach.

"What are we doing with him?" James asked.

"We'll have to bury him," Thatcher said. "We can't let anyone know that he's dead. He's a pirate captain, he's supposed to die in battle after a heroic fight. He can't die like a dog."

About a mile from the dock, they found a spot where the coast was rough and the water ran deep. They found some rocks and put them inside the sheets.

"Here goes," Hammond said. "On three. One, two, three."

They tossed the body into the waves and it sank to the bottom. Captain Wright was laid to rest.

"Nobody can know that he's dead," Thatcher said. "Let them think that he's in Madagascar or something, doesn't matter. I already told that whore that he was our ship's cook, William Strong. We have to keep the secret no matter what. Harold Wright and *Howling Doom* must live on. Understood?"

"Should we say a few words?" Douglas asked.

"Shut up, Douglas. Now listen. Gather the crew, we're leaving."

"Are we going to tell them?" James said.

"No. Not yet. I don't know. We'll figure it out. Right now, we just get our crew and set sail."

The sun was peeking from behind the horizon by the time they got back to the tavern. Thatcher ordered some rum.

"Gentlemen, a toast."

They raised their tankards and drank.

CHAPTER XXIII

Williamsburg, Colony of Virginia

"What do you mean?"

"Sometimes it makes you do things that make no sense whatsoever," James said. "And you do them, even though you don't want to and see no point."

"You're speaking in riddles."

"Yes. Yes I am. Anything else you wanted to ask?"

"I can't think of anything right now. I'll let you know when I have something."

"Just don't become a pirate. You'll wind up right back here."

"But if someone were to quit at the right time…"

"Forget it. You won't leave. You'll keep going until you're hanging in the gallows or floating face-down in the sea."

"What would happen if someone tried?"

"Tried what?"

"To leave. What would the others say?"

"Probably tell you there's another job coming, and it will pay even more. Don't worry about what others think, it's not your crew that keeps you in. You do it yourself. It seems so easy when you're stuck in a prison cell – hey, I'll just make some money and then quit. But when you're out there… There's gold, booze, and whores. Life is so much fun. Why would anyone leave that?"

"At some point you'll want to do something else."

"You said it yourself, whores and rum on the beach, who wouldn't want this?"

"People grow old. Then—"

"Pirates don't. Pirates die young. I don't think I've ever seen an old pirate."

"How old is Heartless Harry?"

"I don't know."

"Not very young, from what I've heard."

"Not old, either."

"But it's possible to make a bunch of money quickly, right? Like if you sack a rich city?"

"Sure. If you survive."

"So it's possible for a man to join a pirate crew, make money, and then leave to pursue other things."

"What other things?"

"Buy a house somewhere nice. Not a mansion, just a nice small house somewhere in the Caribbean."

"And then what?"

"With the remaining money, I'd start investing. I hear a man can make a lot of money in shipping, but you need to have some gold to begin with."

"And then what?"

"Once I have some money, I can find myself a wife."

"And then what?"

"Live happily."

"Rob, you don't need to be a pirate to get all that."

"But it makes everything easier."

"There are better ways to make money."

"Such as?"

"Any job that doesn't involve ships. Except maybe shipbuilding."

"I don't want to build ships."

"Fine, do something else then. Just find something you're good at and put in some effort. All those things you mentioned can be done without robbing people."

"I know. I know I can make money if I work long and hard, and I'm not afraid of hard work, trust me, but… If you had to choose between working hard for years or working easy for months, which one would you take?"

"It's a bit more complicated than that."

"I don't think it's that complicated."

"You could get hit by a musket ball out of nowhere before you even see any gold. I know men who ended up like that. One was seventeen or eighteen when he had his head blown off."

"A friend I knew in Medford was twenty-five when he had a tree fall on him. Can't walk, can't talk. He can move one arm, but just barely."

"So?"

"I might just end up dead walking down the street. People get struck by lightning. Some people just randomly die in their sleep. Some get stabbed by robbers."

"Tell me about it."

"What I'm trying to say is, I could die any day for any reason. I don't want to hope that someday I will have enough money for a house. I don't want to spend decades working in some coal mine in Massachusetts and dreaming about it. I don't want to enjoy the good things when I'm old. And I don't want to spend my days in a coal mine when there's adventures to be had. Sure, it's dangerous, but so is everything. It's still better than getting crushed by a damn tree. I'd rather die storming Vera Cruz. It's better than wasting my youth breaking my back for pennies."

"Jesus Christ, Rob…"

"What?"

"You don't know what it's like out there. You don't know what you're getting yourself into and you don't understand what it will do to you. You think you'll just join a group of jolly adventurers, make a ton of gold, and live like a king? Forget it. You'll live in a dirty old ship reeking of vomit and piss, surrounded by horrible people who will slice your throat as soon as they don't see any use in you. You'll make money, and think you've made it, only to see it disappear in one week, and you'll wonder what happened. And then you're out in the sea again, to make more money, this time it's going to be big, just this one big job, and you'll be rich beyond your wildest dreams, but then you get your share and go to Nassau, and a couple of weeks later the money has disappeared again, and it goes on and never ends. You think working some other job is breaking your back? Piracy is exactly the same. Breaking your back for pennies. You think it's a lot of money, but when you realize that you could get shot any moment, that you could lose an arm or a leg or an eye, that there are people out there trying to kill you, that you cannot even walk down the street in any city that isn't a pirate-infested slum because you'll be hanged… When you realize what kind of things you have to do to get that gold, you– it's not worth it. I look back and none of it was worth it. Those things you want – a house, a wife, some money – I want that too. I wish I could just live peacefully someplace sunny, but that's gone now. That's it. I'm going to be swinging in the gallows in the morning."

CHAPTER XXIV
Tortuga, Saint-Domingue

They went around waking up the rest of the crew. Some were in deep sleep, some were already awake. Everyone was ordered to get back to the ship immediately, as the *Doom* would be setting sail the same evening. Most crewmen were angry, especially ones who had plans to visit the brothel. Hammond had to beat up a couple of men for insubordination.

Several crewmates had to be carried. One was dead. At least a dozen pirates had to stop to vomit. Most of them immediately headed to their beds and fell asleep.

"Let them," Thatcher said. "They'll sleep it off and then we can put them to work. Right now we need to get them all in the ship and get the hell out of Tortuga."

Douglas stood leaning over the gunwale and looking at the gentle waves below. He hadn't said a word the entire morning. Several pirates wanted to talk to him, but he wouldn't even acknowledge them.

As James led two hungover pirates back to the ship, he stopped to talk to Hammond.

"Do we have a plan?"

"We're going to Cayman Islands," Hammond said. "On the way we'll try to catch a few ships. Williams said there's a loaded frigate that should be passing through here pretty soon."

"A frigate?"

"Yeah. He said it stopped here a few days ago, headed for Kingston."

"Can we take it?"

"Williams saw it with his own eyes. He said it's a juicy target. We just need to catch it."

"When do we talk with the crew?"

"Not yet. We talked about it and we both think the best time would be when we're in the Caymans."

"And until then we just pretend that everything's fine?"

"Exactly."

"People will ask questions," James said.

"Come up with an answer."

"What happens when we reach the Caymans?"

"It has sea turtles, fresh water, and fish. And it's close to main shipping routes. It will be our spot to hide."

James looked around the empty deck.

"Exactly how fucked are we right now?" he said.

"It's not that bad. We'll figure everything out. The crew will be the same. It just takes time."

"It won't be the same. We lost Roger, Clarke, Ashborne, Manzanares, Abernathy, Scott, Guimaraes, and a bunch of others. And now there's the possibility we might lose Nassau."

"We're a pirate crew. People come and go. We're still the same crew. We still have the *Doom*."

"I guess."

"And Nassau? Trust me, once we get women and drinks into the Caymans, Nassau will be irrelevant," Hammond said. "New Providence was full of Englishmen back in the day, we made them all move out and Nassau was ours. This time it will happen faster. When the word gets around that there's a new place for pirates, and it's founded by the scariest crew in the Caribbean, everyone will flock to the Caymans."

"Do you really think we're still the scariest crew? After Vera Cruz and Santiago?"

"We'll build our reputation back up. We'll take ships one after another. It's a matter of weeks before sailors start telling stories about us again."

"I really hope so. Right now things aren't looking too good."

"We'll be fine. We survived worse."

By noon, all the men they could find were onboard.

"Time to go," Thatcher said. "The faster we get out of here, the better. Weigh the anchor!"

"Sir, what's the course?" O'Keefe asked.

"For now, Jamaica. Once we catch the ship we're looking for, we'll be headed for Cayman Islands."

"Understood, sir."

Hammond went to wake up more pirates to man the ship. A few men were complaining about not getting enough rest or missing out on a chance to visit the brothel.

James overheard Wentworth and Phillips.

"I don't even know where we're going," Wentworth said.

"Towards Jamaica," James interrupted. "Williams says there's a frigate that came through here, we should be able to take it without an issue. After that we're going straight to Cayman Islands."

"What about Nassau?"

"What about it?"

"Are we going there?"

"No. Apparently, from now on we'll be visiting the Caymans, not Nassau. Captain's decision."

"This is bullshit. Where is he?"

"This isn't a good time to argue with him."

"He's in one of his moods again?" Phillips said.

"Yeah. Leave him be."

Phillips shook his head and walked away.

James looked around. Even after taking a day off in Tortuga, the crew was weary and sluggish. There was no singing or telling jokes.

They raised the anchor and unfurled the sails and let the easterly wind turn the *Doom* around. The voyage began.

The news of the course being changed from Nassau to Cayman Islands spread quickly. Some pirates didn't care, others were disappointed, some were furious.

"What is this bullshit?" Browne yelled. "How come the captain changed the course without telling the crew? And how come we only get one night in Tortuga? This is bullshit and I won't stand for it!"

"Browne, listen to me…" James started, but was ignored.

"We want to go to Nassau!" Browne shouted.

Hammond quickly walked over to him and punched him in the face. The punch knocked Browne off his feet. As he tried to stand up, Hammond kicked him in the ribs several times.

"What you're saying sounds like mutiny talk, Mr. Browne," he said. "Do you know what happens to mutineers on this ship?"

"Yes."

Hammond kicked him again. Browne was lying on the deck trying to catch his breath.

"Yes *what*?"

"Yes, sir," Browne uttered.

"Damn straight. What the fuck are you idiots looking at? Back to work!"

"Good job, Mr. Hammond," Thatcher said as he passed by.

James caught up with Hammond at the stern.

"I don't think we'll be able to keep it going until the Caymans."

"Just pretend that everything's fine," Hammond said. "If we have to deal with it sooner, fine, but that doesn't mean you don't have to keep your mouth shut. And check on Douglas."

"Why? Is something wrong with him?"

"Make sure he doesn't start talking."

James went belowdecks. He found Douglas in his hammock, staring at the ceiling.

"Hey, how are you doing?"

Douglas didn't even look at him.

"Hey, I'm talking to you, dirtbag."

"Fuck off." He was still staring at the ceiling.

"What is up with you?"

"Leave me alone, McDougall."

"Hey, keep it down there!" someone yelled.

"Douglas, what the hell is up with you?" James said, this time quietly.

"We're fucked. We are completely fucked."

"What do you mean?"

"You know exactly what I mean. We're fucked. It's only a matter of time before this is over."

"What's over?"

"Everything. It's done. We're done." Douglas quickly looked around. "This whole crew is on its last breath," he whispered.

"You don't know what you're talking about. Just wait until we reach Caymans, all right?"

"This is the beginning of the end. I know it, you know it."

"Can you promise me you'll keep it to yourself until we reach the Caymans?"

"What difference does it make?"

"Give this crew a chance."

"Sure. It's not like I can leave."

James went back to the upper deck. Everything was as usual. The sky was cloudy and it seemed like it would rain again soon. For a while, the wind was strong and the *Doom* covered distance quickly, but sometime in the evening it began to wane. After James and several others hoisted the studding sails, Hammond came up to talk to him.

"Did you talk to Douglas?"

"Yeah. Don't worry about it," James said. "Although he was acting strange."

"Strange how?"

"He's saying this crew is finished and this is the beginning of the end."

"He's an idiot. He wants to give up at the first sign of trouble."

"I asked him to not give up on this crew until we at least reach the Caymans."

"Did he agree?"

"Yes. I don't think he'll be causing us any trouble."

"Good. At least we don't have to worry about that."

"Jack?"

"What?"

"Do you think Douglas is right? That everything is about to fall apart?"

"Douglas is a coward," Hammond said. "Just wait 'til we reach Cayman Islands. And don't listen to his ramblings. Every time something doesn't go the way he wants it to, he starts crying that the fucking world is about to end."

"All right."

"Just ignore him. He does that all the time. Not sure why we even keep him on this crew, he kills everyone's morale with his bullshit."

"Got it. Do you need anything else from me?"

"No. But stick around, we'll need to trim the sails soon."

Douglas came up to the upper deck in the evening. He worked without complaining, but didn't say a word to anyone. A couple of pirates tried to talk to him, but were told to go fuck themselves.

By dinnertime, the *Howling Doom* was in the Windward Passage and headed southwest. The wind picked up for a while, then slowed down again. A third of the remaining crew didn't show up for dinner.

Around midnight, James went belowdecks, slapped Richards and told him it was his watch, and climbed into his hammock. He didn't want to sleep. James looked at the ceiling and listened to his crewmates calmly breathing, some of them snoring. Someone coughed. He wondered if things were about to go to shit, or if everything had already gone to shit and they were simply buying time, like Douglas said. Eventually he convinced himself that the crew had been through too much to just roll over and die, and with that thought he fell asleep.

In the morning, the sky was cloudy and it seemed it would rain soon. The wind was strong. The *Doom* was making up for the miles lost while becalmed at night.

The crew was starting to get back into routine. Breakfast was just like before, although the crew wasn't as talkative as always and the food was worse than usual.

"Why didn't we restock on meat?" somebody grumbled. "We could be eating fresh meat right now."

"Everyone was drunk."

"Even Beasley?"

"Hammond had to carry him to the ship."

Douglas showed up late, ate little, and didn't talk to anyone.

Hammond looked like he had not slept well, if at all. James went to talk with him after breakfast.

"Hey. Anything new?"

"No."

"Look, I don't think we should go for that ship," James said.

"Why not?"

"There will be questions. Taking a ship is a big deal."

"So?"

"Wouldn't it be better to just quietly make it to the Cayman Islands first, sort everything out, and *then* go hunting for money?"

"We talked about this," Hammond said. "I don't care if we have to deal with this before we reach the Caymans. It's not going to be smooth anyway. But there's one thing that could make everything smoother, and that's gold in pockets. I understand where you're coming from, but no one takes the careful approach on this crew. It's just not what we do."

"Right. Then I guess I have no choice but to follow along."

They were quiet for a while.

"Have you told anything to anyone?" Hammond asked.

"No."

"Good."

"Do we have a plan on how we're going to get out of this mess?"

"Yes. We just need to take that ship and get to the Caymans. Don't say anything to anyone, because you won't be mentioned. There's no need for you to take the fall."

"Thank you. I appreciate it."

"Don't mention it. Just be quiet and let me know if something is up."

"Got it."

The day went by slowly. The *Doom* was doing nine knots. The wind was steady and there was no need for any major adjustments. Ten men were enough to control the ship, and everyone else had nothing to do.

"Sail, starboard bow!" someone shouted.

Thatcher, who was hanging out amidships, ran over to the bow and inspected the ship through his spyglass.

"It's a sloop," he said. "Not what we're here for. Let it pass."

As the ships drew closer, they could see that it was indeed a small vessel. It was flying Dutch colors.

"What colors do we fly?"

"None," Thatcher said. "Just ignore it. Stay on the lookout for a large frigate. That's what we're going for."

The sloop approached. Once the ships were close enough, the pirates saw the Dutch crew waving. A few waved back, but most of them just ignored it.

That afternoon, they caught up with another ship, a Spanish brigantine, going in the same direction.

"Not the ship we want," Thatcher said. "We're going for that frigate."

"That was a nice ship," Mason said.

"The one we're going to take is even nicer. And it's an easier target."

They passed the slow brigantine and left it behind, and its sails disappeared in the distance. The *Howling Doom* was alone again, with nothing but water as far as the eye could see.

Several hours later, as evening approached, someone spotted a third sail.

Thatcher ran to the bow to see it first.

"It's a big one," he said. "Three masts. That's got to be our frigate. Battle stations!"

James ran to the lower deck to get his pistols, powder horn, and ammunition. He returned to the main deck and took up one of the starboard guns. Beside him was Wayland. They loaded the cannon without saying a word to each other.

"Load the chasers with grapeshot!" Phillips commanded. "You two, hurry up!"

"Load your pistols!" Thatcher yelled. "I want everyone ready! Keene, go get the black, but don't fly it yet!"

James felt a raindrop fall on the back of his neck. He saw another one fall on the deck and a third one on the cannon.

"It's starting to rain," he said.

"Yeah, I see that," Wayland answered.

More and more raindrops fell on the deck, and it turned into a drizzle, then all-out rain.

"It's just rain, it's not a storm," Thatcher announced. "The battle is still on. Watch the powder, don't let it get wet. Let's try to get aboard that ship before our guns stop firing."

Some of the cannon crews took off their shirts and laid them on the guns to keep water out of the touchholes. Many of them quietly prayed for the ship to get there faster before the powder got wet, but it was still far away and it seemed like both ships had gotten slower. Twilight was approaching, and it was getting harder to see.

The rain kept coming, and there was no sign of it letting up. Wayland put his hand over the touchhole. James was grasping an unlit slow match in his fist. Several pirates put whatever they had over their pistols to keep the water out, some decided to go to the lower deck and come out once the battle started.

James watched the ship as it got closer and he could tell that it was big, much bigger than the *Doom*. He was worried that a ship like that would have more crew, but he told himself that they were most likely not prepared to fight, especially in rain.

“Mr. Keene, fly the black on the mainmast,” Thatcher commanded. “If we don’t fly it right now, they won’t be able to see it. I want them to know who we are.”

Keene fumbled for a while trying to attach the flag, but once it was secured he raised it to the top of the mast.

The ship was getting closer. There was still just enough light to distinguish colors, the crew definitely had seen the black. The ships were finally within three hundred yards.

All of a sudden, their target adjusted the yards and the wind pushed the ship towards starboard.

“They’re trying to get a broadside on us!” Thatcher shouted. “Turn to starboard!”

As the ship turned and the *Howling Doom* turned the same way, they ended up facing each other broadside.

“LARBOARD GUNS, FIRE!”

Only half of the cannons actually fired, but most of the shots hit the target. The ship answered with twice as many cannonballs. Most of them hit the side, a few flew over the deck and landed in the water, one barely missed Browne and struck the carriage of the cannon next to them. Another shot went through the side of the ship into the galley and killed Beasley.

Pirates came running from belowdecks. The wind carried away the gunpowder smoke and they saw that their target had not one but two rows of cannons. The pirates were dealing with rain while the other ship had cannons on the lower deck, safe from the water.

“White Ensign!” someone shouted. “They’re flying the White Ensign!”

“It’s a fucking man-of-war!”

The pirates reloaded their cannons, but again some of them would not fire.

“We’re fighting for our lives now!” Thatcher yelled. “Give them everything you’ve got!”

The man-of-war fired, and once again multiple shots hit the side of the *Doom,* several went high, two took out Mason and Hart, and one smashed into the mainmast.

As the ships drew closer, James saw a tall silhouette standing on the quarterdeck. It had to be the captain. He drew one of his pistols aimed and fired, but the shot missed, as the man was still standing. James aimed slowly and carefully with his other pistol and pulled the trigger, but the gun just clacked.

His crewmates were firing their pistols and muskets into the man-of-war, but many of the guns misfired. Meanwhile, rounds of grapeshot took out Johnson and Hammond. Phillips took a shot to the arm.

James took cover behind the mainmast. He watched as another round of grapeshot hit the ship. Douglas was hit twice in the chest. Thatcher took one to the head. James looked back at the cannon he had just manned and saw Wayland lying dead on the deck.

Anderson ran up to him.

"I need your help with the guns," he said. James nodded and followed him. They ran towards one of the cannons, keeping their heads down.

"Make sure you keep the powder dry!" Anderson yelled through the noise.

A fistful of grapeshot hit the side of the *Doom* right where James and Anderson were, and one ball made it through the gun port and went through Anderson's abdomen. He fell down, crying in pain and grasping the wound. James pulled his hands off to look at it, and saw there was nothing anyone could do. Anderson was done.

Everyone on the *Howling Doom* was either dead or unwilling to fight. No one was firing the cannons. No one even reloaded their pistols. Everyone just hid belowdecks or behind the bulwark, hoping that the man-of-war and its crew will somehow decide to just mark it as a victory and move on. But the captain wasn't done yet. Their guns kept firing cannonballs into the *Doom*, tearing holes and occasionally hitting a pirate.

The rain kept coming. It was too dark to make out anything except the terrified pirates and dead bodies on the deck.

The wind was picking up, and one strong gust pushed the damaged mainmast too far. It cracked and fell forward, and everyone rushed to get out of its way. The mast got tangled in the rigging and was leaning against the foremast.

James heard cheers coming from the man-of-war.

Another strong gust came, and this time the foremast gave up under the weight of the mainmast. It broke just above the deck and fell towards the larboard. More cheers came from the British man-of-war.

Both masts were still partially attached to the *Doom*, and some of the rigging still held. The weight of the masts made the ship lean towardlarboard, and she started taking water. A starboard cannon broke off and rolled to the other side. The larboard gunwale was in the water. She was still floating, but the damage was too much. The *Howling Doom* was starting to sink.

Dead bodies slid and rolled down into the water and were carried away by the waves.

Some of the pirates jumped in the water and were swimming towards the man-of-war.

"To hell with it," James whispered to himself. He let go of the gunwale and slid into the sea. The deck seemed wide, but James was underwater in a blink of an eye. The water was freezing cold. He fought to the surface and started swimming. Someone else was swimming beside him but quickly disappeared.

It was a long way to the ship, and James had never had to swim through big waves. He was cold and tired, but the fear of drowning kept him moving. It seemed like he was splashing in place, and the ship wasn't getting any closer. He kept swimming and prayed for the ship not to sail away.

Little by little, the distance disappeared, and eventually James reached the ship. The crew had thrown a cargo net. He grabbed it with his numb hands and held on. He felt the net being pulled, and then somebody grabbed his hand.

Two men helped him to the deck, but before James could say "Thank you," something hit him in the abdomen and forced him to his knees.

"Enough," a voice said. "Leave the rest to die. Return to the original course."

James looked around. He was surrounded by British sailors. One was holding a lantern. In the front stood the captain, a tall, broad-shouldered man in perfect Royal Navy uniform.

He looked to his left and saw six other men kneeling beside him. His crewmates.

David Burroughs. George Arlington. Joshua Lawrence. Thomas Henderson. Pedro Murillo. Walter Sheppard. James McDougall. The only remnants of the *Howling Doom*.

"Gentlemen," the captain spoke. "Welcome to His Majesty's Ship *Fife*. I am Captain Charles Howard Forsyth. These are my men. And you are filthy pirate scum, and you will be treated accordingly. Now, which one of you dirtbags–"

A sailor ran up to Lawrence and stabbed him in the abdomen several times before his crewmates pulled him away. It took three men to hold him.

"How do you like that, you cocksucker?!" he yelled.

"WOODSON!" Forsyth shouted. "Fifty lashes! Boatswain, if you don't mind…"

"Yes, captain."

"I don't care!" Woodson yelled. "Those fuckers killed my brother, I don't care what you do!"

The boatswain and three others took Woodson away.

"Not a good first impression," Forsyth said. "But back to business. Which one of you horse turds want to talk? How about you?"

He was looking at Murillo.

"*No comprendo, señor, yo no hablo ingles…*"

Forsyth drew his pistol and shot Murillo in the head.

"Throw him overboard. The other one too."

Two sailors picked up the body and threw him out, then did the same with Lawrence, who had already bled out.

The captain reloaded his pistol.

"You've seen what we do with liars," he said. "Better start telling the truth."

He aimed the gun at Sheppard's head.

"What is the name of your ship?"

"Don't tell him anything!" Arlington yelled. One of the sailors walked up behind him and slit his throat.

"I'll say it again. What is– I'm sorry, what *was* the name of your ship?"

"Fuck you and fuck your–"

Forsyth pulled the trigger and Sheppard's brain splattered. Two of the sailors tossed Arlington and Sheppard overboard.

Forsyth was looking at James.

"Are you going to talk?"

"Yes, sir."

"What was the name of your ship?"

"*The Albatross.*" James was looking at Forsyth, but he could almost feel Henderson and Burroughs sigh in relief.

"Who is your captain?"

"He's dead."

"What was his name?"

"Will Ashborne."

"What was your destination?"

"Cartagena de Indias."

"Were you going to attack it?"

"I don't know."

"What do you mean you don't know?"

"We're new," Burroughs said. "We joined the crew a month ago. The captain didn't tell us his plan."

"Well, whatever the plan was, I seem to have ruined it. Instead of Cartagena, you're going to Virginia Colony with us. Mr. Rossington, take these worthless sacks of shit to the lower deck. Treat them the same way you would treat any criminal, or worse."

Three men pointed their pistols at Henderson, Burroughs, and James, and led them to the hold. Every sailor spat on them as they passed.

The three pirates were chained up and locked in a small room. It was quiet.

For a while, they didn't say anything.

"How did we end up here?" Henderson said after a while.

"We should've taken that brigantine," James said.

"What?"

"That Spanish brigantine we saw. We should've taken it. It would've been a good prize. But no, Thatcher wanted something bigger. We could've had two ships."

Burroughs and Henderson didn't say anything.

"Hammond wanted to start his own crew. He once asked me if I would be his first mate. We had a chance with that brigantine. Now it's gone. It's all gone. Everyone is underwater now. Including the *Doom*."

James lay down and looked at the ceiling. He was going to prison. He was a prisoner now. Hammond was dead. So was Thatcher. So was Douglas. So was Wright. The *Howling Doom* was sunk. It was all over. They were captured, and now they would be executed.

Hours went by, but James didn't want to sleep. He was still thinking about the fact that their ship had been sunk and the entire crew that sacked Porto Bello and Vera Cruz and retreated from Santiago de Cuba – his crew – was gone. It was just him and two other men, on their way to execution.

Everything was gone.

Everything was gone, and soon he would be too. He would be hung like the pirate that he was.

James heard Burroughs moving around. Then there was a weird gargling sound. He tapped Henderson on the shoulder.

"What the fuck is going on?"

"Burroughs?" Henderson said. "Burroughs, what's going on? Shit!"

"What is it?"

"Blood. I think he slit his throat with something."

"Fuck, is he dead?"

Henderson grabbed Burroughs's shoulder and shook him.

"Yeah. He's gone."

"Shit."

The crew shrank to two, James thought.

For a couple of hours, he and Henderson tried to fall asleep, but neither of them could. They didn't have hammocks, and the ship's rocking kept them awake.

"McDougall?"

"Yeah?"

"Do you ever have those dreams?"

"What dreams?"

"When… when we took Bedford's ship, I shot one man in the chest. Then… I recognized that it was Waterstone. We used to get drunk together in Nassau. I wouldn't have killed him, but it happened too fast. Now… I have this dream where he and I are in Nassau, standing on the beach, and he asks me why I killed him. And I can never come up with an answer."

They both were quiet for a while.

"Do you ever get dreams like that?" Henderson said.

"No."

"I get them a lot."

"Goddammit, Henderson, we're on a boat on our way to be hanged, and all you can think about are some fucking dreams?"

"You don't feel bad about anyone you killed?"

"No."

"If they asked you why you killed them, what would you say?"

"Enough. Don't talk to me."

But as James lay on the floor in a rocking ship with his eyes closed, the question kept coming back.

If they asked you why you killed them, what would you say?

He tried to push it out of his mind, but it kept coming back.

If they asked you why you killed them, what would you say?

James was cold, and he was starting to get nauseous. Probably because of the rocking. He wished he had a jug of rum.

If they asked you why you killed them, what would you say?

CHAPTER XXV

Williamsburg, Colony of Virginia

"James?"

"What?"

"I'm sorry."

"Don't be."

"You've led a hard life."

"Well, that's about to change."

"It's a shitty way to go out."

"I know."

"Is there anything I can do for you?"

"Are you still thinking about becoming a pirate?"

"Yes."

"Promise me you'll be a good, law-abiding citizen and will never get into piracy."

James could hear Rob's breathing.

"Rob?"

"Look…"

"Damn it, Rob, what is it that you don't understand?"

"I just think it doesn't have to be the way it was for you."

"What are you talking about?"

"It would be possible to make good money out of it and escape before… you know…"

"Stop it."

"All it takes is one big job."

"There's no such thing."

"There is! All it takes is some smarts and a little bit of luck."

"It will take you a lot of luck to last a week."

"Just hear me out. If I could make my way to Nassau, I would join a pirate crew going for a big prize, then during the battle I would stay behind and avoid getting into the fight as much as I can. With all that going on, no one would notice. We win the battle, I take my share, and abandon the crew in the nearest port. I would hardly have to do anything. It would take some luck, of course, and some wise money management. And willpower, to abstain from having too much fun in Nassau."

"You don't listen, do you? You hear what you want to hear."

"I'm only in it for the money. I know this is possible. I understand that not every prize will be a big one, but it could be a huge opportunity. I know it's dangerous, but who wouldn't want to sail alongside one of the legendary pirate captains, like Bedford, or Whitaker, or Heartless Harry

Wright… Who could refuse that? A life of adventure, fame, riches, of combat… I don't have anything against bankers or businessmen, but to me, that is not real work. Scribbling on some paper and playing with money is not what a man should do. Combat, that is where men are tested, where they can show what they're made of. In battle, you see who is courageous and who is a damn coward. There's no pretending. That's the beautiful thing. You can't buy your way into glory, you have to prove your worth."

He paused and waited for James to say something, but only heard silence.

"Aren't you going to say something? James? Fine. Be like that. You know what I think? I think you wouldn't be saying those things if you weren't stuck in gaol with me. But you ran out of luck. It just happens that way sometimes. You had some rotten luck, and you ended up getting caught. And now you're here, when you should be sailing the seas and living the dream in the company of legendary men like Heartless Harry Wright. It's awful. I'm sorry this happened to you. I wish I could help you in some way. If I wasn't locked up here with you, I'd break you out. You're a good man, you deserve better than this rotten hole. I'm sure those bastards here would realize it if they gave you a fair trial. I don't think they'll do that. They'll just see you as another criminal. It's a damn shame."

Rob closed his eyes and soon fell asleep. He dreamed of sunny Caribbean beaches and glistening gold coins.

www.ingramcontent.com/pod-product-compliance
Lightning Source LLC
LaVergne TN
LVHW010653110826
845149LV00014B/3071

9781966625704